The Case of
the Sin City Sister

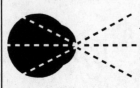

This Large Print Book carries the
Seal of Approval of N.A.V.H.

A DIVINE PRIVATE DETECTIVE AGENCY
MYSTERY, BOOK 2

THE CASE OF
THE SIN CITY SISTER

LYNNE HINTON

THORNDIKE PRESS
A part of Gale, Cengage Learning

GALE
CENGAGE Learning·

Farmington Hills, Mich • San Francisco • New York • Waterville, Maine
Meriden, Conn • Mason, Ohio • Chicago

GALE
CENGAGE Learning®

LIBRARY OF CONGRESS CATALOGING-IN-PUBLICATION DATA

Hinton, J. Lynne.
 The case of the Sin City sister : a Divine Private Detective Agency mystery / by Lynne Hinton. — Large print edition.
  pages cm. — (Thorndike Press large print Christian mystery)
 ISBN 978-1-4104-8145-0 (hardcover) — ISBN 1-4104-8145-X (hardcover)
 1. Nuns—Fiction. 2. Private investigators—Fiction. 3. Missing persons—Investigation—Fiction. 4. Large type books. I. Title.
PS3558.I457C37 2015b
813'.54—dc23   2015015562

Published in 2015 by arrangement with Thomas Nelson, Inc., a division of HarperCollins Christian Publishing, Inc.

Printed in Mexico
1 2 3 4 5 6 7 19 18 17 16 15

This story is about the bond between sisters, so since I have the best sister in the world, it only makes sense that I would dedicate this book to her.

To my sister, Sharon Bender, I am grateful and blessed to have you in my life. If you ever go missing in Vegas, I will find you.

PROLOGUE

April 19, 1889

Caleb Alford stood on the rustic, wood-paneled porch of his childhood home and placed the small piece of turquoise in the front pocket of his jacket. The air was still, quiet. He took in a long breath, strapped on his canvas pack, and stepped down. He walked down the front steps and along the dirt path all the way to town without ever looking back.

It was four o'clock in the morning as he set out, the darkness thick, stars and moon barely lighting the way, the night a long woolen blanket pulled across the eastern North Carolina farmland he had called home all of his life.

His pack was heavy, making the walk a bit slower. He had everything he would need: an extra pair of work pants, two winter shirts, thick wool socks, a leather vest, a new pair of long johns, biscuits, dried beef, two small apples, and the roll of dollars he had saved for fourteen months. He had a few tools — a small pick and two tin pans — roped to the bottom of the pack, along with a lantern given to him by his father, a sleeping mat, a pair of gloves, and a map drawn and labeled by Judah Gardner that included every detail the old man could recall. Mr. Gardner, a comrade of his uncle, had just returned from the mines. He had quite a story to tell, and Caleb Alford wanted to hear it all.

The young man had been prepared for this trip for a long time, but now that the day had arrived, he felt weighted down, hesitant. He walked at a slow but purposeful pace. Claire had known about his plans before she realized she was pregnant. It had been discussed by the newlyweds for months, Caleb having been completely forthcoming even before they married. He'd learned of the mines in the West from his uncle Jonathan. His mother's younger brother had been a soldier in the Confederate Army who traveled as far as the territory known as New Mexico, fighting the Union soldiers in a region fed by the Pecos River known as Glorieta Pass.

The Confederates had planned to break the Union possession of the West along the base of the Rocky Mountains. After they pushed the Union force back through the pass, they had to retreat when their supply train was destroyed and most of their horses and mules were killed or driven off. Eventually, the soldiers had to withdraw entirely from the territory back into Confederate Arizona and then Texas. Uncle Jonathan had returned to North Carolina, wounded and defeated. The light in his eyes was all but snuffed out, except for the fantastic stories he'd tell of the intricate Indian jewelry he had seen in the hills near the battle site.

"Turquesa" and "chalchihuite," his uncle called the Turkish stone that was deemed better than gold, a stone more profitable than silver because the Persian mines where the ore was usually found were being emptied. Out in the desert hills of New Mexico, however, just east of Santa Fe, where the Union soldiers had pushed out the Confederates, there the ore was plentiful. And unlike the gold mines of California and the silver mines in Colorado, there weren't that many who knew about the turquoise or of its increasing value in Europe and the Americas.

Caleb was not quite a teenager when he heard his uncle's tales, but he knew even then that he would head west. All he needed to do was earn enough money to cover the wagon fare and, once the railroad line was completed, the train ticket as well as the mining fees that he expected to be charged when he arrived in the territory known as New Mexico.

Caleb had planned for his new bride to travel with him, and once they arrived she would find a job in the mining town of Cerrillos, waiting tables at the local diner or taking care of the townspeople's children. Claire, like Caleb, was resourceful. And she shared his dream, making it her own, feeding their love for each other and their desire to marry. But then, even though they had been very careful since their first time together, she had gotten pregnant.

He stopped and looked behind him, wondering if he should have awakened her before he left. The sun was beginning to light the sky, which meant Claire was awake. He could see her in his mind's eye, standing at the bedroom window, her hair long and unbraided, her eyes and nose still red from the night's tears. She was already showing by the time he was ready to leave — her dresses now pulled tight across her belly. She had less than three months to go before the due date, and when he had seen what was really happening, what it all really meant, he almost stayed.

Claire hadn't asked him, but he'd come close to using the money they had saved for his mining trip to pay for the crib and stroller in the Sears catalog, almost took the job at the tobacco warehouse, and almost started clearing the land behind the barn, down near the creek, a nice spot for a little house. But when it came time to stake off the building site and drop by the warehouse and ask Mr. Moore when he would start; when he was standing at the counter at the general store, flipping through the catalog, pointing out the desired baby furniture, the store owner's wife adding up the deposit, he just couldn't pull the money from his pocket. He just couldn't settle when he had gotten so close.

Claire had urged him to go on. He should go ahead with his plan, find a nice place for the family to live, make some money, and send for her. She would be fine, she had told him, her words hardly convincing. She would stay with his parents and have the baby, give the boy or the girl a good start, a strong name, and then she would join him. His uncle, now recovered and restless after the scars of war, had even volunteered to travel with her and the child. It was a good plan B. It was a solid and good plan B.

Now was the best time for mining. That's what Judah Gardner, the old man who was a friend of his uncle, the one passing through, the one who had just returned from panning turquoise, had said. The only reason he had come back was because his mother had taken ill, and he was the only one left to take care of her. "I'd head back out there in a skinny second," he had said. "A skinny second," he had repeated, smiling at the young man paying for the map he had drawn, grinning with every detail he added. "Rich and ready for the taking."

It had been all that Caleb needed to hear.

"Caleb Alford," the driver of the stagecoach parked at the edge of town called out when he spotted the man walking in his direction, looking back over his shoulder. "Are you Caleb Alford?"

The young man turned his sights away from home and toward the voice calling out his name. "Yes, sir, I'm Caleb." And he walked over to the coach, making his way to the side of the driver.

"Then I guess you're going with us," the wagon master responded, jumping down to take his pack.

"Yes, sir, I guess I am." And he handed him his things and walked around to the door of the coach.

"You can sit back there if you want, or you can ride up front with me. Just the two of us until we get up to the state line, then there will be a family of three joining us all the way to the train station in Richmond. You'll likely want to claim a seat inside then. Looks like rain."

Caleb headed past the door of the coach, grabbed the hand extended in his direction, and pulled himself onto the front seat. The driver waited a minute, letting his passenger settle, then made a clucking noise and shook the reins. The horses moved forward, and the coach shifted and was quickly pulled along.

The sky was full of light. Caleb reached into his pocket, rubbed the small smooth stone between his fingers, nodded once more, and didn't look back again.

ONE

Sister Evangeline remained in the chapel even as the altar candles were extinguished and all the other nuns and monks had gone to their chambers for the night. She knelt in the dark on the hard oak bench before her and remained quiet, her head in her hands, her eyes closed, for more than an hour, waiting for something she wasn't sure would come. She wanted an answer from God — a sign to show her the way — and every night and every morning for the last three weeks, she had stayed in the chapel for hours at a time, waiting for God to tell her what to do.

She listened, but there was nothing. All she could hear were the birds, the flapping of the wings of the pigeons that came and went from their nests along the eaves of the chapel. She also heard the telltale sounds from the habits of her sisters in the hallway, the kind of swishing noises that the long skirts made, and she knew they had gone first to the kitchen to make sure the breakfast supplies were out and now were on their way to bed. She waited another twenty minutes without an answer and was about to leave when she heard a voice from behind her.

"This has gone on long enough, Sister."

She swallowed hard. She had not heard him come in.

"It's been almost a month."

It was Father Oliver, the monk in charge of the monastery where she lived, and hearing him speak made her wonder how long he had been in the chapel and sitting behind her.

"You need not pray any longer for wisdom. You have prayed for that long enough. It is time for you to obey what is being given to you. Your path is clear to everyone here, except perhaps to you."

She rose from the bench and sat back against the pew but did not turn around to face her superior. She dropped her hands into her lap, the rosary draped across her fingers, her face down. "But I don't know," she replied. "How can I be sure?"

"Your heart knows," he answered.

There was a pause. She did not respond.

"How do you feel when you think about

16

the work you have done with your father, Captain Divine? How was it to solve that murder?"

Eve closed her eyes and thought about the case she'd helped to figure out working alongside the Captain. She took in a deep and full breath, her heart opening, as she considered what it was like when she made the educated guess as to who had killed the Hollywood director. The satisfaction of it — the completeness of closing the case — it was true; her spirit soared in those days unlike it ever had before.

"I am right, yes?" he asked. "This work as a detective, it fulfills you."

She did not answer at first. She considered what he said, understanding exactly what he meant, knowing in earnest it was true. She felt something so different when she had worked at the detective agency. She felt connected to the world in a way she hadn't experienced before. She felt useful and engaged. Alive. The monk was right, and as much as she didn't want to admit to her passions, she knew it.

"But how do I know to trust those feelings? How do I know that the feelings aren't just my temptation, something I should surrender and let go of, not trust? How do I know this urge should be honored and not resisted? How can you be sure I'm not just being willful and disobedient?"

Father Oliver poured out a long breath. Eve felt him then, just at her back, close but not threatening, not hovering. She was glad to have him near her this way, behind her, not in front of her, not looking into her eyes. It was a bit like the sacrament of confession, with a thick veil, a wall, separating the confessor from the one offering redemption.

"We are told by the psalmist that God meets the desires of our hearts. Even Saint Paul wrote to the church in Galatia that 'it is no longer I who live, but Christ who lives in me.' "

Eve was confused. She was not following his explanation, but she didn't interrupt. In more than twenty years as a nun she had learned some skills about listening and about silence; and as she bit her lip, holding back another question, holding back her impatience, she realized this was one of the skills that had benefited her in solving the mystery of the dead Hollywood director. She had known how to listen to what was being said as well as to discern what was being shown. She had solved the mystery because she understood what it meant to listen carefully, to pay close attention to the details.

Oliver waited a bit and continued. "If you are a true disciple, Sister, and I believe you are, then Christ lives in you. If this is so, then the desire that is in your heart can be trusted. It is the truth for you to live by."

Eve relaxed. It was the news she had wanted but had not expected to hear from her superior. She knew that what he was saying was certainly true, that working at the detective agency energized her in a way she hadn't felt for a long time. She knew being in the role of detective fed her spirit, engaged her mind and heart, and fulfilled her. It was everything she had been searching for at the monastery for years, even years she had not realized she was looking for something.

"Who will watch the animals?" she asked, suddenly remembering the stray cats and dogs she had been housing and feeding at the monastery. She was the only resident who took care of them. She worried that to leave would mean the animals would more than likely be neglected. Not knowing who would step up and take over was one of the reasons she had been using for her decision to stay.

"I have spoken to Sister Mary Edith and

Brother Stephen. They are both dedicated to caring for all the residents here, the four-legged creatures as well as those of us with two. We will continue the good work you began."

Eve smiled. It warmed her heart to know that he had understood this would be important in her discernment process to leave the monastery. He knew what caring for the animals meant to her, and with his reply, it was clear that he had already managed this matter of concern.

She nodded and thought about the man sitting behind her and understood how she had come to love and respect Father Oliver over the years. He was not one who spoke frivolously or one who used his authority as a means of power over the others at the monastery. Even in times of disagreement, and there had certainly been a few of those, Eve had always found her superior to be kind and fair in his leadership. She trusted him.

"I just want it to be a leave of absence," she said. "I am not ready to leave for good. I just need a couple of months to sort through things, help my dad again, and be back in Madrid and just have time to think about things."

She felt his hand on her shoulder. It was

warm and strong.

"It is just a leave of absence," he agreed. And then he removed his hand. "But Sister Evangeline, you must use these six weeks as the opportunity that they are. You must still your mind and listen to your heart. If you do that, if you seek in truthfulness to know what it is you are to do with your life, you will know the truth."

"And the truth will set me free," she added. She reached her right hand across her opposite shoulder and held it there, waiting. She didn't wait long before his hand clasped hers and squeezed. She dropped her head, said a prayer of thanks, and felt the release of his hand on hers. When she stood up to leave, she turned around to thank Father Oliver, to tell him what relief he had given her, to let him know what his counsel had meant to her, how she had been praying for what he had given to her, but the chapel was empty. There was no one else there. The one who'd provided her the answer had already gone.

TWO

"There's no time to take anything." Her husband rushed into the bedroom, trying to hurry her along. "There's no room for those," he said, nodding at the two framed pictures she'd just pulled from the nightstand. "Just essentials."

She turned to him and started to argue but realized it would just take time — time they didn't have. She put the pictures back and opened a small drawer to pull out a few things she didn't want to leave behind: a small angel given to her by her mother when she moved to Vegas, a bracelet with silver charms, a tiny seed pot from a potter living on the Acoma Pueblo. She closed the drawer without removing the small book she hoped would not be picked up by the wrong person.

He swore. "I hear a motorcycle," he said and darted from the bedroom into the kitchen.

A motorcycle, she thought. Wouldn't that be great if it was her sister arriving and not the man terrorizing the two of them? But her family was nowhere near the town she was in. She shook her head and glanced around, wondering what she needed and if she would ever be back, if she'd ever recover these things that she had treasured.

There were so many other items she wanted to take, including a necklace from her mother, a Navajo squash blossom design of turquoise and coral, the one she wore all the time, the one given to her just before she died. There was the painting found in the back of an old church — the sisters Mary and Martha sitting at the feet of Jesus — and a book of prayers she'd received from her parents on her sixteenth birthday, a book she had never been without. She picked it up and couldn't help herself; she fanned through the pages, remembering when it had been given to her, the way her mother smiled, as though she thought it was the perfect gift for her teenage daughter, a gift she seemed to think might save her — from what, she would never say.

"I need more time," she said to no one in particular.

"What?" he called from the other room. "What are you saying?"

"I said I need more time," she repeated, speaking up this time so her husband could hear her. "I like it here. It took us a long time to find this apartment, and I don't like leaving all our stuff like this. I don't like worrying that somebody will take it."

"Don't worry about it. I called next door. They have the extra key. They'll make sure nothing gets stolen while we're gone. I took care of it," came the voice from the other side of the wall.

"Right," she said under her breath. "Just like you took care of everything else." She stuck the book of prayers in one of the side pockets of the suitcase. She hobbled over to the closet, her ankle still swollen and sore, and grabbed a few blouses, along with a jacket since it was still chilly in the evenings.

"We'll buy clothes. Don't worry about clothes."

"Buy clothes?" She looked at him. "How are we supposed to buy clothes when we don't have any money?"

"I'm going to get the money," he said. He walked over to where she was standing and put his arms around her. "It's going to be okay, I promise."

She closed her eyes and dropped her face into his shoulder. She took in a whiff of his cologne and was somehow comforted by

24

the familiar smell. He was trouble, always had been, but she loved him, and she was going to do what he said.

Suddenly he yanked away. "I hear it again. It's him for sure. He's here." His voice had dropped to a panicked whisper.

"Okay, okay," she said, leaving the closet and grabbing the suitcase from the bed. "Let's go." She hopped to the bedroom door and glanced around once more at everything she was leaving behind. "I hope it's enough," she said, but her husband did not hear her.

THREE

Carlos and Joseph Diaz had been four-wheeling on every trail in the Santa Fe National Forest since their twelfth birthday. Mary, their mother, thought her twin sons too young to have the ATVs, but she had been outvoted by her husband and her brother, a dealer in Santa Fe who'd gotten them a great deal on a matching set.

They rode on the marked trails where motor vehicles were permitted, the ones their father had pointed out the day they got their new toys, and they rode on the ones where they were not allowed and had not been authorized to ride by a parent or adult. Since federal lands were rarely patrolled, the chances of their being discovered and punished were slim, and so for three years they had been running up and down the mining trails as though they owned the land. Sometimes they even parked and entered some of the abandoned and closed mines they drove past, something they had promised never to do. One mine in particular had captured their attention on an earlier ride, and on this day, they'd brought flashlights and a few supplies, determined to go into the mine and stay a little longer than they had when they'd first discovered it.

The brothers drove from the back side of Madrid all the way beyond the Cerrillos Hills, out past the marked trails and old mining roads. They rode on private land, but the fence that bordered the property had been cut and pushed aside long before they'd arrived the first time. It was Carlos who had noticed the opening the previous Saturday morning, providing them with a new territory to ride, a new area to explore, and he had hurried to stop his brother and turn back to drive across the unfenced border. He knew he wouldn't have any trouble convincing his brother to follow him because Joseph was usually the first one of the pair to break any trespassing laws.

When they found the old mine the first time, it was late in the afternoon, the sun was setting, and they couldn't see past the boarded-up opening. Having heard all too often the stories of collapsing mine roofs and how the mines were often dens for mountain lions and rattlesnakes, they'd pulled aside a couple of the boards but decided to come back another day with more time and better supplies to see and discover what lay within the small hillside opening.

"You sure it was this far out?" Joseph asked when they stopped along the trail, neither one of them completely sure of the exact spot where they'd crossed.

"Yeah, it was way past those switchbacks and just before we usually cross the arroyo." Carlos peered out into the desert landscape before them. "I think it's just past that old sign." He raised his chin to point out where he thought the fence was cut and headed out again. Joseph pulled out behind him.

Sure enough, Carlos was right, and the two of them picked up speed as they rounded the far hill and headed toward the abandoned mine they had only recently found. When they got to the opening, they slowed and parked, turning off their engines at the same time.

"You got the hammer?" Carlos asked, remembering that they had pulled off only two of the top boards so they could peek inside. They had tried to pull off the others but were unsuccessful. That was the other reason they had decided to come back. They knew they could cross over the old boards, but neither one of the brothers wanted to be the one pushed up and over without knowing what was on the other side. It would be easier, they decided, to go in together, and to do that, more of the boards needed to be pulled away.

"I got it," Joseph answered, reaching inside the small toolbox he kept attached to the back of his four-wheeler.

"You brought Dad's good one?" Carlos asked, sounding both impressed and a little nervous at what his brother had done.

"We'll get it back before he needs it," Joseph replied. "Here," he said and threw him the flashlight while he walked over and started pulling nails out of the boards.

"What kind of mine is this, anyway?" Carlos asked, turning on the flashlight and beaming light in between the boards.

"Silver, I think," Joseph responded. "Up front they were mining for placer gold, but back here I think it was silver."

"It could be turquoise," Carlos noted. "We studied that in history last year. There were a lot of people digging for turquoise in the early 1900s. Cerrillos was almost picked as the capital of New Mexico."

Joseph yanked out another nail and pulled at a board from the center of the opening.

"I know, Professor. We're in the same grade. I take State History too." He turned back to his brother. "Are you going to just give history lessons or are you going to help?"

Carlos turned off the flashlight and stuck it into his back pocket. He walked over next to his brother and yanked at a loose board until it came free. He threw it off to the side. "You want to get that last one?" he asked, pointing to the board near their feet.

"We can just jump over that one," Joseph said. He dropped the hammer at his side and took a step inside. "Man, it must be twenty degrees cooler in here," he commented.

Carlos paused and then walked in behind him, turned on the flashlight, and began to throw light inside the old mine. He shivered. His brother was right — it was very cold inside. He was glad he had worn a long-sleeved shirt.

"Here, let me see that." Joseph reached over for the flashlight.

Carlos handed it to him.

"Look, it goes way back," Joseph noted, pointing the light in front of where they stood. "You ready?"

Carlos shrugged. "How do we know there's no rattlers back there?"

Joseph grinned. "Guess we don't until we

hear them."

"Or get bit by one."

"We'll just go a little ways," Joseph said, trying to persuade his brother. "That's why we came back, right?" He turned to Carlos and shined the light in his eyes.

Carlos turned away. "Geez, Joe, you trying to blind me?"

His brother laughed and started toward the back of the mine. "Looks like it gets a little smaller," he commented, pointing to the opening. He knew his brother was claustrophobic. "You can wait out there if you want," he added, prodding him.

Carlos followed. "I'm not scared, if that's what you think."

"Okay then, why don't you go ahead?" Joseph stopped and waited.

Carlos paused. "No, you go first. That way if the snake or cat jumps out, you'll be lunch and I'll have time to get out."

The two brothers walked in a few steps farther.

"Just looks like the others," Carlos said as he followed close behind his brother. "I think it would be boring being a miner. Never seeing the sunshine, breathing in all this dust and dirt."

"Yeah, but if you found the gold or the silver or whatever thing you were looking for, well, then you would be set for life," Joseph noted. "You could be a millionaire."

"I don't think that really happened to most of those guys. A lot of them were on the payroll for the big companies. Most of them came out here, spent all their hard-earned money, and went home broke and without a piece of gold or silver or turquoise to their name."

"And probably they were the lucky ones." Joseph stopped. The flashlight was shining straight ahead of them. "Some of the other ones may have ended up like him."

Carlos's gaze followed the beam of light.

There, straight ahead of Joseph, about ten feet from where they stood and propped up against the side of the wall, was a pile of bones, along with a skull and a rib cage — a human skeleton. The two boys didn't speak.

There was a scratching noise from farther down in the mine and then a long, high-pitched cry.

Joseph dropped the flashlight as Carlos pushed past him and didn't stop running until he was astride his ATV. He glanced behind him only to make sure his brother had made it out, and then he cranked the engine and took off. Joseph was only a few yards behind, leaving the entry wide open, the boards thrown to the side, hiding their father's favorite hammer as it lay abandoned in the thin weeds, and the flashlight still on, rolling across the dirt floor, casting shadows across the walls of the old turquoise mine and across the old bones of someone who had died inside.

Four

Evangeline waited for the prompt to leave her message. "Dorisanne, it's your sister. Again. Why aren't you returning my calls?" She waited as if she thought there might be a response, then continued. "Well, look, I'm calling because I was cleaning out some of our old stuff and I found that Zuni bracelet you used to wear all the time. The turquoise-and-silver one, the one with the old needlepoint stones. I polished it up and it looks real nice. Anyway, I thought you might like to have it. So let me know if you want me to send it to you." She paused and was about to add something else, something like she was praying for her or missed her or hoped she was okay, but the beep sounded and she was disconnected. She returned the receiver back to the cradle.

"She still not answering?" The Captain was sitting across the room at his desk, drinking coffee and reading the morning paper.

Evangeline shook her head. "I've been leaving messages for three days." She got up from where she sat behind the narrow, fold-up table that served as her desk, walked over to the coffeepot, and started to pour herself a cup. But there was no coffee left. She turned to her father, holding the empty carafe in the air as witness. "How many cups have you had this morning?"

"I don't know the answer to that." He turned the page. "How many cups does that thing make?"

"Probably more than you should drink," she answered. She reached down and petted Daisy, the cat she'd adopted the last time she stayed in Madrid. The cat yawned and raised its head, purring as Eve scratched underneath her outstretched chin. She glanced back at the Captain, and he was watching her.

"Look in the checkbook," he said, seeming to know what she was thinking. "I sent her some money after I talked to her last. It should be in there. That will tell you what day it was."

His suggestion was a welcome surprise. She gave Daisy one final pet and walked back over to her table-desk. She reached into the box on top and retrieved the checkbook from under some files. She flipped through the transaction records. Eve knew practically all of the deposits and withdrawals because in addition to taking care of her father, she was also the temporary bookkeeper and administrative manager for the Divine Private Detective Agency, the Captain's business.

"I knew that boy was trouble. I tried to tell your sister, but she was so convinced he was changed. Yeah, five thousand dollars changed . . ."

Eve blew out a long breath; she hated to hear him start in on her sister. She stopped listening to him and found the entry. He had sent her two hundred dollars almost six weeks ago.

Seeing the date, Evangeline vaguely recalled her dad telling her a little bit about the conversation. Dorisanne was late on the rent and said her hours were docked at the bar where she was a waitress. She had missed a few days because she'd sprained her ankle. At least that's what she told him when she called in May. When she was a child, Dorisanne was always falling and getting hurt, but Evangeline thought she had moved out of that accident-prone stage. Once Dorisanne had become a dancer as a young teenager, she wasn't as careless or awkward.

"Did she say how she injured herself?"

"What?" He wasn't paying attention; he had moved from the front page on to the sports section.

"Dorisanne," Evangeline answered. "Did she say how she sprained her ankle?" She was still looking through the entries in the checkbook ledger. She couldn't help herself — she was adding and subtracting, checking the numbers as she flipped through the pages.

"Fell down the stairs at the apartment, she said," he replied.

"I thought she lived in a downstairs unit," Eve noted.

"Then maybe she lied about that too."

"What do you mean, 'lied about that too'?"

Captain Jackson folded the paper and placed it on the desk in front of him. He studied his daughter. "Your sister isn't exactly known for her honesty."

Evangeline was surprised. "What do you mean by that?" Dorisanne had her flaws, but lying had never been one of them. She had always been one of the most truthful people Evangeline knew.

Her father shrugged. "I checked on some

things," he answered.

"What kind of things?"

"On Robbie, his job, their bank accounts, things like that."

Evangeline shook her head. "I should have known you'd be playing private detective with your daughter."

"A man has to look out for his own interests."

"She's a human being, not an interest," Evangeline replied.

"Whatever. Let's just say she's not been as forthcoming about how things really are as you think."

Evangeline closed the checkbook. She tallied up the days again and confirmed that it had been more than a month since she had heard from her sister. They usually spoke every other week, and the length of time since their last communication bothered Eve. She was just about to comment about the month without contact and her father's recent detective activities in Las Vegas when the front door opened, the small chime sounding as a tall, gray-haired stranger entered.

FIVE

"Is this Mr. Divine's office?"

"It's *Diveen,*" Evangeline and the Captain answered at the same time.

The man glanced from one Divine to the other and then to a small card he held in his right hand. "Private Detective Agency?"

"That part you got right," the Captain responded, putting down his paper. "What can I do you for?"

The man moved into the office, shutting the door behind him. He turned in the direction of Jackson. "I'm searching for someone," he said.

"Okay," the Captain responded. "Do you expect they're here in Madrid?"

The man appeared confused. "Seems like I have that one wrong too. I thought it sounded the same as the city in Spain, Madrid," he noted, placing the emphasis on the second syllable.

"Common mistake," Jackson replied. "Just

like the last name. We appear to be something we are not."

The man waited, taking all of this in. He sneezed.

"Bless you. This is my daughter Eve. No tricky syllables there. And I'm Jackson, sounds just like it's spelled."

The visitor looked over at Eve, who was still holding the checkbook in her hand. He took out a handkerchief and blew his nose. "Sorry," he said.

"Good morning," she said, wondering who in his life had gone missing. She noticed that there seemed to be no sense of urgency about his search; rather, he seemed more concerned about correct pronunciation. "You got a cold?"

He nodded at her and smiled. "Allergies," he answered. "I'm Caleb Alford," he added, walking over and holding out his hand. He looked around the office. "Do you have a cat?"

She shook the offered hand. "Nice to meet you. And yes."

He turned back to Jackson, moved in his direction. "Caleb Alford," he repeated, his hand out again. "That's it then. I'm allergic to cats."

Jackson reached forward. "Jackson Divine," he responded, saying his name again

40

as well. "Here, have a seat," he said and motioned over to the empty chair placed next to his desk. "Eve, get that cat out of here." He pointed to the corner where Daisy, the stray cat, was sleeping.

Mr. Alford sneezed once more and sat down.

There was a pause as Eve walked over, petted the animal, and picked her up. She held Daisy under her arm and carried her out the door.

"So who is it that you're looking for?" Jackson wanted to know.

"My great-grandfather," came the answer.

Captain Divine glanced over at his daughter, who had returned and was wiping the cat hair from the front of her jeans, then back to the man sitting next to his desk. "When did your family first notice his absence?"

He was careful with the words he chose, but Eve could read her father. She could see the same thing he did. The man sitting in their office had to be in his sixties. His great-grandfather was surely long gone from Madrid or anywhere else on the earth for that matter. This would definitely be classified as a cold case. She took out a pad of paper to write down a few details.

"It's been a while," the man replied,

understanding the question. "Eighteen ninety, to be exact. But I read about the skeleton that was found in the mines by those boys."

"Did that make national news?" the Captain asked.

"Not exactly. I've been reading the news of this place for a while. My search has been a hobby for a number of years, but mostly from home."

"You think your great-grandfather came here?"

The gentleman nodded. "He came here to mine for turquoise, left his pregnant wife back in North Carolina. He wrote letters." He reached into the pocket of his jacket and took out a clear plastic bag, placed it on the desk. "The last one is dated November 13, 1890."

Eve watched as her father took the plastic bag, opened it, and took out a small stack of yellowed papers. He unfolded one and began to read.

"I was named for him. Caleb," he explained. "His name was Caleb Alford. His son and grandson were both named Jessie. I was given his name, and for some reason I don't know, I've just always felt connected to him somehow." He was talking to Eve, since the Captain was reading the letters and appeared not to be listening. "When I read about the skeleton, I finally decided to quit just reading stories from home at my computer. I decided I needed to come and see for myself if it was him."

Eve nodded. "Are you from North Carolina too?" she asked.

He shook his head. "Virginia," he answered. "I'm from Norfolk, Virginia. Moved out of Carolina after college. Just retired from teaching school," he volunteered. "I was in the Navy for a while, then got my teaching certificate. History and math," he continued.

"This the last letter he wrote?" Jackson interrupted.

"It's the last one I have," he answered. "I don't know if there were others after it."

"These are in good shape," Captain Jackson noted. "You can still make out every word."

Caleb nodded. "My great-grandmother kept them in a cedar chest and then passed them on to her son, who passed them on to my father. He always talked about driving out here to find out what happened to his grandfather, said it was the great heartbreak of the family. But he was not well for much of his life; he died when I was a teenager. Anyway, I was given the letters at that time, and I guess when he passed them on to me, he also passed on that desire to find answers." He leaned back in the seat. "It's taken a while, but I finally got here."

"You could probably do the search by yourself," the Captain explained. "You don't really need a private detective for this. You could just go down to the courthouse, search the mining records; there's probably information there. And as far as the identity of the skeleton, you can ask for a report."

He nodded. "I made a call to the medical examiner's office. I told them I'd like to submit an example of my DNA to see if there is a match."

"And did they agree?" Captain Jackson asked.

"Yes," he answered. "I should have a report in a couple of weeks."

"So, again, you don't really need a private detective. While you're waiting for the results from the DNA test, go over to the courthouse."

"I did that too. I went to the Santa Fe County Courthouse, found the old mining books, even found his name. Caleb made a minerals claim with a group of six other men — about thirteen miles from here — had it staked off, legally recorded, and everything. But that's all there was. That's all I could find."

"What was the date?" Eve asked, jumping back into the conversation, pen in hand.

"Eighteen eighty-nine," he answered. "July 2, 1889. That's three months after he left, about a year and a half before his last letter."

"Who were the other six men?" the Captain wanted to know.

The man pulled a sheet of paper from his front shirt pocket. "Claude McCaskell, Deming Dixon, Paul Hernandez, Louis Wiggins, Jose Gonzales, and Philip Lucero." He folded the paper and placed it back in his pocket.

"A few of those names are familiar," Jackson noted. "Some of the families are still around." He studied the man sitting near him. "What does your family think happened to your great-grandfather?"

Caleb turned to Jackson, thought about the question. "Is that information important to your job?"

Jackson shrugged. "Maybe, maybe not. Maybe I just want to know the story you've been believing all your life. Maybe it might help me understand what it is you're looking for."

"I'm looking for the truth. Shouldn't matter what I was told." He paused for a minute, thinking. "But to answer your question, I was told the same thing that my father was told, the same thing that his father was told: that Caleb died in the mines. That he came to New Mexico in search of turquoise, had plans to bring his wife and newly born son out here when he got settled. He was doing what every miner did, trying to strike it rich and make a good living for his family. And then something happened along the way to seeing that dream come to pass, that he fell and broke his neck or had some unforeseen accident that ended his life. That's the story I was told."

Jackson and Eve waited. They glanced at each other, and it was Eve who made the comment they were both thinking.

"But that's not the one you believe."

And Caleb turned quickly to look her in the eye. He shook his head. "No, you're right. That is not the one I have ever believed."

Six

"The story sounds logical enough to me," the Captain noted. "Lots of families got the same story yours got. And it was the truth. Those boys dealt with explosives and rattlesnake dens, and that doesn't even call into account all the thieves and robbers that showed up in the mining heyday. It was dangerous work. Well, you got the proof with that skeleton." He studied the man sitting in front of him.

"What makes you think your great-grandfather's story is different? What makes you think he didn't come out to New Mexico, crawl into one of those shoddy mines, and get killed in some sort of accident?"

Caleb fidgeted in his chair, appearing as if he was trying to decide what to say, how to explain, and then he reached up and began to unbutton his shirt. Around his neck was a long strand of turquoise beads. Even from where Eve was sitting she could see how beautiful the blue stones were. He lifted the necklace over his head and placed it on the desk in front of Jackson.

"About forty years ago, not too long after my father died, in fact, just a year or so before my son was born, this came in the mail delivered to North Carolina, addressed to 'The Family of Caleb Alford.' At the time the Alford family farm was being tended to by my cousins. I was the only Caleb they knew, so they forwarded the package up to Norfolk to me." He nodded at the beads. "This was in it. No note, no explanation, no return address, just this piece of jewelry, wrapped in a piece of old handkerchief that had the initials CA sewn into a corner. I kept it, and I never told anyone except my wife about it." He watched as Jackson held up the necklace, eyeing the stones.

"It's a nice strand," the Captain commented. "Looks like the turquoise from around here, over at Cerrillos. Stones are a little greener. Where was the package postmarked?"

"Madrid, New Mexico," he replied, mispronouncing it. "I mean, Madrid," he corrected himself.

"CA?" Eve called out, joining the conversation. "Caleb Alford?"

The man turned to her and nodded. "Seems like it," he replied. "I remember my great-grandmother was known for her embroidery work. She added a lot of intricate details. My grandfather had a set of pillowcases she made for him and my grandmother; the threadwork looked the same."

"You still have the handkerchief?" Jackson asked.

Caleb nodded his head. "Yes, but it's back at the hotel. I brought it along on this trip, just not with me today."

"You said you have a son?" Eve phrased it more like a question than a complete sentence, even though she wasn't really sure why she was asking.

"Richard," he replied. "He's thirty-nine."

There was a pause.

"I don't see much of him since his mother died six years ago."

Jackson glanced up.

Caleb shook his head. "In fact, I'm not even sure I know where he is. Last time I heard from him he was working on a pipeline, somewhere off the Gulf of Mexico, Louisiana or Texas, I'm not sure."

Father and daughter looked at each other.

Caleb noticed the exchange. "I guess you think it's weird that I'm searching for a long-dead great-grandfather and not my son." He reached for the strand of beads that Jackson was holding out in his direction. He placed them back around his neck and began to roll the stones between his fingers.

Eve watched, noticing how he handled them much as she would the beads in a rosary, and she wondered if that was what this necklace was to him — some symbol, some form of prayer.

"I don't think it's weird at all," Jackson noted.

"My son and I never really got along," Caleb explained as if he had been asked. "He was more of a mother's boy. And I, well, after coming back from Vietnam, I wasn't much of a father."

"You fought in Nam?" Jackson asked.

"Signed up for the Navy so I wouldn't be drafted into the Army. That's how I ended up in Norfolk." He looked at Jackson. "You?"

"Frog, underwater demolition. Naval Amphibious Base, Coronado. But I got out in '59, before the war."

"You guys were crazy," Caleb responded.

"True, some of them were," Jackson replied.

"You see any action back then?" Caleb asked.

"Nothing I really want to talk about," Jackson replied, glancing over in his daughter's direction.

Caleb nodded.

Eve didn't comment. She knew her father had never talked much about his time in the service. He'd served a few years, met her mother, married and became a police officer, and settled in the Desert Southwest. She hardly remembered him talking about his time as a Navy UDT Frog as she was growing up. She had practically forgotten about it.

"But I never had to deal with what a lot of men dealt with. I consider myself pretty lucky." Jackson began rubbing his leg, something Eve had noticed him doing since the amputation whenever he felt uncomfortable.

"War is hard," Caleb responded. "Especially that one." He shook his head. "It took me a while, but I got some help and I got better. I think it just came too late for my son. He mostly remembers me messed up."

Jackson nodded and cleared his throat. "So you want us to find out what happened to your great-grandfather, a miner who was here mining for turquoise in the 1890s. You want to know how he died and where he's buried." He was guiding the conversation back to the business at hand.

"That's what I want," Caleb answered. He placed the beads back underneath his shirt and fastened the buttons. "And I'd like to know who sent the strand of turquoise. Forty years ago Caleb Alford had to be long gone. So, somebody here in" — he paused, hoping to pronounce the town name correctly this time — "Madrid . . ." He looked at Eve, who smiled. "Somebody here sent this back to North Carolina, so somebody here knows something."

"Where are you staying, Mr. Alford?" Eve wanted to know.

"Santa Fe," he replied. "And please, it's Caleb."

"Okay, Caleb," she responded.

"So, Caleb, Eve here will go over the fees for our service. If it's all right, I'll keep these letters for now." Jackson held up the stack Caleb had taken from his front pocket earlier in the conversation. "I can make copies and then I'll give them back."

He nodded. "That's fine. If you can't trust a Frog, I don't know who you can trust." He smiled at the Captain and turned to Eve. "And I can see that the apple doesn't fall far from the tree. The two of you seem to make a good pair."

Eve began sorting through the papers, found a contract, and slid it over to their newest client. As she did that she glanced over at the Captain and, for a second, thought she saw him smile.

Seven

"I'm home." Eve placed the bags of groceries on the counter in the kitchen of her childhood home. She pulled out a few things and placed them in the old refrigerator near the row of dark cabinets the Captain had built when her parents first moved in. She yelled toward the back of the house. "Captain? I said I'm home."

Trooper, her father's dog, an aging but cheerful yellow Lab, hurried in to give the proper welcome and began dancing around Eve's legs.

"Hello, girl." She bent down and gave the dog a good rub on the top of the head. Trooper sat, enjoying the attention.

When Eve stood up, the Captain was making his way up the hall. He was on his crutches, having already taken off his prosthetic leg. He said the leg still bothered him, that it bit into the skin where it was attached, so he took it off when he was home and just got around the house without it.

"You got anything else to bring in?"

Eve studied her father. She wondered how he expected to go down the front steps, take the other bag from the passenger side of the truck, and walk back up the steps and into the kitchen, this act performed entirely on crutches, but she didn't dare ask. He would do that very thing just to prove he could. "I'll get it," she replied, proud of herself for avoiding a fight.

Things had eased between them lately. He didn't pester her anymore about when she was going back to the Benedictine monastery she had taken a leave of absence from, and she didn't nag him about the desserts he sometimes ate, taking his medicines, or getting the rest she thought he needed. It wasn't a perfect setup with the two of them, father and daughter, living and working together, but it was no longer difficult and had actually become comfortable. It was as if they had both made a decision to steer away from the subjects that created tension and conflict and enjoy instead those matters and things about which they agreed and that they shared. For Eve, the years she had spent living in community had taught her more than she'd realized about finding harmony at home.

Eve headed out the front door to retrieve the last bag of groceries. When she returned the Captain had taken a seat on the sofa with Trooper resting on the floor beside him.

"Epi Salazar called again," she said, remembering the message she'd taken before she left the office to run errands. "Does he still live out there on that big ranch by himself?"

"Yep, he's lived there since he was a boy. His father bought all that property from a mining company, paid them cash. Nobody ever figured out where Mr. Salazar made that kind of money, but some folks think he did a little mining on his own before he got the deed for the land. Epi still wanting to hire us?"

Eve placed the bag on the kitchen counter next to the others. She waited before answering. It was the first time she had ever heard her father use the word *us* when speaking about his private detective business. The significance of the chosen pronoun made her smile.

"He's convinced somebody buried gold up there. I told him he didn't need a private detective, he needed a handyman or one of those metal detectors."

Jackson grinned. "What did he say?"

"He claims you're better than a metal

detector. He said that you had the best nose for missing items in all of Santa Fe County."

He shook his head. "I don't know what he thinks I can find walking around his property with one leg. And if I remember the old Mr. Salazar right, he would never have allowed any gold to stay underground on his property. He would have dug up anything he found and gotten the money. He lost a fortune trying to keep cattle up there on that hillside."

She started unpacking the bags, putting things away. She put the canned foods in the cabinet next to the sink, bread in the bread box on the counter beside the refrigerator, and two cereal boxes, Cheerios for her, Grape-Nuts for him, on a shelf in the pantry next to the kitchen. "Well, he found some papers, a map or something. He said he wants you to have it; he says with this you can definitely figure out where the gold was hidden."

"Did you tell him what we charge for locating missing stuff?"

Eve took out the milk and placed it in the refrigerator along with the yogurt and butter. She turned toward her father. "I've never billed for locating a missing treasure. Is it the same as for a person?"

He stretched out his leg in front of him.

57

"Same hourly rate, same success percentage. Buried gold or a dead miner, they cost the same for me to dig up."

Eve finished putting away the groceries and headed into the room where her father was sitting. She carried two cans of diet soda and a bag of grapes. She handed him one of the drinks and sat down in the chair across from the sofa. She held the bag of fruit up, an offer to share, but he shook his head and opened the can of pop.

"I'm worried about Dorisanne," she said, taking out a grape.

"I know you are," he responded.

"Well, do you think I should try to call someone else to make sure she's okay?"

He took a drink of his soda and set the can down on the table. He shook his head. "I don't know, Eve. Since she left home twenty years ago she's been out of touch more than in touch. I figure she's busy and she doesn't need us right now. I wouldn't be too concerned about her just yet. Give her a few more days, another week, and then we'll start calling neighbors and casinos."

Eve nodded. "You're probably right. She isn't one to check in on a regular basis. I know that." She waited, ate another grape, and sat back.

"What?" he asked, as if he knew something

was wrong.

"I don't know. It's just a feeling," she answered.

"What kind of feeling?"

"The bad kind, you know, the kind you can't shake."

He blew out a breath. "Okay, tell me again when you talked to her last."

Eve smiled and sat up, grateful to be able to talk about her concerns. "You talked to her last. It was May 14. You wrote her a check that afternoon. Remember?"

Jackson appeared to be counting. "It's a little over a month," he acknowledged. "That's not a long time for her."

"I know," Eve replied. "It's just that she's not returning any of the calls I've made this week. She may not call us regularly, but she's always called me back when I've left a message."

"Are you sure she's getting the messages?"

"What do you mean?"

"Doesn't she change out her cell phones all the time? Isn't that one of the bills she can never pay?"

Eve considered this. "Yeah, but why would it still be her voice, her message, if they discontinued the number?"

"Maybe they don't turn it off right away; maybe they hold on to the number expecting payment."

Eve shook her head. "That just doesn't make any sense."

He waited. "Check the bank records," he said.

"What do you mean?"

"Check the bank statement, see if she cashed the check."

Eve sat up. "That's a great idea. At least that will tell us if she got the money."

She hurried into the kitchen and picked up the phone. She had called the bank before to check on outstanding checks. It was an automated system, and even though she didn't recall the check number, she did remember the date it was written and the amount. She was sure that was enough to see if it had cleared.

She dialed the number written on the phone book she kept in the top kitchen drawer and pulled out the account information she kept in her wallet. After punching in a series of numbers and having answered more than a few questions, the check numbers were called out. They were all in sequence and all of them had cleared. All but one. Check number 2052. The one written on May 14. The one written in the amount of two hundred dollars. The one written to Dorisanne Divine Miller.

She hung up the phone and walked back into the den.

The Captain looked up from the television program he had turned on. He didn't have to ask because he knew the answer just by reading his daughter's face. He switched off the remote. "We'll call her boss first," was all he said.

EIGHT

"Right now, I'm short three waitresses. One is pregnant, the other got a job at the Poker Table, and Dorisanne with her bum foot. She said it'd be four weeks, this makes the fifth. You tell her to call me when you see her."

"Haven't you talked to her?" Eve asked.

"She called a week or so ago, just to say she was going to need the whole medical leave, the whole month. At first, she thought she might be able to be back, but she called then to say she was still on the crutches. That was before Jackie and Harriet left me. You tell her I need to hear from her right away."

"I can't get in touch with her," Eve tried to explain. "That's why I called you, to see if you've talked to her recently."

There was a pause.

"The staff here doesn't tend to call me just to chat. This ain't one of those kind of places. I hear from them when they're pregnant, when they're hung over, and when they've sprained their ankles. They don't even call when they ask for a transfer to the gambling tables. I get to hear that from the supervisor. So, no, I haven't talked to your sister since she first called to say she couldn't come in. She left a message with the bartender a week ago to say it would be another week before she came back."

"Did he say she sounded okay?" Eve wanted to know.

She could hear the sigh pouring across the phone line. "She said she needed another week before she could come back. That was the message. I didn't get no mental health report."

Eve waited. It certainly seemed as if the manager didn't have any additional information, but she was not satisfied. She still didn't know where Dorisanne was and if everything was fine with her. "Can you give me his name?"

"Whose?"

"The bartender's. Can you give me his name and maybe I can talk to him?" Eve realized that some of the skills she had observed in the Captain were actually quite useful in getting information. She'd learned by watching that he would never hang up on a call until he at least had been given another contact.

"Jason, can you talk to this woman?"

Eve heard shuffling noises as if the phone was being moved, and then there was another voice on the other end.

"Hello?"

"Is this Jason?" Eve asked.

"Yep," came the answer.

"Are you a bartender there?"

"Yep," he replied again. "What's this about?" he asked.

"Jason, I'm Dorisanne's sister, and I haven't been able to get her on the phone lately. I'm worried. The manager said she called the bar last week. I'm not sure if you answered that call or not. But I assume since he passed the phone to you that you did. Was that you? Did you talk to her?"

"You the nun?"

The question surprised Eve a bit. "Um, yeah, I'm in the Benedictine Order. She told you about that?"

"Yeah. We talk some."

There was a pause.

"So last week when she called, did you talk to her?"

"Yep, she called while I was on."

"Did she sound okay? Is her phone still working?"

"She sounded like Dorisanne."

Eve waited. *Surely,* she thought, *that can't be all he has to say.*

He continued. "She just said her ankle was still swollen and she couldn't be on her feet for an eight-hour shift and to tell Darrell. So I did."

Another pause.

"I think she got that whole money thing sorted out."

"What money thing?"

"Oh," was his only response.

"Was she in some kind of financial trouble?"

He seemed to hesitate. "I think she and Robbie got it worked out. You should probably talk to her."

"Well, that's what I'm trying to do," Eve explained. "I just can't reach her."

"Yeah, she got a new phone," was the reply.

"Do you have a number?" Eve picked up a pen. She couldn't help herself, she felt a little hopeful.

"Nah, I don't have that."

She put down the pen and dropped her forehead into her hand.

"But when I talk to her, I'll tell her you called. I'll tell her you're looking for her."

"Thanks, Jason." She waited. "Do you

think she'll call?"

"Look, I gotta go. I got three customers sitting here waiting for their vodka tonics. I'll let her know."

And Eve heard the phone line go dead. She sat for a second just holding the receiver in her hand, halfway expecting Jason or Darrell or someone from the bar at the Rio to pick it back up again and tell her what she wanted to know. After a couple of minutes, she hung up.

She glanced across the room at her father, who had been watching the entire exchange. He was still sitting on the sofa.

"She talked to someone at the bar a week ago."

He nodded.

"They said she asked to be out of work another week because her ankle is still swollen," she said.

He waited.

"He said he thought she had gotten the whole money thing sorted out."

The Captain reached up and scratched his chin. This meant nothing to him either.

"She got a new phone." Eve shrugged. That was all the news she had to report. "What?" She noticed the way he was eyeing her.

"You sounded like a detective."

The comment surprised her. "Is that bad?"

He smiled. "Not to me," he answered. "But I'm not sure what your Brother Oliver will say when you go back to the convent and he hears you answer the phone. You don't sound like the kind and gentle nun anymore."

Eve didn't respond. She walked over to the kitchen sink, grabbed the dishrag, and began wiping off the counter.

"Speaking of professional leaves and calling in . . ." He didn't complete the sentence.

"I have a couple more weeks," she said. She retrieved the letters written by the missing miner from the far corner of the coffee table and walked down the hall. "If you need me, I'll be in my room, reading."

NINE

The next day Eve dropped the Captain off at the office and then drove his old truck to her favorite coffee shop, the Java Junction, to finish reading the letters. She pulled into a parking place in front, put the gear in Park, and turned off the engine while glancing around at the shops on the main street in Madrid. She couldn't help but smile. It felt good to be there, good to be driving the truck, good to be getting a cup of coffee in the morning, good to be home. She got out and headed inside.

"Good morning, Sister Eve." Twila was washing dishes at the sink that faced the door. She wiped off her hands, turned behind her, and grabbed a mug that read "Life's too short to drink bad coffee."

"We've got the French roast today," she announced, handing her customer the cup. She was accustomed to Eve dropping by for coffee in the late morning hours. "You and the Captain got a new case?"

Eve took the cup. "Not sure I'd say it's new, Twila. Missing miner from the 1800s. Came from North Carolina to dig for turquoise. Never made it home."

"That skeleton they found?" Twila glanced down at the folder Eve was carrying under her arm but didn't ask about it.

"Yeah, starts there," she replied. "But even if the skeleton isn't his family member, our client wants to know where he is."

"Well, he ain't here." She winked. "You got the place all to yourself. But if he stops by later, I'll tell him you're looking for him." She handed Eve the pitcher of milk and pointed her to the coffee carafe on the table next to the counter. "By the way," she said as Eve was pulling out cash from her pocket, "I finally did it. I e-mailed the adoption agency that handled my case."

Eve waited. She knew her friend had been on a search for her sister. Apparently the two siblings had been separated when they were very young, both of them having been given up for adoption by their mother.

Twila hadn't even known she had a sister until a few months before when a family member had visited her in New Mexico and happened to mention it. Twila, excited about the possibility of having a sister, asked the Captain for help in searching for her not long after hearing the news. Eve had also assisted. After a few weeks they'd finally tracked down the name and location of the adoption agency that had handled Twila's adoption, but for some reason, after she received that information, Twila seemed to lose interest. After asking her several times how she wanted them to proceed and receiving no reply, the Captain and Eve just backed off and were giving her the space and time she seemed to need before continuing the search. It had been so long since working on it, Eve had almost forgotten about the search for Twila's sister.

"I think I just got nervous for a while, started worrying about what it could mean to find a family member I never knew, a sister of all things . . ." She shook her head. "But then I decided I was being stupid. I want to know what happened to her. I want to know who she is. So I sent the e-mail yesterday."

Eve nodded. She wasn't sure what to say to her friend.

"It's good to have a sister, right? I mean, how could that be bad?"

Eve forced a smile. She wanted to tell her how bad it could be, how having a sibling could cause you worry and sleepless nights, how she was spending endless hours trying to find her own sister, and she wasn't sure whether to keep searching for Dorisanne or just do what the Captain said and wait to hear from her. She didn't say any of those things, however; she just kept that smile in place. "That's good, Twila," she finally responded. "Will you let me know when you hear back from them?"

"You betcha I will," Twila agreed. The phone rang in the back and she left the counter to answer it. "Duty calls," she yelled as she walked away.

Eve stuck some dollar bills in the tip jar and walked over and poured herself a cup of coffee, topping it off with some milk. At the table in the far corner of the café, she sat down and opened the folder. She took a long sip from her coffee as she gazed out the window in the direction of her house, southwest from Twila's and the other downtown businesses. She watched a hummingbird flit around a feeder and thought about Twila's latest news, wondering what or who she would find, how it would be for her to be reunited with a sister. This made her think of Dorisanne again, and when she felt herself start to worry, she pulled out the miner's letters. She clearly needed a distraction. The first one was dated May 19, 1889:

71

Dear Claire,

It is one month today since I left you. I wonder if the baby was born, whether it's a boy or a girl, and how it is for you. I wish I had not left you. I see now that I should have waited and traveled when we could all come together.

It's cold in New Mexico, but I have the wool coat and I have purchased a few things to keep me warm. You were right to tell me to pack as if it were still winter because it is still winter here.

I have met some other miners, and there are several companies that have already claimed certain parts of the hills for mining. I am still trying to find out how to stake a claim and how to proceed in finding the stones. It is not as easy as I thought.

I will write again in a few days. Know that I am thinking of you and love you. I am making a place for you and our family. When you are able, write me and let me know our baby's name. You can send your letters to this post office station. They give out mail to all the miners and people in town.

Yours,

And it was signed, *Caleb*.

Eve drank some of her coffee and pulled out another. This one was dated June 21, 1889:

My Dear Claire,

I have taken work with the Tiffany Miners. They own a lot of the mineral rights to the hills and mountains where we have been told that there is silver and turquoise. Right now, the blue-green stones like the one I showed you are becoming more and more valuable, just like the old man said, but most of the miners are still trying to find gold and silver.

I rent a room above one of the general stores in Cerrillos. I share it with a man from Oregon who is a little older than me and knows a lot more about mining than I do. He says we need to put our money together and then we can make our own claim. I've told him all about you and the baby and the folks back home. He never seems to talk too much about himself. All I know about him is that he's called Red. I guess that's because he's got a head full of red hair.

I am glad you named our son Jessie Ray Alford. It is nice that both of our fathers are honored in the naming. I hope that in a few months, maybe after this summer, I will have money to pay for your trip here and the room for our family but everything seems to cost more here. I am trying to save as much as I can, but I had to buy new tools, pay a mining tax, and there's the rent and food. So far, I have not found out how to make more money but I'm working on it.

I long for the day we can be together again. Thank you for the letter and for the beautiful handkerchief. I only use it on Sundays when I go to church.

Always yours,
Caleb

Eve pulled out a couple more letters and glanced over them while she drank her coffee. They all seemed to say the same kind of things, how expensive it was to be in Madrid and Cerrillos, how the mining was mostly governed by the big companies who had rushed in and bought up a lot of the mineral rights, how much he longed for his wife and son, and how he hoped they would soon be able to join him. He occasionally mentioned the roommate from Oregon, Red, but there wasn't much about him either.

So far, Eve thought, there was not much

there to explain what had happened and why he was not able to send for his family to join him in New Mexico. In the few letters she had read or looked over, there had been no mention of the danger of his work or any illness to which he might have succumbed. All she could see was news from a young man writing to his wife every two weeks, longing for his home, and still searching but not finding the break he was looking for.

She pushed the letters back into the folder and finished her coffee. The loneliness of the missing miner had only worsened Eve's mood and caused her to ask the question that had been bugging her for days: What if Dorisanne was gone like the miner, leaving no trace behind?

TEN

Sister Evangeline knew what would help her sour mood. She drove the truck back to the house, parked, and headed to the garage for her bike. She needed to take her mind off Dorisanne, the missing miner, and the imminent date for her upcoming conversation with Brother Oliver at the monastery, and taking a drive on her bike was just the thing that would help her do that. Riding on the Harley always calmed her, always relaxed her, always helped her think more clearly; and after the unaccommodating conversations with her sister's colleague and boss, the Captain's questions about whether or not Eve was going back to the monastery or staying in Madrid, and the double dose of caffeine she had just enjoyed at Twila's, she needed a little calming. She needed a little relaxation. She needed to think a little more clearly. She needed a ride.

Eve's first great love had been horses, and

she'd competed in barrel racing and rodeo events from the time she was tall enough to reach a pair of stirrups. She was a natural, they had said, and she enjoyed the competitions, enjoyed riding the horses. She won a number of ribbons and awards. She was comfortable and relaxed in her rides.

But when she was a young teenager, the Captain had bought a small motorcycle as a gift for his daughters, and from that moment on, Eve left the horses and the stables and the rodeos and started racing in motocross events. Dorisanne never got a chance to try out the bike, but it hadn't really mattered. She was more of the girly-girl and Eve was the tomboy.

Right away Evangeline seemed addicted to the speed and the way it felt to take a curve or drive along the barren desert hills. She loved the motor and the weight of a bike, the control she felt gripping the handlebars and changing the gears. She had not won as many awards in the sport as she had with the horses because her mother made the Captain put a governor on her bike's speedometer, and Eve was never able to push the bike enough to get ahead of the other competitors. She complained about this her entire time racing, but her mother would not budge from her position. It was enough, she had told her daughter and husband, that she let Eve ride the motorcycle, let her race. She was not about to let her child manage her own speed. And no matter how hard Eve or her father fought, claiming this restriction put her at a terrible disadvantage, her mother toed that line. It was racing with the censored speed or no racing at all.

Eve still managed to win from time to time. Even though she wasn't the fastest, she learned skills the other riders didn't. She knew how to maneuver easily around the obstacles on the path and how to move in and out of the race traffic without being in or causing an accident. What she lost in speed she made up for in her reaction times and in her ability to veer from trouble. Still, her inability to move as quickly as she wanted in a race remained difficult for her. Oddly enough, this lack of patience showed up in other areas of her life as well.

No matter what she dealt with, Eve always felt like there was some governor on her emotions, on her spirit, that was curbing her, holding her back. It was one of the reasons she had trouble at the convent, one of the spiritual lessons she was forever forced to learn. Slow down, she had been told by her mother. Show patience, she was being taught as a nun. And riding her Harley in Madrid, away from Pecos and the monastery, away from a mother and a priest's watchful eye, finally old enough to set her own speed, go her own distance, free and out on the road, was the one place where she felt unbridled and uncensored.

Eve cranked the engine and took off. She was glad winter had finally passed and she could ride comfortably with just a jacket and jeans. She rode year-round, but it wasn't as much fun in the cold.

She started up Highway 14 and headed west toward the little town of Cerrillos. She thought she might drive around the Silver Cross Corral, up the old mining trails where John Ewing took his riders and where the body of the movie director Charles Cheston had been found. She hit fifty miles an hour, settled into her ride, and thought about her first case working with the Captain, how much she'd enjoyed digging for information and finding clues about the murderer.

She breathed in the fresh air, felt the afternoon sun on her face, the breeze in her hair stirred by the bike's speed, and remembered how it had been for her solving the mystery, how it was to have felt so alive, so passionate about something; and she remembered that it had been those feelings that had eventually led her to take this second leave of absence.

"You seem so engaged in life," Brother Oliver had first commented when she talked to him about the murder investigation in which she had been involved. "I see that your relationship with your father has deepened and become more satisfying for you both; but this time away that you have had, this medical emergency that took you home for all these weeks, has been more than just an opportunity to care for your parent."

Eve was taken aback at the time. Her own animation in her conversations about the private detective work surprised her. It wasn't until Brother Oliver made mention of her passionate descriptions of her work in Madrid that she came to realize that the search and the mystery and the solutions and the analyzing and the data gathering, even the relationships, fed her in a way that her vows and her life in the community had not. And once this had been brought to her attention, she had been deeply bothered. She went back to the monastery and secluded herself from everyone. Although Brother Oliver had not chastised her about it, Eve had felt ashamed of her excitement, disappointed that she had been lured into the things of this world so easily, troubled that she had made such a confession to her superior and to herself.

How could she have a desire to leave the monastery? It was her home. The church had been her constant companion. Falling in love with her father's profession was an accident — an unintended consequence of her stepping in to help. Now she realized that this work, this life outside the monastery, had to be considered, had to be looked at more closely. If she intended to stay as a nun, she must work through this discernment process honestly and truthfully. It was difficult work, however, unnerving to her; and even halfway through this leave of absence she had been given, she was still trying to understand what was happening with her, trying to figure out what she truly desired and felt called to. She knew as she drove along the desert highway that she was just as confused as she'd been when she and Brother Oliver made the decision that she should come back to Madrid and be with her father a while longer.

In the beginning, the call to the order, the decision to enter the monastery and become a nun, had not been difficult at all for Eve. Once she had spent some time as a novice, learning the rules and the expectations, once she had become accustomed to the gentle routine of prayer and work and worship, the hours of silence and the services that arranged the days and nights for the monks and nuns, it all had felt so natural, so right. Only in these latter years, she thought, only in the seasons since her thirty-fifth year, had she become bothered and unsettled, suddenly longing for something she had not ever felt she had missed before.

She was making the turn into Cerrillos when she saw the blue lights in her rearview mirror. She recalled seeing a police car when she'd passed the turnoff to Galisteo and had slowed down. Since she hadn't been followed, she had believed in the power of her good luck and sped up. Now, as she turned left and pulled into the parking lot of the Cerrillos Clinic, she realized her luck wasn't all that good, and she hoped that — with all the interpersonal skills she had learned from both the superiors at the convent and the Captain — she still remembered how to talk herself out of a ticket.

Eleven

Eve grinned as she saw the officer get out of the car and walk in her direction. It appeared that she wouldn't need any special skills to handle this after all. She wouldn't have to say a word.

"Sister Evangeline, if I have told you once I have told you a thousand times, wear your helmet!"

Eve jumped off the bike, kicked out the stand, and hurried over to the officer. Daniel was her friend and the Captain's former partner. He was tall, broad-shouldered, and Eve had to step up on her toes to embrace him. She felt his strong arms around her and it made her smile. He was the brother she never had and she cared deeply for him.

"Daniel, it's so good to see you! What are you doing out here?" she asked.

"Slumming," he answered, adjusting his belt after the hug.

"Yeah, well, you must be if you're having

to drive that old cruiser." She motioned with her chin toward the police car he had just exited.

"Hey, she looks big and slow on the outside, but there's some muscle under that hood."

Eve laughed.

"I caught up with you, didn't I?"

"Only because I slowed down when I saw you a couple of miles back," she noted. "I helped you out a lot."

Daniel shook his head. "You were going seventy," he said and pulled out a small leather pad from the inside of his coat jacket.

It looked as if he was going to write Eve a ticket. She pulled back and watched as he reached for a pen and clicked the top, acting as if he was starting to write out a summons. He put the pen to paper and glanced up.

"Gotcha," he said, flashing his wide, perfect grin.

She punched him hard in the arm. "That's not funny."

Daniel put away the pen and pad of paper.

"Seriously, what are you doing out here?"

"Came out to the country to see the old man," he answered. "Things are slow at the office, so I decided I'd drive out and take him to lunch. He called about some old files yesterday. I did a little digging and came up with some stuff. I thought he might like to hear it in person and have a green-chile burger at the same time."

"He'll like that," she responded. "What was he having you look for?"

"Murders from the 1890s. I assume you're working a cold case."

"A real cold case. A man came in the other day who is trying to find out what happened to his great-grandfather, a miner from North Carolina."

"This guy think his family member was that skeleton those boys found in the mines? He think the guy was murdered?"

Eve thought about the questions. "He is interested to see if the skeleton is his kin, but nah, I think the murder idea comes from the Captain. You know how he always heads down the dark path first."

"Well, it may be the right one. Seems like there were lots of murders in those days. I guess there's something to calling this the wild, wild West." He glanced into the car. "I got a box from the 1890s, homicides, most of them never tried. Looks like it was a crazy time."

"They needed good lawmen like you," Eve said, winking.

"I suspect a black man wouldn't have had much luck arresting white folk back then," Daniel said. "But your daddy" — Daniel smiled — "he'd have a jail full of those outlaws."

Eve laughed.

There was a pause. Eve could feel Daniel's eyes studying her.

"You troubled?" he finally asked.

Eve shook her head, even though she was well aware that her father's former partner knew her as well as anyone. He knew she liked to ride when she needed to clear her mind.

He studied her, appearing as if he didn't believe her or was waiting for more.

"Okay, a little, yes," she confessed.

Daniel waited. "The Captain acting up?"

She shook her head. "No, he's actually behaving himself these days," she replied. "Takes his insulin, comes to the clinic in Cerrillos, eats pretty good. He hasn't even picked a fight in two weeks," she added.

Daniel reached up and rubbed his chin as if he were perplexed. "Your father?" he asked. "In two weeks?" He paused. "You slipping him something in his sugar-free milk shakes?"

"Nah. I know," she responded, "doesn't sound like him, but he's mellowing."

"Well, I'm glad I came today to see this. I'd say you've got your own hometown miracle out here. You think the Pope will come and bless him?"

"I didn't say he was a saint, just that he had mellowed. He's still the Captain."

"Right," Daniel agreed.

He waited.

Eve shrugged. "It's Dorisanne," she said.

He frowned. "What's little sister gotten herself into now?" He leaned against the car.

Eve moved next to him. "I just can't reach her is all."

"Well, from what I remember, your sister was never one to make herself easily available. Wasn't she missing her entire senior year of high school?"

Eve smiled. "Yeah, I know. That's what the Captain says too. But I've just got a bad feeling about her. I'm worried something's wrong."

"You try the Rio?" He knew where Dorisanne worked.

Eve nodded. "They said she called in last week. She fell about a month ago, sprained her ankle. She's been out of work since the accident."

"But somebody's talked to her?"

"Yeah," Eve answered.

There was no response and she stood up away from the car. "I know. I know. She's fine. She has never been good about staying in touch. She'll call in a couple of days."

"She will. I'm sure," Daniel responded.

Eve was not convinced, but she didn't say as much. "Enjoy your time with the Captain, and don't let him get dessert," she said. "I know how he likes the pie at the Tavern."

"Green-chile burger, fries, no pie," Daniel noted.

There was a pause as the two friends watched a few cars travel past them on the highway, most of them slowing down when they saw the police car.

"So, are you giving me a ticket or not?" she asked.

He shook his head and smiled. "No, there's no ticket."

She turned and headed toward her bike.

"Get a helmet on your head," he instructed as she walked away.

"Okay," she replied. "When I get home."

And she jumped onto her bike, cranked up the engine, and drove away, thinking that just like herself, Daniel seemed a bit bothered about something too.

TWELVE

After reading police files all evening, Eve slept fitfully. The Captain had retired to his bedroom before ten o'clock. She tried going to bed herself around eleven but was unable to quit thinking about what she had read and what had been on her mind all day, so she eventually got back up, threw on her old terrycloth robe, and headed for the kitchen. She took down her favorite mug, the one her mother had liked best, the thick one with a bear's claw painted on the front that she had bought at a thrift shop. After filling it with milk, she stuck it in the microwave and waited. She leaned on the counter, her chin resting in her hand, and looked out the window above the sink. The night was a typical New Mexico night with a sky full of stars and an easy desert wind. When the microwave dinged, she walked over, retrieved the mug now filled with steaming hot milk, and headed back to the living room to continue looking over the contents of the box that Daniel had delivered to the Captain.

She read more missing person reports filed in Santa Fe County in the year 1890 by concerned family members across the country, as well as the homicide reports filed in that decade. Based upon what she'd found, it seemed to Eve that there must have been lots of folks like Caleb Alford from everywhere in the country who came to New Mexico to strike it rich and who never returned to or contacted folks in the hometowns they had left.

It surprised both Eve and Jackson that there was such a complete set of files from so many years ago. The Captain had commented that the box and the files therein were more thorough than the last bunch of reports he had worked on before retiring from the police force. Daniel had explained to them that there had been an entire collection of old reports from a century before that had been kept at the home of a history-buff sheriff named Tom Jaramillo in Santa Fe County. Jaramillo had come across them in the courthouse basement, and since they were old even when he found them in the 1940s, he was permitted to take them home, sort through them, and find a way to secure them. It had apparently become quite a project for the lawman, and the evidence of his meticulous care and work was clear.

They learned that the files had originally been kept in a dry, cool, dark environment, the center storage area of the courthouse underground department, so they were in good shape when he first discovered them. And then, when he became their caretaker, he took extra precautions, filing the reports in low-lignin storage containers with corrugated acid-free spacer boards. He put them in chronological order, making the collection easy to read and easy to follow. Except for a bit of yellowing on the edges, the papers were in excellent condition.

Reviewing them was like taking a step back in time, and the father and daughter had spent most of the evening reading some of the more interesting files to each other. It had been an enjoyable night for them both, a sort of crash course on the justice system in the western part of the country during a time when there wasn't much federal assistance in the outlying areas like the territories of New Mexico and Arizona. There were still skirmishes between the Indians and the white settlers, still struggles between the Spanish landowners and the Americans coming down the Santa Fe Trail. It truly was a wild and raucous time in the nation's history.

The two learned that Sheriff Lawson Carson was the central lawman in Santa Fe County, taking office in 1886 and staying in the position until he was shot and killed by a band of bank robbers in 1910. This information Eve found on the Internet, hoping to uncover more about the writer and keeper of the files they had started reading. The reports kept in the files were mostly written by him. Each incidence of a homicide or violent death was documented in a one-page report; missing person reports were documented in the same way. Names, dates, short descriptions, and then a longer, more in-depth summary of what Sheriff Carson did in response to the incident or concern was the standard content of each file. Eve wondered out loud to the Captain if the sheriff did all of the police work in those days, if he was officer, prosecutor, and judge for those charged with criminal offenses since there seemed to be no other names on any of the files, both those that had been closed as well as those that had remained open and unsolved.

Some of the missing person reports had the words *Found Alive* written across the top of the page. Others had *Found Dead,* all of them dated and signed by the sheriff. Some of the homicide reports had the word *Hanged* written across the entire page; others were left without a conclusion or follow-up report, appearing to Eve as if the punishment for criminals was swift and brutal or simply overlooked. All evening her mind was filled with the cowboy images from the many Westerns she'd watched as a child. She even remembered some of the stories she had heard of Kit Carson, who was known to have traveled extensively through Madrid and Cerrillos and Santa Fe County on many occasions, and she wondered if the sheriff was any kin to the brigadier general and Indian agent or if the last name was just a coincidence.

Most of the missing persons, all men, were reported to have been working in the mines, and most of the homicides had to do with fights over stolen money and property or mineral rights. None of the files, those dealing with missing miners or those dealing with murder, cited the name Caleb Alford. Although the reading was interesting, it was not proving to be beneficial to the case. Even with all of the files from the year the North Carolina miner went missing, all of them easy to read and easy to follow, it didn't appear as if there was any official report of the whereabouts of their client's great-grandfather. They'd come up empty when it came to finding any information that would be helpful to the man trying to find answers about his family member.

After going through the last files and finishing her warm milk, it was late, after midnight, and Eve tried once again to go to sleep. The milk did not help. She tossed and turned. And when she finally did fall asleep, her dreams were chaotic and overwrought with cowboys and saloons and fights and restless women searching for the men they loved and lost. Brothers, husbands, boyfriends, fathers, the images of family members trying to find someone filled Eve's mind until finally she found herself in one of the dreams, searching and searching for somebody, for something.

In the dream Eve was wearing a black scapular and her hair was short. She had just taken her first vows, and she was walking down a long hallway, opening doors on both sides, looking for something or someone. Behind the first door was a beautiful scene from her home in Madrid: Her horse from her early childhood stood at a stall window eating hay. She longed for the horse, longed to ride him again, but something else was calling her and she kept moving, opening doors and seeing people and things from her past, from before she became a nun, before she entered the convent in Pecos.

A favorite teacher, several nuns praying, a room of books, stacks of gold and silver, her mother sewing, her father — the Captain — his back turned toward her, building or repairing something placed in front of him. She stopped for a second, just as she had at all the doors, almost entering, glad to see the people she loved, eager to speak to them, but still drawn to something else, something she couldn't explain. She moved on. She opened and observed and then closed the doors, felt the delight at seeing her loved ones, felt curiosity at seeing the rooms containing money and books, and she kept moving down the hall, searching for something or someone she hadn't yet found. She felt frustrated and a little anxious, even though she didn't know what was missing.

Finally, she arrived at the end of the hall. She stopped, took in a deep breath, and understood that there was only one last door standing in front of her. She reached for the doorknob and started to turn it, but she was suddenly halted by a voice calling her from the other end of the hall.

"Eve." She heard the voice but could not tell who was calling.

"Eve." She heard it again.

"Eve! Wake up!" And then she realized the voice belonged to the Captain, and he was standing at her bedroom door, the phone in his hand.

"It's Dorisanne," he said as she finally tumbled out of bed.

THIRTEEN

"Hello," Eve called into the proffered cell phone.

There was no response.

"Hello . . ." She waited. "Hello," she called out again. "Dorisanne, are you there?"

There was only silence from the other end and then finally a dial tone. Eve looked at her father, who was leaning against the doorframe. She wondered but didn't have time to ask how he had gotten from his room to hers so quickly. His crutches were nowhere in sight. She only shook her head.

"What, she's not there?" he asked, a look of surprise on his face. "I just talked to her," he added. "Let me see," he said, and he reached out for the phone.

Eve shook her head again as she handed the phone back to him. "She's not there," she said.

The Captain took the phone and began

calling out, "Hello, Dorisanne. Hello, are you there?" He held out the phone to study it and turned back to his daughter. "I swear she was just there. I talked to her."

Eve walked past her father toward his room. "Here," she said when she returned, handing the crutches to him that she had retrieved. "Come into the kitchen. I need a glass of water." She turned down the hall and he followed behind.

In the kitchen, Eve took a pitcher of water from the refrigerator and poured herself a glass. Jackson sat down at the table. Trooper had joined them both and was lying next to his chair. The loyal companion dropped her head onto her paws.

"You want something?" she asked Jackson.

"No, I'm fine," he answered.

Eve drank some of the water and joined him at the table.

He was shaking his head, still staring at the cell phone in his hand.

Eve reached for it and he gave it to her. She scrolled through the recent calls but could not place Dorisanne's number anywhere on the list. "Your last call was from Daniel," she noted, handing the phone back to him.

He looked at the list. The call from his

former partner had come in at eleven thirty that morning; he had called just before he came into town for lunch. He snapped the phone shut. "Well, I don't care what the phone says — she called, woke me out of a deep sleep. I heard it ring, picked it up, answered it, and she said, 'Daddy, can I speak to Eve?' And I got up, hopped over to your door, and got you."

Eve didn't know what to think. Captain Jackson Divine was not one to make up tales of people calling who had not called. Even when he was in his worst state of confusion following the surgery, following too many pain medications, he had never hallucinated. This kind of behavior was like nothing she had ever experienced with him before. And yet, there was no record that Dorisanne had placed a call to him. Besides, Eve thought, she never called his cell phone, only the landline at home.

"When did she get your cell number?" she asked.

Jackson thought about the question. "I don't know. I figured you gave it to her."

Eve shook her head. "No, when I got you the phone last year, you told me not to give out the number to anybody. You didn't want it, remember, and then when I bought it I told you just to keep it for emergencies. I didn't even know you kept it on at night."

"Well, of course I keep it on at night. How else would I use it for emergencies if I didn't keep it on?"

She didn't answer. It was the middle of the night, and she was certainly in no mood to argue.

"You don't believe me?"

She shrugged. "I don't know. I was sound asleep, having some weird nun dream, when you yelled and woke me up. She wasn't on the line when you handed me the phone."

"Well, that doesn't mean I've made this whole thing up!"

Eve leaned against the back of the chair.

Neither one of them spoke for a few minutes.

Eve rose and looked at the Captain again. "Tell me what she said one more time. And how many rings were there before you woke up and answered?"

"I don't know," he replied. "It's loud, though. I can't believe it didn't wake you. And there's a stupid jingle instead of a normal ring. It sounds like a car horn."

Eve raised her eyebrows. "Could it have been a car horn?"

"A car horn with your sister's voice at the end of it?" He blew out a breath and shook his head. He started to get up from the table. "Well, this is a waste of my time. If you don't believe me, I don't need to try and persuade you."

"Sit down," she pleaded. "It's fine. I believe you. I just don't know why she called your cell phone and why she called in the middle of the night and why she asked for me and why she hung up."

"You got a cell phone?"

"Sure," Eve answered. "You know that. I got ours at the same time. I bundled," she added. "Or whatever they call it. It was cheaper that way."

"Your sister got your phone number?"

Eve thought about the question and then nodded. "Yes, I gave it to her when we got them."

"But you didn't give her mine?" He had stayed in his seat.

She shook her head. "You asked me not to."

He placed the phone back on the table and scratched his head. "Do you think I'm going crazy?"

She smiled. "I have thought a lot of things about you in my lifetime, but I have always thought I'd be the one going crazy long before you," she said.

She finished her glass of water and reached down and petted Trooper. "Did you help

101

him out of bed?" she asked, not expecting an answer but wondering how Jackson had managed to get from his bed to her door without assistance.

"I was dreaming about her," he confessed. "I was dreaming that she was calling and I couldn't get to her."

Eve suddenly thought of her own dream, wondering if that was what or rather who she was searching for as she opened and closed doors, walking down the dark hallway. What Jackson was saying somehow resonated with her, and she figured they must have been having the same dream. She was just about to ask him for details when a car horn started to sound.

FOURTEEN

"What was that?" Eve turned to Jackson. They both looked down at the phone and then toward the front window.

"It's not this thing, that's for sure," the Captain answered. "It's out there." He motioned with his chin. "It's somebody out there."

Eve waited. She was still only half awake from the first disturbance of the night and was having some difficulty tracking what was going on.

"Well, go see what it is," Jackson bellowed.

Eve shook her head, trying to get her bearings, and headed to the front door. She opened it and peered outside. The noise had stopped, and there was no one parked in the driveway or close enough on the street below to see. She was about to close the door when the horn sounded again. She pulled the door open wide and stepped outside onto the porch. After trying to determine the source of the sound, she was fairly certain that it was coming from the direction of their closest neighbors, Michael and Sarah Parker, artists who had moved to Madrid in the early nineties and who lived a couple of miles away.

She turned and walked back into the kitchen. "It's from up the road," she announced. "Sounds like it's at Michael's." She closed the door and locked it. "Should I call them?"

The Captain cleared his throat. "No, don't bother. He told me a week ago that the horn on his old truck was getting stuck, asked me then if it had bothered us." He shook his head. "That's all it is. Just that old truck horn."

Eve headed to the table and sat down across from her father. "It still could have been her," she said, referring to the phone call and to her sister trying to make contact.

"There's no record that she called. You didn't talk to her. You didn't even hear the thing ring."

"I didn't hear the car horn either; that doesn't mean anything." She started to reach out and take his hand but hesitated, thinking better of it. The Captain was not one who appreciated gestures of concern.

"I'm going back to bed," he announced

and started to get up.

"Wait," she responded. "Let's talk about this."

He sat back down. "Talk about what? That it's finally happening, that I'm starting to lose my mind?"

"Now you're just being dramatic. I never said that. You heard something. You heard Dorisanne calling. Maybe that noise out there was just a car horn, but maybe you heard everything you say you did."

"You calling me psychic now?" He studied his daughter.

"Is that better than crazy?"

There was a pause.

He shrugged. "Probably not."

"Tell me again what she said." Eve wasn't sure where she was going with this line of thinking, and she was mostly certain the Captain would have nothing to do with believing in telepathic communication, but it seemed important that he thought he'd had a call from his youngest daughter. It seemed important in a way she wasn't able to articulate.

"I picked up the phone and said hello and she said, 'Daddy let me speak to Eve.' " He glanced down at the cell phone on the table in front of him. "It wasn't her. I was just dreaming."

"Then tell me about your dream," she said, suddenly thinking about her own.

"I'm not telling you about my dream," he replied.

"Why not?"

"Because it's of no concern to you. It's just a dream, bad clams or something."

"When did you have clams?" She smiled, trying to lighten the mood.

He glowered at her. "You know what I mean. It was just something I ate or just the stuff we were going through, those files. It's nothing. It was a silly dream, and I thought it was real but it wasn't."

"Just tell me about the dream," she repeated.

He blew out a breath. "She was little, ten or eleven, had those pigtails she always wore. And she was stuck in some cave, a well, or probably a mine, since that's what I've been thinking about. And I heard her calling and I couldn't get to her, couldn't find her."

"Who was she calling?" Eve wanted to know, though not sure why it mattered.

"For me," he answered, glancing down at the phone. "She was calling for me, calling out 'Daddy,' which she hasn't called me since she was about that age."

"And then you heard the phone ring?"

"And then, apparently, I heard Michael's truck horn."

"Whatever," Eve responded. "But then you heard the noise and then she said for you to get me?"

He nodded. "Then I answered the phone and she said, 'Daddy, let me speak to Eve.' "

"And then you got out of bed and jumped to the door and called for me?"

"Yes, Detective Divine, that's exactly how it went down."

Trooper raised her head and then lowered it back to the floor.

"Don't call me that," Eve said. "And don't be so grouchy. I'm just trying to understand what happened."

"There's nothing to understand," he explained. "I had a dream. I got carried away in my dream and confused my subconscious ramblings with reality. It's not that complicated."

"Why do you do that?" Eve asked.

He seemed confused. "Do what?"

"That," she replied. "That way you have of blowing off anything other than what you can prove. Why couldn't this have been a call from Dorisanne? Why couldn't this have been some way of her trying to reach out to you, to get your attention? Why does everything have to be so scientific and factual with you? What happened to believing in hunches and intuition?"

"I believe in hunches and intuition. I don't believe in people contacting me through dreams."

"Well, I do," Eve noted. "I believe that people are connected to each other on many levels and in many ways, and sometimes those connections are not the ones we expect. Sometimes we are connected in our spirits or in our thoughts."

"You're a nun. You're supposed to believe that stuff."

"Well, you're a parent. You're supposed to believe that stuff too."

"That was your mother's role in the family."

"See there, you do believe it then, don't you?"

"I believe your mother had those kinds of connections with the two of you. She always seemed to know when you were bothered or upset, always seemed to know when something was wrong."

"So maybe now it's you that has the connections." She looked over at her father.

He glanced up.

Eve smiled. "I mean, I know it seems like a real stretch that you could have that kind of a relational gift with your daughters and all, but who's to say?" She shrugged. "Who's to say Dorisanne isn't in trouble? Who's to say she didn't send every bit of psychic energy available to her in your direction to ask for help or that Mama didn't send some message from heaven to advocate for her daughter? Who's to say they weren't both moving heaven and earth to get your attention so that they could get your help?"

He shook his head.

"What?" Eve asked, unsure of whether he was disagreeing or there was something more.

"It just seems odd is all."

"Yeah, well, anything that can't be proven with science or facts is odd to you." She picked up her glass and took it over to the sink. When she turned back around, he was still shaking his head. "What?" she asked again. "I get it. You have a hard time believing this spiritual stuff."

"It isn't that," he explained. "If she wanted my attention, why did she wake me up to ask for you?"

FIFTEEN

Caleb Alford was at the detective agency office on Firehouse Lane first thing the following morning waiting for the Captain and Eve. The sun was up, the sky a perfect blue, and there were songbirds singing, perched high in the branches of the cottonwood tree to the east of the long, rambling row of shops and offices next to the fire station.

Their client, dressed in a pair of khaki pants, a light jacket, and hiking boots, was sitting on the small wooden bench beside the front door, his back leaned against the wall. He was eating a pastry — a doughnut maybe or one of Twila's famous cinnamon buns — and a cup, probably holding coffee, Eve thought, was situated near his feet. She saw right away that the man's breakfast came from the Java Junction, and it made her wonder how long he had been in town. She glanced down at the clock on the dashboard of the truck and saw that it read ten minutes before eight. Mr. Alford was about six hours early for his scheduled appointment. She was a bit disappointed because she wanted to continue her conversation with the Captain about the events of the previous night. He had not wanted to talk about them over breakfast earlier.

"Good morning, Mr. and Ms. Divine," he called out as Eve and Jackson exited their vehicle. He stood up with his greeting.

"Div-een," the two of them replied at the same time.

"Right, sorry."

"Good morning, Mr. Alford," the Captain said. He had already slid his legs out of the truck, so he righted himself, stood up, and shut the door. "You're out bright and early."

Eve smiled and waved as she shut the driver's door and headed toward the office. She was wearing jeans and boots, and when she got to the door, she glanced down, noticing the scratches in the dirt around the front of the building. She thought about Daisy and hoped the cat was okay, safely inside, and that she had not run into trouble with some wild animal during the night.

"Yeah, I just couldn't sleep last night. I found out the skeleton isn't Caleb." He put down his pastry, wiped his hands on the front of his pants, and held out one to Eve.

"That didn't take long," Eve noted. She quickly shook his hand, stuck the key into the door lock, and hurried inside.

"You sure you want to come in here?" Jackson asked the client.

He seemed surprised by the question. "Oh, the cat," he said. "No worries, I took a pill," he noted.

"Oh good," Eve commented, not as a part of the conversation of the men just outside the door but because Daisy was waiting for her when she walked into the office. The cat was fine and Eve heaved a sigh of relief. She bent down and gave the cat a good scratch under her chin.

"They were able to tell that my DNA and the mitochondrial DNA extracted from the skeleton bones weren't a match," she heard the voice behind her say.

The two men walked in behind Eve as she picked up Daisy and moved farther into the office. She put the cat back down by her small desk, turned on the light, and then headed straight for the coffeepot that was on the table near the window. She took the empty pot into the back bathroom, rinsed it out, and filled it with water, then walked back to where the men were standing. She poured the water into the machine, put a filter in the basket, and measured out the coffee. She slid the pot back into its place and turned on the maker.

Caleb waited until Jackson made his way around his desk. The detective removed his hat, hung it on the rack beside the file cabinets, and sat down. He motioned for his client to take a seat in front of him, and Alford did. He was holding his cup, having already discarded the small pastry bag.

"I still want to find out what happened to him," Caleb said. "I'm going to hang around a while."

Eve made her way to her desk. She was choosing to let the Captain be in charge of this conversation.

"You don't have to," Jackson replied. "I can call you back in Virginia if I hear anything."

Caleb shifted in his seat. "Actually, I've met someone."

Eve glanced up.

"Oh?" the Captain responded.

"She's an officer," Caleb added. "Rochelle Kent." He crossed his legs, appeared a bit more comfortable. "We met when I first got into town."

Jackson nodded. "I know Officer Kent," he responded. "She's a fine police officer, a nice person."

There was an awkward pause.

"I'm sure it seems odd that I've met someone since I've been on this trip. I wasn't expecting anything like that. I wasn't looking for this kind of thing." He took a sip of his coffee.

"Nothing's odd about meeting someone," Jackson replied. He looked over at Eve. "That coffee ready yet?" he asked gruffly.

"Not yet," she replied.

"I know it seems weird that I want to find out what happened to a family member from more than a hundred years ago, but I just feel connected to him, and I want to find out what happened. I feel like I've been called to this search. Do you think that's possible?"

Jackson didn't respond right away. "Sure it's possible. Look, I don't believe in that hokeypokey stuff, but she does. You need to be talking to her," he finally commented and raised his chin in Eve's direction. "She's your gal when it comes to feeling called to something."

Eve rolled her eyes. "It's hocus-pocus, not hokeypokey."

Caleb turned around in his chair to get a better look at Eve. "So, you think it's possible?" he asked. "Do you think we can find out what happened to my great-grandfather?"

"I think lots of things are possible," she responded. She got up and walked over to the coffeepot. She waited a few seconds until it had finished brewing and then poured two cups. She handed one to the Captain. "You want a refill?" she asked their client.

He shook his head and repeated, "You think we can find out what happened to Caleb?"

Eve returned to her seat. "I don't know, Mr. Alford. Probably not," she said.

Jackson smiled and nodded his approval.

"But there's no harm in doing a thorough investigation," she added.

The smile faded from Jackson's face. Clearly, this was not a case he was interested in pursuing.

"I was actually planning to leave town this weekend because it seemed I had done everything I could do here. I figured you could just call me if you found anything. But then I met Rochelle, Officer Kent. It just seems like a sign that I'm supposed to stay. Does that make any sense?" He looked first at Jackson and then turned so that he could face Eve. "Does it?"

Eve looked at the client and then at her father. "It makes perfect sense. You have to read the signs."

"Then maybe you'll take me out to the mine?" he asked.

The Captain looked puzzled. "Why do you want to go out there? The skeleton wasn't your family member."

Caleb shrugged. "I'd just like to see the place, and you both know your way around out there; maybe you could drive me out?"

Eve shook her head. "That request you'll have to take up with him because actually I'm leaving town this afternoon," she said.

Jackson looked up. "And just where are you going?"

"Oh, you should know the answer to that one, Captain. I've read the signs. I'm going to Vegas."

Sixteen

"I don't know, Eve." Daniel had stopped by the office with some more police files for Jackson from the late 1800s. He had secured another year's worth from the station in Santa Fe. "Vegas?" He dropped the box onto Jackson's desk and glanced over at the Captain. He looked around. "I thought your client was here."

"He's gone down to Golden to get some gas. He wants me to drive him over to the mine where they found that body."

"That was way out past Cerrillos, wasn't it?" Daniel knew some of the details of the recent find but had not been on the team to locate the remains or manage the scene.

"Out on the Martinez property," Jackson replied.

Daniel nodded. He knew as much about the territory around Madrid as his former partner did. The two of them had spent a lot of time hiking and exploring the hills together when they were younger. He turned back to Eve. "Vegas?"

"Yes, Vegas," she answered. "How did you find out so fast?"

He tapped his forehead. "I'm just smart that way," he said.

Eve smiled. "He told you when you called to say you were stopping by."

Daniel sat on the edge of the Captain's desk. "Well, that too. You needing to blow off some steam?" He grinned.

"No, I don't need to blow off steam. I told you yesterday I'm worried about Dorisanne. I can't get any information from the people she works with. She doesn't answer her phone, and I don't know how to contact her landlord."

"Which isn't out of the ordinary," Jackson piped up.

"Which isn't out of the ordinary, that's true," Eve agreed. "But I just feel like I need to see things with my own eyes."

"If you want, I can get the police to send someone over to the apartment. I know one of the detectives out there." He looked at Jackson. "Beefy guy who used to work with us and moved over to Nevada about ten years ago."

Jackson seemed to be thinking.

"James Drennan," Daniel noted.

"Drennan," Jackson repeated. He shook his head. "I don't remember him."

Daniel turned to Eve. "He's a good guy. You want me to call over there and ask a favor?"

"No, I feel like I just want to go there myself."

Daniel nodded as if he understood. "You got your ticket yet?"

"Ticket?" She sounded surprised.

"Airline ticket. You do realize this is Las Vegas, Nevada, and not Las Vegas, New Mexico?" Daniel crossed his arms over his chest.

"Of course I realize that. But I still thought I could take the bike. What is it, eight or nine hours?"

"It's about six hundred miles," Jackson answered.

"Then I was right, it's about eight or nine hours," she responded.

Daniel and Jackson exchanged a glance.

"Are you going to tell her or am I?" Daniel wanted to know.

"You tell her," Jackson replied. "She doesn't listen to me."

"Tell her what?" Eve asked.

"That you are not driving that bike all the way to Vegas," Daniel answered. He stood up. "It's an hour flight from Albuquerque."

"I don't want to fly," she explained. "I want to drive."

"You're not driving that bike to Vegas," he repeated.

"Then I'll take the truck," she said in compromise.

Daniel shook his head. "I got some vacation days stored up, and since we're slow, I'll just take off the rest of the week."

"I don't need a driver," she exclaimed.

"No, you need a babysitter," the Captain noted. "You shouldn't be in Vegas by yourself. You're a nun for heaven's sake."

"Exactly," Eve responded. "That makes it even safer for me."

"Where do you plan on staying?" Jackson asked.

"There's a shelter there run by the Catholic diocese of the city. Some of the monks told me about it. I'll stay there."

"In a homeless shelter?" Daniel was the one asking.

Eve nodded.

"In Vegas?"

"Yes, in Vegas," she replied, incensed by their questions and their assumptions that she couldn't manage this trip alone.

"Yeah, see, that ain't happening," Daniel replied. "I'll make the hotel arrangements and I'll pick you up first thing tomorrow.

Pack for three or four days."

Eve threw up her hands and slumped back into her seat.

Daniel turned to face Jackson. He patted the top of the box he had brought in. "So, here's everything from the 1890s. There's even some stuff from 1900 in there. I thought I'd give you an extra year. I didn't look in them so I don't know exactly what's there. You think it's still the same lawman?"

Jackson reached up, pulling the box of records toward him. "Sheriff Lawson Carson is the man of the times, and it appears as if he liked to write reports."

"Yeah, what's he reporting?"

"Who stole a horse, who shot a miner, who started a fight in the bar."

"Sounds about the same as your reports." Daniel grinned.

"You're still a funny guy." Jackson opened the box and pulled out some of the files.

"Are you not giving me any choice about going with me to Vegas?" Eve was still in shock that decisions were being made without her input.

Daniel turned around to answer her. "You can pick where we stop for lunch." He turned back to the Captain. "So the man is coming back and you're driving him out to the Martinez place?"

"What's it been? A couple of weeks since they found the skeleton?" Jackson asked.

Daniel nodded. "It's probably fine. But if you want, I can go over there and check it out first."

"It's all right. I'll just drive out and see. If we can't get to the scene at least I'll have shown this guy the area around the old mine. He seems determined to check the place out."

"Okay then," Daniel said, "I'm heading back to Santa Fe and try to do some police business." He knocked on the Captain's desk, a gesture of farewell, and then walked over to Eve.

"Don't worry, little sister. I'll not get in the way of your drinking or gambling. See you in the morning." He winked and before she could respond, Daniel was out the door.

SEVENTEEN

"That's all you're taking?" Daniel took the small duffel bag from Eve's hand and placed it in the open trunk of his car.

"Why? Should I have packed more?" She walked around to the trunk and immediately noticed Daniel's large suitcase inside. "How long do you think we're going to stay?" she asked.

Daniel shut the trunk. "I just like to have the right clothes," he answered, heading over to the driver's side. He opened the door.

Eve walked to the passenger's side and then turned back toward the front door of the house. "Let me just make sure he's okay," she said and headed up the stairs.

She was met at the door by Jackson's booming voice. "I have the insulin. I know there are meals in the freezer. I can drive myself to work and I will not drive out of town. I know how to call you on your cell

123

phone. GET OUT OF HERE!" he bellowed.

"Don't forget to feed Daisy and give her some milk. She likes milk," she said as she backed away from the front porch, down the steps, and got into the car. "He's fine, by the way," she said to Daniel, who was grinning.

He started the engine and they made their way down the driveway and out onto Highway 14. They headed south, where they would pick up Interstate 40 and drive west. It was early, just after dawn, and they knew they had a full day's drive to get to Las Vegas. Eve took out her rosary and began to pray. Daniel turned to his passenger, saw what she was doing, faced the highway, and did not interrupt. After finishing her morning prayers, she wrapped her rosary around the rearview mirror and reached for the cup of coffee she had placed in the holder between the seats.

"When was the last time you were in Vegas?"

Daniel shrugged. "It's been about six months. I usually go twice a year."

Eve was surprised. She didn't know her father's former partner made the trip that often. "You like the tables or the ladies?" she asked, smiling.

He shook his head. "No, it isn't for the gambling," he answered. "Or for the women," he added. "Well, maybe just one." He turned to Eve and winked.

Eve didn't respond. She thought about what he was saying and soon caught on. "I can't believe it. You go out there to check on her," she surmised.

Daniel glanced back in her direction. He didn't respond at first.

"How long have you been doing this?" she asked.

He shrugged. "A while. It always worried Jackson that she was out there without anybody watching over her. And it worried him even more after she married that boy. So, I got nothing better to do and I've always enjoyed a road trip. I figure Vegas is as good a place to visit as any."

Eve placed her coffee back in the holder and leaned back in her seat. The news surprised her at first, but then it seemed exactly in the man's character. She even wondered whether he had driven over to Pecos to check on her. "Do you visit with her when you go? Does she know you're in town?"

"Sometimes," he replied. "I used to take her out for dinner, give her a little extra money. She seemed to like the company.

But a few years ago, after she got married, it seemed like she resented my trips. She said I was a spy and that I shouldn't waste my money driving down there just to go back to Madrid and give a report to the Captain. By then I was sort of enjoying my little getaways and decided to keep going. I found a great hotel at the end of the Strip, a cheap dinner buffet that serves the best crab legs you can find in the Southwest, and a few stores where I like to shop. I relax when I'm there. I told her that, but she didn't believe me. So since then I haven't called her or tried to meet her for a meal. I just go to the lounge where she works, eyeball her, make sure she looks okay."

"And the last few times, was she okay?"

Daniel chewed on the inside of his bottom lip. He shook his head. "I couldn't tell. She's talked to me less and less in the last couple of years. She acts jumpy a lot of the time. That boy, Robbie, he's a troublemaker, that's for sure."

Eve thought about her sister's husband. The truth was that she didn't know much about him. Dorisanne had met him when she moved to Las Vegas, and since Eve didn't travel so much while living at the monastery and Dorisanne never came home, she had only met her brother-in-law a couple of times. Once at the wedding and the other time at her mother's funeral. He was polite in his conversations with the Divine family, but their interaction certainly wasn't anything close to intimate.

"She told me once that he had money problems," she said, as if to prove to herself that she knew a little bit about her sister's life. It was the only thing she could say with certainty.

Daniel laughed. "That's an understatement if I've ever heard one."

"Why?"

"He has a gambling problem, and he borrows from the wrong sort of people. Dorisanne keeps finding ways to bail him out."

Eve thought about this and began to wonder how much money the Captain really had given to her. There were a lot of things about her sister's relationship with their parents that she never knew.

"Of course I tried to tell her that she can't keep doing that. And she told me that she gave him an ultimatum, but it's like a woman in an abusive situation. She keeps making excuses for him, saying he's getting help, that he's stopped." He shook his head. "I don't understand you women."

Eve looked in his direction. "Excuse me?"

"Oh, I'm not talking about you. I never worried about you getting hooked up with the wrong guy. You were always too smart for that."

"How do you know that?"

"Girl, I've been watching you and your sister since the time you were in pigtails and braces."

"Yeah, but how come you never worried about me?"

"I didn't say I didn't worry about you. I said I didn't worry about you getting hooked up with the wrong guy. You brought along your own set of issues for me to worry about."

"Like what?" This conversation intrigued Eve.

"Like you on them horses and then on the bikes. You about drove your mama crazy with how fast you would go."

She knew her mother's concern, but hearing this made her wonder about something else. "What did the Captain think?"

Daniel smiled. "He worried a little, but for some reason he figured you would be okay. He thought you were more like him — strong, tough. He always thought you could handle the hard stuff."

Eve considered this explanation regarding Jackson's parenting. When her mother

would complain about her recreational out-
ings, when she would try to make her
husband curb Eve's enthusiasm for speed
and danger, and when he would shrug off
the worry, Eve had simply thought he was
ignoring her, didn't really care about her.
Now she was hearing that he did notice
what she was doing, that he did keep up
with her activities, he just thought she was
smart or not as vulnerable somehow as her
sister. She felt surprised and a little pleased
at learning this.

"What made you think I wouldn't get all
girly and date bad boys like Dorisanne?"

Daniel looked over at Eve. "I guess I was
like Jackson. I could always see you were
too smart for that kind of thing. You never
seemed to care too much about what people
thought about you."

"I cared," she responded.

"Yeah, I know. Everybody cares about that
at some level. But you just always seemed
to know yourself better than most kids. You
always seemed to know what was important
to you, what you wanted, and you went for
it. You never waited for somebody else's approval. Barrel racing, dirt bike contests, going overseas for that semester, joining the
convent — you always seem to know what's
right for you."

Eve thought about her friend's assessment and wondered if that's how her life appeared to others. She also wondered, if that was true, when it had all changed. She was certainly not nearly so confident in her desires or choices at the present time. She wondered if Daniel could see that as well, and she was just about to ask when the phone in her pocket began to ring.

EIGHTEEN

"Hello," she answered as she flipped open the phone and took the call.

Daniel glanced over at Eve as he drove and then reached inside a plastic bag that had been placed between them. He took out a handful of trail mix and began snacking.

"It's me," came the loud and gruff response.

"Jackson?" Daniel asked.

Eve nodded. "Yes, what's wrong?"

"Nothing's wrong," he yelled.

"You don't have to talk so loud," Eve explained. "I can hear you fine."

"Right," he yelled again.

"So why did you call?" she wanted to know.

"The files Daniel brought," came the answer.

"Yes, what about them?" She'd gone to bed reading the files from 1891 but had not found any mention of the miner Caleb Alford. She had put those back in the box and left the box on the kitchen counter. She told the Captain that before she left. He must have started his reading of them right away.

"I found something," he reported.

"Is it a police report?" she asked.

"No, not anything like that. This was in a different set of files, a book, a county record book."

"Okay," she responded, waiting for the rest of the news.

"The record book of marriage licenses," he explained.

"Caleb Alford was already married," she responded.

"Yep."

"So what did you find in the book?"

There was a pause. Eve realized he was waiting for her to figure it out on her own. And in a few seconds she did.

"You found his name in there?"

"Yep."

Eve considered this bit of news. "So he came to Madrid telling his family back in North Carolina that he would send for them, and instead he came out here and married somebody else."

"Yep," was the repeated answer.

"Huh." Eve was surprised. Suddenly, she thought of the man who had hired the two of them, the man from Virginia who was hoping to find out how his great-grandfather had died, what had happened to him that prevented him from ever returning to his family. She wondered how he would take this bit of news, and she wondered how the Captain planned to tell him.

"I'm going to let you break the news," he said as if he had read her mind. "When you get back from Vegas, you can tell him his great-grandfather was a polygamist. I figure you'd be the better one to offer that bit of information than me."

"What makes you think that?" She turned to look at Daniel, who was watching the road and eating.

"You should be able to figure out how to wrap it up nice. That's what you religious people seem to know how to do real good. Wrap up the bad news in a nice package and make it sound not so bad."

Eve shook her head. "I'll tell him when I get home," she said. "In the meantime, you need to call Epi Salazar and find out what he wants us to do about finding that gold. He's still trying to hire you, and I told him you'd call him today. It sounds like there might be more than gold buried out there, so be careful."

"Right," the Captain noted. "I'll drive over

there later and talk to him in person."

"Okay."

"How far have you gotten?" he wanted to know.

Eve dropped the phone away from her mouth. "He wants to know how far we've driven," she said to Daniel.

"Tell him we're in Gallup," Daniel replied. He dusted off the crumbs from the front of his legs and held out the bag to Eve, offering some of his trail mix.

She shook her head. "Gal—"

"I heard him," Jackson interrupted her. "Call me when you get to Nevada," he said, and then, before she could reply, he hung up.

She looked at the cell phone in her hand. "Well, it doesn't appear as if the cell phone has improved his telephone manners."

Daniel laughed. "Made him talk louder," he commented.

"There's that," she said.

"So the old miner had two families." Daniel had overheard the report. "Hey, can you hand me a soda from the cooler?"

"Looks like it." Eve closed the phone and placed it in her pocket before bending down to open the cooler at her feet. She took out a drink and handed it to Daniel. "He thinks I should be the one to tell his great-grandson," she added.

"Heard that too," he said, popping the top and taking a swallow.

He turned to face her. "You up for that?"

Eve shrugged. "I don't know," she answered. And then she studied him. "How about you? How do you break that kind of bad news?"

He placed the drink in the holder near the console and turned back to face the road. "You mean the kind of bad news that says your family member, your loved one, isn't the person you thought he was? You talking about that bit of bad news?"

"Yeah."

He shook his head. "Just the facts, ma'am," he answered and smiled. "Just tell them the facts."

Eve hoped there was more advice coming. And there was.

"They usually don't believe it at first, want to see the proof. So then you show them the arrest warrants or the explicit photographs or the confession document, whatever you got, and then they usually ask that you leave them alone."

"And do you?" she asked, curious about this police procedure.

"Sometimes, I mean I do if I can. But sometimes if you're up against a deadline, you have to ask them some questions. 'When did you see him last? Do you know where he is? Did you have any idea about this behavior?' That kind of thing. But yeah, mostly I try to give them a day to sit with the bad news and then come back with the questions. But it's hard," he admitted. "Nobody likes to know they've been duped."

"Duped," she repeated. "That's a nice way to put it."

"How would you put it?" he asked.

"Betrayed, lied to, deceived . . ."

"Duped doesn't sting as much," he noted.

Eve nodded. She thought about the client from Virginia. Mr. Alford had never expressed a great loyalty for his long-lost family member, but she figured he hadn't thought the worst about him either. Even if he was a few generations removed, the news that his great-grandfather had left his young wife and soon-to-be-born son, moved to another state, waited a brief time, and then married again, was not news anyone would want to hear.

"What do you think about that?" she asked.

"About what?"

"About having a second family, about never getting a divorce, never breaking

136

things off with the original family, but just starting up all over again as if you were single, as if you didn't have another wife and child?"

Daniel reached up and pulled on the shoulder strap of his seat belt. "It happens more often than you think," he responded. "People can pretend a lot of things about themselves — that they're single, that they're in love for the first time, that they're faithful, that they won't get caught. I've been doing police business a long time, and I've seen people make choices I can't figure out for the life of me. Maybe your boy got out here and learned things about himself he never got to know back home. Maybe he realized he wasn't really the guy he thought he was and he didn't want to face it so he just started over. Maybe he got away from his mama and daddy and the childhood sweetheart he'd married and realized that all he really wanted was to get out of the South, not to start a family and run a farm, not even to mine for treasures; maybe all he really wanted was just to get away."

Eve turned away from him and faced ahead. Something about what Daniel said rang true and felt somehow a little too familiar. She gazed out the window. The New Mexico sky was bright blue with only a few clouds moving across the horizon. The hills were a bit more green because of the recent rain, and she drew in a deep breath, watching the land she loved, the desert, as they sped past.

NINETEEN

"Two rooms," she heard Daniel telling the clerk at the front desk. "And it's Divine," he said, pronouncing her name correctly. "Not Divine," the way it was usually voiced. Eve was standing in the small lobby looking out the window in the direction of what Daniel had told her was "the Strip." There was a small sitting area near the counter with an overstuffed sofa, two chairs, and a long table situated in the center. The lobby appeared to have been recently renovated and painted, the walls were bright and without blemish, and the furniture showed no wear.

The clerk was wearing a blue blazer and a red tie, and suddenly Eve felt a bit underdressed. She looked down at the outfit she had been wearing most days since leaving the monastery, old jeans and a long-sleeved Western shirt. She noticed the mud on her boots and looked around, hoping she hadn't tracked dirt onto the clean tan carpet. She wondered if she should have just worn her habit, if wearing the jeans and snap-button shirt didn't set her apart even more than the long robes. She still felt so unaccustomed to the ways of the world.

She turned back to the view out the window. It was late, and yet there were so many neon flashing lights you couldn't even tell that night had fallen. On the way to the hotel, Daniel had driven right through it all, giving her a close look at the entertainment center of the town. It was like nothing she had ever seen. She knew Daniel drove that way just so he could watch her jaws drop.

Dorisanne had sent pictures and Eve had certainly heard lots of stories, but Las Vegas was bigger and brighter and more of everything than Eve had ever imagined. It was like an amusement park or the midway at the New Mexico State Fair, only flashier and bolder. She stood at the hotel lobby window and remembered a conversation with her sister in which she had asked her what it was that she liked about the gambling town set down in the middle of the desert, why it was she had chosen it for her home.

Dorisanne, back in New Mexico for some holiday or short vacation, had thought about the question, and then her face had softened into a big grin. "It's just so wide open," she had answered Eve. "There's nothing that you can't find or do or try. It's like anything's possible there."

And according to what Daniel had explained as they arrived at the outskirts of the city, over the last ten years it had only gotten wider. She turned just as he was heading in her direction.

"You want to grab something to eat?" he asked.

"I want to go to her apartment," Eve answered. She was antsy after the long trip, and even though she was tired, she didn't want to prolong her search. The city was bigger and probably more dangerous than she had imagined.

Daniel nodded. "Okay, let's put our bags in the room and we'll head out," he said. He handed her a key.

Eve looked at the thin card, not sure if she knew how to use it, but she didn't worry because she figured Daniel would help her get into her room. She was glad that he had come with her. Now that she was in Las Vegas, she understood that she would never have been able to navigate such a place on her own.

She followed him out to the car, stood at the trunk, and when it was opened, pulled out her small duffel bag, sliding the strap across her shoulder. She watched Daniel as he yanked out his large suitcase and set it next to him.

"You need some help with that?" she asked, teasing him.

"Funny girl," he replied, shutting the trunk. "This way." And he headed back into the lobby and over to the elevators, pushed the button, and held the door while Eve walked in. He moved in behind her and reached in front of her, hitting the button for the top floor. She looked at him with raised eyebrows.

"What?" he asked.

"You must come here more than you say," she answered. "Top floor?"

"The manager has a soft spot for police officers. She likes to take care of me." He winked.

Eve smiled. "I don't really need to hear anything else."

The doors opened and Daniel led her to her room. He took the key from her, and she was able to see how the key slid into the lock. When it opened and she walked in, she couldn't help herself, she dropped her bag at the same time her mouth fell wide open. "Are you sure this is just for one person?" she asked as Daniel came in and stood beside her. There was a huge king-size bed with a dozen pillows meticulously placed near the headboard, a long narrow chest of drawers with a flat-screen television situated on top, and a large desk and rolling office chair near the window. She saw the open door to the bathroom and could see from the door that it was bigger than the one all the nuns shared at the monastery.

"I'll be right next door," he replied, smiling, seeming to enjoy Eve's first response to their lodging. "We have adjoining rooms," he explained. He walked over and opened the curtains, and the flashing lights from the Strip poured through the window. "Great view," he said as he walked back to the door. "Just let me throw my bag in and freshen up and I'll be ready to go."

Eve felt her head nod up and down. She was still in a state of shock over the size of the hotel room and the glare of the city below her. She heard the door close behind her, but suddenly, all she could hear was her sister's voice.

"It's so beautiful, Eve," Dorisanne had told her after she first arrived in Vegas. She had called the convent and Eve had answered. "It's like a party all the time, a glorious, spectacular grown-ups' party twenty-four hours a day."

Eve moved closer to the window as she recalled the conversation she'd had with Dorisanne just after she had relocated to Nevada. Eve had recently taken her final vows and had been received as a nun in full standing as a member of the community. Just as her sister had fallen in love with Vegas, she was in love with Pecos and Our Lady of Guadalupe Abbey.

"Do people want to be at a party all the time?" she had asked, knowing that she couldn't imagine life without order, without silence and prayer and quiet worship.

Dorisanne laughed. "You've been brainwashed by those monks," she replied. "Most people, yes," she answered. "Most people want to think that their lives are exciting and brilliant and something that they have to stay awake for. Most people want their lives to be like this. Vegas is amazing. It twinkles and shines all the time."

Eve had thought about what her sister was saying. She thought about Dorisanne and how she had always been drawn to things that were bright and flashy. Since she was a little girl she had loved the lights of the stage. This discovery had occurred at a very young age when their mother had taken her two daughters to a show at a concert hall in Albuquerque. It was some kind of a Disney production about a princess; Eve didn't recall the details. She did remember, however, that there were fancy costumes and big dance numbers, and while Eve ended up sleeping through most of the performances or trying to read the entire program, her little sister had come to life.

She stood on her seat the entire time, oohing and ahhing over every singer and dancer. As soon as the houselights went down and the curtains were raised, it was easy to see that Dorisanne was hooked. And from that point on, she made sure that she was signed up for every dance class they offered in Cerrillos and Madrid, even making the Captain drive her to Santa Fe when she was old enough to take classes at a dance studio that held elaborate recitals at the end of every year.

As a young girl, Eve had taken to horses and fast bikes, wanting the dirt paths and twisting mining roads of the high desert, while Dorisanne had wanted only to be onstage. Lights and action and music and applause, that was what she craved. And after all those years of thinking it was just the desire to get away from the small town of Madrid or just that she had a good job or later because she was married to a Vegas man, Eve now understood the real draw of this town for her sister. It was like living on a stage. It was all Dorisanne had ever really wanted.

"You ready?" Daniel had returned and was standing at the door.

"It's something, isn't it?" he asked as she remained at the window. "It's like Disney World for grown-ups."

"And Dorisanne thinks she has finally become the princess." Eve turned around and headed out of the room.

TWENTY

It didn't take Eve long to realize that not all of Las Vegas was as bright and beautiful as the section of town where they were staying. Once Daniel turned the car in the direction of Dorisanne's address, the shine of the famous desert city quickly faded.

"Wow, I can actually see that it's night," Eve commented as they drove into the darkness. "I was thinking I needed to get out my sunglasses driving down that street. It's like Hollywood Boulevard or something." She turned to Daniel, who was suddenly grinning. "What?" she asked.

"What do you know about Hollywood Boulevard?"

"I went to L.A.," she told him, a bit offended at his question. "The cabdriver took me to some of the famous places before I left town."

"Well, Hollywood Boulevard doesn't have anything on the Strip," he commented.

"Yeah, that's true," she agreed.

There was a pause.

"You didn't really ask a cabdriver to take you to Hollywood Boulevard, did you?" he questioned her.

She glanced away. "Well, maybe I just happened to see the famous road while I was on my way somewhere else."

Daniel grinned. "The cathedral?"

"Harley-Davidson store," she replied.

Daniel laughed. "Should have known. You didn't happen to buy a helmet, did you?"

"No. I looked at them, though."

Daniel eyed her. "Are you telling the truth?"

"Yeah, I saw them on a shelf when I walked in." She smiled. "Anyway, enough about that. Vegas is one lit-up city, that's for sure," she said, having had all of that conversation she wanted. "It's like they don't want you to know it's night. It's as if they don't want you to be able to tell what time it is."

"That's the strategy in the casinos," he noted.

"Why?" Eve wanted to know.

"So you won't realize how long you've been standing at the tables or sitting at a slot machine," Daniel answered. "No clocks, no reality," he added. "The whole town is an illusion, a place to think you're somewhere that you're not."

"Or somebody you're not," she added, wondering if that was part of the draw for her sister.

"Yeah, I guess we all have our little escape fantasies," Daniel responded.

"You talking about our boy from the 1800s again?"

He shrugged. "I don't know. I guess I'm talking about anybody. Aren't most people looking for a way out of the life they've made for themselves?"

Eve was surprised. "I don't think so," she answered. "I figured most people liked their lives."

Daniel turned to look at her. "You actually think that?"

"Yeah, I guess," she responded. "Why? Don't you?"

"Don't I what?" he asked. "What are you wanting to know? Don't I think that most people like their lives, or don't I like mine?"

She thought about the question he was asking. "I don't know, how about both?"

There was a pause.

"I think most people like their lives okay, but if they had an out, if they could escape even just for a weekend or if they were allowed out for a month, they would take the opportunity. They do." He reached up and rubbed his chin, then placed his arm on the side of the door. "That's why this town is so popular," he added. "That's exactly what most of those people walking down the Strip are doing."

"Escaping?"

He nodded. "Exactly. They're trying to imagine what their lives might look like if they were in a totally free zone."

"Only nothing about that place looks free," she commented. "I saw the price of our hotel rooms. Speaking of which, I want to help pay for this trip."

"It's not a problem," he said, waving away her offer. "But I'm not talking about this place being financially free."

"Then what?"

"I'm talking about being judgment-free. No consequences, no rules."

"But that's not real life," she argued. "Nobody can live without consequences, without rules. Even Vegas has rules."

"Well, let's just say they're a little more lax than the kind of rules and consequences that most people are used to and expect."

"That explains why people come here for a weekend or a bachelor's party, but why would somebody want to live here? Why does Dorisanne like it here so much?"

"She's a dancer," Daniel answered.

"Yeah, that part I know." Eve sighed and studied the scenery outside her window. There were a few houses, a strip of run-down motels, and a few pawnshops. She turned back to Daniel. "And she loves the bright lights and the drama of a place like this. I get that. But I don't think of my sister as being so hedonistic that she doesn't want rules and boundaries. She did get married, after all. That's a relationship with certain rules and boundaries, right?"

"Yes, I suppose it is." He paused a moment and then continued. "I think she likes the allure of a fantasy life too. I think she likes the thought of being away from reality as much as the next person. You know, if you think about it, it's not very different from the choice you made."

"What?" This comparison surprised Eve. "How can Las Vegas be anything like taking vows and living in a religious community?"

He didn't reply right away. She waited as he signaled and made a right turn.

"Oh, I get it," she answered herself. "You think that choosing to join an order is a kind of escape just like coming to Vegas can be. You think I did it to get away from reality?"

He lifted his shoulders slightly. "In that long view, they are both paths different from most people's realities. You two are very different women, but in some ways, you have both done the same thing."

"We both left Madrid," she said. "We both left the small town where we were born and raised."

"And you both landed in places where most everyone else just visits once in a while."

"Except more people visit Dorisanne's place than visit mine." She looked ahead and noticed they were coming to an area with several apartment complexes. There were names like Desert Sun Apartments, Desert Wind Luxury Townhomes, and Desert Sky Condos. She wondered if they were getting close to where Dorisanne lived.

"When are you expected back to your place?" he asked, raising the issue she had avoided for the entire trip.

"Three weeks," she answered.

"You want to talk about it?" He started slowing as he made a turn onto a small side street.

She shook her head and he didn't push.

The two were quiet as he pulled into an apartment complex parking lot and stopped. She noticed the sign as they entered, "Desert Home Place," and she looked around at the mostly nondescript large brick buildings in front of them, thinking that the complex looked nothing like the desert home she and her sister had grown up in. The parking lot was well-lit but mostly empty, and Eve wondered if everyone who lived there worked late hours.

"This is it," he said as he put the engine in Park. "Welcome to your sister's world."

TWENTY-ONE

Dorisanne's apartment complex appeared to be made up of eight or ten brick buildings, each one three stories high. There were thick, wide sets of cement stairs in the center of each building, and it appeared as if there was a unit in each corner and two apartments side by side on the main walkways. "Well, what do we do now?" Eve asked.

"I go in," Daniel answered, shutting down the engine.

Eve studied the place. It was not a bad-looking housing area, but it was also not anything she would consider to be high-end. She wondered how much Dorisanne paid to live there but then realized it would mean very little to her. She hadn't paid rent or utilities or insurance or even a car payment since she was in college. And even then, she didn't really pay the bills. Those all went to her parents and she simply lived on an allowance.

Dorisanne may have had trouble managing her money and often relied upon the assistance of others to help her make it month to month, but she still knew a lot more about living in reality than Eve did. Maybe Daniel was right, she thought. Maybe the convent was a kind of escape. She certainly never had to worry about her own financial security and well-being as a nun.

"Do you know which one is hers?"

Daniel glanced around. "It's around back, south side." He unfastened his seat belt and pulled the key out of the ignition and handed the set to Eve. "You wait here. I'll go knock on the door. If she answers, I'll come and get you. If there's no answer, I'll come and tell you, and then I'll try to find the manager and see if he'll let us in. Lock the door behind me."

Eve didn't respond, but when Daniel got out of the driver's seat and walked around the car, she was waiting there.

"I thought I told you to wait."

She shrugged. "I'm not that kind of girl," she answered, smiling.

Daniel shook his head. "Well, give me back my keys."

She handed him the set and he locked the car. He started walking toward the build-

155

ing, and Eve hustled to catch up.

They walked around the corner of the first building and up the stairs in the back. "She lives on the second floor," she said softly, recalling the conversation she'd had with the Captain about Dorisanne's fall and his thought that she was not telling the truth about how it happened. She had been wrong in thinking her sister's apartment was on the ground floor, and Dorisanne hadn't lied.

Daniel waited until Eve was next to him, and they both stood in front of the unit right at the top of the stairs and looked at the door marked with a large F. The curtains in the front window were closed, and there were no lights on inside.

If she's in there, thought Eve, *she's asleep or hiding.*

Daniel knocked.

They waited.

He knocked again, this time calling out her name. "Dorisanne," he spoke to the door. "Dorisanne, it's Daniel. You in there?"

There was no response.

"Maybe we should have gone to the Rio first," Eve suggested.

Daniel knocked again.

Eve stepped away and tried peeking through the front window. There was one narrow opening between the curtains and she cupped her hands, pressing her face against the glass, trying to see inside.

"She ain't here," came a voice that startled Eve, causing her to jump back, right into Daniel. She quickly looked in the direction the voice had come from. Suddenly, Daniel was beside her, his arm shielding her. They were both staring at someone peering at them from the unit next to Dorisanne's, A woman, blocked by the door, was standing there, the chain lock in place, her face and body barely visible. "She ain't here," the woman said again.

"Do you know when she'll be back?" Daniel asked, dropping his arm away from Eve, no longer perceiving a threat.

"You a cop?" The door closed a little more.

"I'm a friend," Daniel answered.

There was no response.

"I'm her sister," Eve spoke up. "I'm Dorisanne's sister."

The door opened again slightly.

"You the nun?"

Eve wondered if Dorisanne told everyone that her older sister had taken vows. It seemed that every time she met someone who knew Dorisanne, they always knew of her chosen vocation.

"Yes," she answered, hoping it would bode

well with her sister's neighbor.

"You don't look like no nun," the woman noted.

"Yes, well —"

Daniel interrupted. "When was the last time you saw Dorisanne?"

The woman pulled the door closed a bit more and Eve rested her hand on Daniel's arm, a kind of restraint on his participation in the conversation.

"We just got here from New Mexico," Eve volunteered. "We've been worried about Dorisanne. We haven't heard from her in a couple of weeks, and so we came down here to make sure she's okay."

She waited. The door in front of her was still only slightly opened.

"She's been gone all week," the woman responded. "I ain't seen her in about a week."

There was a voice from behind the woman, a man's voice, asking who she was talking to.

She yelled back, "There's some people here looking for Dorisanne!"

The man said something in reply, but Eve couldn't make it out. Abruptly, the door closed. Eve turned to Daniel, who stood watching. She was about to knock when the door opened completely and the woman came out onto the landing very quickly and closed the door behind her.

She was wearing a thin robe that was open and barely covering a skimpy one-piece outfit. It was gold and studded with sequins. Her blond hair was in curlers and she had on a pair of large fuzzy slippers. She had long red fingernails and dark red lips that had stained the end of the cigarette dangling from the corner of her mouth. Her makeup appeared fresh, and Eve assumed she was getting ready for work.

"Dorisanne and Robbie left last week. It seemed like they were in a hurry. She told me they were going on a trip and would be back soon and not to let anybody in their place." The woman took out the cigarette and blew a puff of smoke above Eve's head and looked nervously toward the door behind her.

"She didn't tell you where they were going?" Daniel wanted to know.

The woman looked up at him. She seemed to be studying him. "I've seen you here before," she said. "You're the cop that worked with Dorisanne's old man."

"I'm Daniel," he introduced himself.

She didn't respond but rather eyed him suspiciously. She took another drag from her cigarette and gave a slight nod.

The man's voice yelled from inside the apartment. "Pauline! Where you at?"

She jumped. "Look, I got to go. I ain't supposed to be talking to no cops," she said and turned back to her apartment.

Eve caught her by the arm. "Is there anything else you know?" She knew she sounded a little desperate.

Pauline pulled her arm away and shook her head. "Just a trip, they said." And she opened the door and headed back inside, leaving Daniel and Eve standing at the closed door.

Twenty-Two

"Let's go get something to eat," Daniel suggested.

Eve glanced once more at her sister's locked apartment and the one next door, feeling torn about wanting to try to have a longer conversation with Pauline. She blew out a breath, chose not to knock once more on the neighbor's door, and followed him down the stairs to the car. They got in and he started the engine. They both sat watching the building.

"She knows more than what she's saying," Eve finally said, shaking her head.

"Yeah, well, I don't think we'll hear anything else while her boyfriend is in there." He pulled out of the parking place and stopped at the end of the driveway and looked in both directions before pulling out onto the street. "Did you see the bruise under her eye?" he asked.

"Yeah, and the ones on her arms," she

answered, thinking about the blue-black marks covered with a thick layer of makeup on her face and the other ones forming a kind of chain around both wrists. Eve had noticed them when she took the drags off her cigarette, the sleeves of the robe dropping away for a clear view of the wounds.

Eve pulled at her seat belt, stretched out her legs, and slid down a bit in the passenger's seat. "We have a lot of abused women come to the convent. I guess since we're right off the highway, we're an easy place to get to. We usually try to bandage them up and get them to the hospital or the shelter, but sometimes they stay with us for a while." She shook her head. "When we offer to call the police, most of them ask us not to."

"Yeah, even when we're called, a lot of the women don't want to file a report. Of course, now New Mexico has an ordinance in place that if the police are called to a domestic dispute, somebody's getting in the backseat of a cruiser. We're taking somebody to jail. It's helped a lot, but still, in the end, usually the victims won't follow through." He tightened his grip on the steering wheel.

"How can a woman stay in a relationship like that, especially in this day and time where there are more options for victims?"

She crossed herself as she thought about the girls who showed up and left the monastery. "I just don't understand," Eve confessed.

"Well, most people don't," Daniel explained. "But once you get in a relationship like that, it's really hard to get out. It's like the women get stuck or their brains freeze. I don't know what it is, but I've seen more women stay with the guys who beat them up than I've seen leave." He paused, seemed to be thinking. "Sometimes if there are children or somebody else gets beat up, they'll find what it takes to leave, but even then . . ." His voice trailed off.

Eve thought about the women who arrived at Our Lady of Guadalupe in the middle of the night. The calls she had received from somebody at the front gate, the women standing there, begging to be let in, claiming that they were running from a husband or a boyfriend that everyone at the convent hoped hadn't followed them to Pecos.

Since she had been in community there, she had probably opened that gate after midnight a hundred times, sometimes even to the same women over and over. She had tried talking them into going to a shelter or getting them a bus ticket to go somewhere to be with family, but most of them would

163

nurse their wounds for a day or two, and then, before one of the sisters or monks could meet with them to discuss their options and make a plan of action, they would leave. Secretly, during a worship time or when most everyone was sleeping, they'd sneak away without any of the help they needed. They would exit in the dark of night in the very same way they had arrived.

Eve thought about one girl, Trina, who came to the religious community at least three times one year, each time more bruised, each time requiring more care, the abuse growing more and more severe. Several of the sisters and even Brother Oliver had tried to talk her out of going back to her abusive boyfriend, promised her a place to stay, help in finding work, money, anything to keep her away from the man who beat her. But Trina would always go back. Finally, Sister Mary Edith had discovered Trina's name in the obituaries. She had taken her last beating. She had been killed.

"Wait a minute." Eve spoke up, trying to shake the memory of Trina from her thoughts.

Daniel quickly turned in her direction.

"You don't think Robbie beats Dorisanne, do you?"

Daniel glanced back at the road and didn't respond right away. Eve could see that he was driving slowly and carefully back to the center of town.

She waited, hoping for some confirmation that her sister wasn't another statistic, wasn't in a domestic abuse situation, wasn't like her neighbor Pauline and spending her evenings trying to cover up the wounds and scars. She closed her eyes and then felt Daniel's hand on her shoulder. She looked up.

"I don't think so," he finally replied. "I've seen them together, and she doesn't seem afraid of him. She doesn't have that look in her eye that you usually see." He pulled his hand away and shook his head. "The look that Pauline had when the guy from the back of the apartment yelled her name. You saw that, right?"

Eve nodded.

"But I'll be honest," he continued. "There's really no profile for an abuser. I can't tell you how many times I've been surprised by the men I've brought in and even more surprised by their victims. So I can't really say for sure," he said. "But I don't think he's threatened her or hurt her. I don't think he's made her go with him. I just think he's in money trouble again, and she's taken off with Robbie for her own safety."

Eve agreed. At least what Daniel was saying felt like some reassurance. And yet, even as she felt some comfort in Daniel's opinion, when she thought about it, it didn't really seem to matter at this point whether Dorisanne was in a physically abusive relationship with her husband or not. Because even if he didn't beat her, it certainly seemed as if he had brought her into something dangerous, some kind of unsafe situation; and whether he meant it to be this way or not, he had put his wife at risk. Eve didn't know the details, but it appeared as if he was responsible for her quick departure from their home and her lack of contact with her neighbors or her family. She leaned back against the seat and closed her eyes.

For the first time since she'd actually begun to worry about her sister, Eve felt a sudden rush of anxiety, her hands starting to sweat. She wished it wasn't so, but her intuitions had been correct: Something was terribly wrong with Dorisanne.

She reached up and removed the rosary from the rearview mirror and began reciting the familiar prayer: "Hail Mary, full of grace . . ."

TWENTY-THREE

They stopped at a diner on the edge of the Strip, a place Daniel knew and liked. They ordered their meals and sat in silence. Eve was at a loss. She realized she didn't know anything about Dorisanne's life in Las Vegas, and without any knowledge of Dorisanne's friends or hangouts, she had no suggestions as to where they might search for her sister. At least Daniel knew where she lived and how to get to her place of work, but it was feeling like they were quickly coming to a dead end.

"We can go to the Rio when we're finished eating," Daniel said. He seemed to read Eve's thoughts. "Or I can drop you off at the hotel if you don't want to go," he added. "It's late. I don't mind going by myself."

"No, I'd like to go," she responded. She shook her head. "But I doubt anybody there has anything new to add to the fact that she's been gone a week. The guys I talked to on the phone didn't seem to know much more about where she might be." She stirred some sugar into the cup of coffee the waitress brought. She took a sip.

"She might have called," Daniel suggested. "She might have called her boss again to tell him exactly when she'd be back. You never know."

Eve could tell that he was trying to sound encouraging, and she smiled at her friend. "You're right," she agreed. "We don't know until we ask."

Eve watched as a few more customers entered the restaurant. A young woman wearing a warm-up suit came in by herself, but with lots of makeup and her hair teased and sprayed, it didn't appear as if she had just come from the gym. Eve assumed she was either going to or coming from work at a casino or bar. She sat alone on a stool at the end of the counter, ordered something from the waitress as they chatted like old friends, and then she pulled out her phone and appeared to make a call.

Eve glanced away.

"I feel awful that I don't know where Dorisanne could be," she confessed. "I don't know her friends. I don't know her daily routine, whom she trusted, or where she went for dinner." She looked back over at the woman sitting alone. "Now that we've gotten to this place where she's lived for more than a decade, I realize I know nothing about her life." She shook her head and glanced out the window. The streets and sidewalks were full of cars and people. "I've never visited her here, not once."

"You've sort of been busy," Daniel commented.

Eve turned to him. "I should have come to see her place," she said. "She tried to get me to come out here, and I always found a reason not to come."

"You're here now," Daniel said.

"It's a little late."

He shrugged. "I'd say it's the most important time."

"I don't know anything about what she does, where she might be."

"There's no need to beat yourself up about that," Daniel responded. "Most adults don't know much about the lives of their siblings. I mean, unless you live in the same town. And even then, sisters don't always know all the details of each other's lives. That's the way it is for most people." He reached for the sugar and poured two packs into his glass of iced tea. He stirred it and took a long swallow.

"You still close to Thomas?" she asked,

remembering that Daniel had a younger brother living in Texas. She had met him on several occasions when he came to visit.

Daniel smiled and nodded. "I don't know if I could find him if he went missing," he said. "We're close, talk on the phone every week, but that doesn't mean I'd know where to look for him on a Friday night."

Eve studied him. "You'd know," she said. "You'd have a better idea than I do about Dorisanne."

He glanced away and she knew it was true. Daniel probably had phone numbers and contact information for his brother's friends and coworkers. He more than likely had gone with Thomas to his favorite hangouts, helped him move, visited his place of employment. He probably knew his neighbors, where he played ball, and where he went for groceries. She knew he'd have a much easier time tracking down Thomas than she was having trying to find Dorisanne. She thought he was going to say something more, but before he could give some reassuring remark, their meals arrived.

Eve bowed her head for a short prayer and started eating. She didn't realize how hungry she was until she took the first bite and then remembered that she hadn't eaten since the late breakfast they'd had just as they crossed the border into Nevada. The clock on the wall by the kitchen read ten o'clock. *No wonder I'm hungry,* she thought, reaching for the basket of rolls.

"What do we do after the Rio?" she asked, shaking aside her disappointment in herself. They were in Vegas to find Dorisanne, and that's what she intended to do.

Daniel grabbed the salt and pepper and seasoned his food. "We'll figure that out tomorrow," he replied, taking a bite. "I think Pauline could tell us more. Maybe in the morning the boyfriend will be gone and she'll talk to us." He wiped his mouth with his napkin.

Eve nodded. "I think she'll talk to me before she'll talk to you," she noted. "Maybe you could just drop me off there."

"That's fine. I'll try to find the apartment manager, see what he knows, see if he's gotten a rent check for the month or whether or not he heard from Dorisanne before they left."

"Sounds like a good plan," Eve responded, feeling a little more encouraged.

They ate their dinners and when they finished Daniel went to the restroom. When he left, Eve picked up their check and walked over to the register to pay. While she stood waiting for the waitress to come and take her money, she again noticed the woman sitting at the counter.

She was young. Probably not much older than twenty-one, Eve thought. And she was pretty, reminded Eve of Dorisanne from a few years earlier. She wondered if the girl was in Vegas trying to fulfill a dream like her sister. Maybe a dancer or actress who'd come to Vegas to try to make it big.

She turned to Eve, who was staring. "Hey," she said.

"Hello," Eve responded.

As the girl shifted on the stool to face Eve, her jacket opened a bit so that Eve could see what she was wearing underneath. It looked very familiar. Where had she seen that design?

"You visiting?" the girl asked.

Eve nodded.

"You like the city?"

"I don't know," Eve answered. "I just got here."

The girl smiled. "I bet you'll like it," she responded and turned back to her meal in front of her.

Eve was still staring. Suddenly the thought came to her of where she had seen the same gold-sequined top. "Do you mind if I ask where you work?" she said.

"Caesar's," the young woman replied. "On

the casino floor," she added. "It's not the showroom, but at least I'm inside. I started out poolside. It was terrible in August."

"I bet," Eve responded.

The girl seemed to be waiting. "You need a job?"

"What?" The question surprised her.

The waitress walked up before she could answer and took the receipt from Eve's hand. "You could still sling cocktails," she said, having overheard the conversation and taking a long look at Eve. "I had to quit last year because of my feet." She rang up the meals and Eve handed over cash. "Couldn't wear the heels," she added. "But you look like you could still do it."

"Yeah, those are killers," the girl at the counter agreed. "But I'm trying to get in practice because if I get in a show I'll have to wear even taller heels."

Daniel came out from the back and walked to where Eve was standing. "I was going to get that," he said, referring to the check.

"That's all right," the girl said with a smile. "She's going to get a job serving drinks and stay here. She'll have lots of money then." She winked at Eve, who blushed.

"Take care," Eve said as she headed for

the door with Daniel following.

"What was that about?" he asked as they reached the car.

"She serves drinks," Eve answered, not revealing what she had just discovered. "At a casino on the Strip. She thinks I'd make a good cocktail waitress."

Daniel grinned. "Well that would be something."

Twenty-Four

Eve could hear the loud music coming from the lounge at the Rio before she could see the place. They stopped at the door situated down a hall from the machines and tables. There was a line of people ahead of them, all waiting, it appeared, to go in. There were lights flashing and a strong bass thumping. It was like nothing Eve had ever experienced, and as she looked around at the others in line, the women dressed in short cocktail dresses and high heels, she suddenly felt completely out of place. Daniel, noticing her discomfort, told her she didn't have to hang around, that he would ask the workers about Dorisanne and she could head back to the car and wait, but she stuffed the ends of her shirt in her jeans, slid her fingers through her hair like a comb, checked her boots to make sure they were clean, and said that since she was there, she might as well stay.

They decided to try to find a table, be actual paying customers, and start asking their questions of the server who waited on them. That actually took longer than they expected. It seemed the manager was still having difficulty filling the positions of missing cocktail waitresses. They paid the cover charge when they entered and walked through the large crowd. The noise was so loud, Eve was unable to hear Daniel asking her where she wanted to sit. She just kept walking toward the front where there was a small stage. A couple got up from a table near the stage and Daniel headed for it, beating out two college-age girls who weren't quite fast enough. He pulled out a chair and Eve sat down. She looked up at the stage, saw the instruments of a band, a few bottles of water sitting near a stool beside the set of drums, and figured that the performers must have taken a break. She glanced around the busy lounge as the two of them waited. It was about fifteen minutes before a server finally arrived.

She was pretty, Eve thought. She looked to be about Dorisanne's age, mid-thirties, and it was easy to see that she was trying to take care of too many customers. She arrived just about the time the singer was heading back to the stage to play.

"You know what you want?" the waitress asked. She had a tray full of empty bottles and glasses she had bused from the tables. Her blond hair was pulled back in a long, tight ponytail. She was tall and wore a skimpy black-and-white one-piece uniform. It looked like a tuxedo shirt, but without sleeves and very tight across the chest. The bottom of the outfit was shiny and black and rode high up on her thighs. To complete the ensemble, she wore fishnet stockings and tall, black studded heels. Eve tried to imagine her sister in the costume and she smiled. Dorisanne would love it.

Daniel waited for Eve to order. When she didn't speak up he ordered for them. "Two cokes," he said.

"That's it?" the waitress asked. "No rum or whiskey in there?"

Daniel shook his head. "Just straight-up cokes," he said.

She nodded. "You'll like him," she said, motioning toward the stage and the singer who was strapping on his guitar. "He won the *American Idol* show a couple of years ago. He's good. All the ladies love him." She grinned at Eve, who was staring at the singer and paying no attention to either one of the people at her table.

"Thanks," Daniel said, smiling at the

woman. He read her name tag. "Misti."

Her smile widened and she walked away.

"Taylor Hicks," Eve said, watching the man onstage.

"Who?" Daniel turned to look at the singer.

"Taylor Hicks; he won on *American Idol,* season five."

Daniel appeared surprised.

"It was a good season. Katharine McPhee, Chris Daughtry, Kellie Pickler. Several of them have done real well. Daughtry has a rock band. Pickler is a country star, won that dancing show." She was watching Hicks and she turned back to find Daniel staring at her. "What?"

"You watch *American Idol*?" he asked.

"Sure," she answered. "Don't you?"

"You live in a convent," he said. "You told me once you never went to the movies."

"We have a television in the lobby."

"And you watch *American Idol*?"

"Yep. We even vote for our favorites."

Daniel shook his head.

"I voted for him," she said, lifting her chin in the direction of the stage. "Dozens of times." She blushed a bit. "He's better-looking in person."

"Well, I see now why you didn't want to stay in the car," Daniel commented.

"What? No," Eve said, realizing the implication. "I came with you to find out about Dorisanne. I didn't know he was playing here."

"Uh-huh," Daniel said in a teasing way. "Right. And since we're here, we might as well enjoy the music." He grinned.

"Two cokes." Misti had returned. "You want to start a tab or pay for those now?"

Daniel eyed Eve. "Looks like we might stay a while, so we'll just start a tab."

"Got it," Misti answered and was just about to walk away.

"Wait, Misti."

She turned back.

"We're trying to find someone."

"Well, I'm sure you'll find just the right someone in Vegas." She winked.

Eve didn't understand the innuendo. "We're looking for my sister, Dorisanne. She works here."

"Oh . . . well, not anymore she doesn't," Misti responded. She arranged the drinks on her tray. "Darrell said she was fired."

Eve remembered talking to Darrell when she'd first called looking for Dorisanne. He was the manager of the bar. He was the boss.

"When was that?" Daniel wanted to know.

Misti glanced down at the two of them.

179

"A couple of days ago. She called in and he told her she shouldn't plan to come back. That's why I'm working doubles. He can't find any help. They keep quitting."

"Was she fired because she had missed work? Because of her ankle?" Eve wanted to know.

Misti looked around. "I think it was something else, but I don't know anything for sure. You should ask Darrell or maybe ask your sister."

"Is Darrell here tonight?" Eve asked.

She shook her head. "He's off until next week, had to take his wife to her parents. Her dad is sick or something. Talk about bad timing. Jill is managing tonight. She's the lead bartender." She pointed, and they both looked to see an older woman fixing drinks behind the bar. A young man was working beside her, and two other waitresses were standing at the corner, waiting on their drinks. "We are so shorthanded," she added, shaking her head. "No good tips tonight, I know."

"Is that Jason?" Eve asked, recalling the bartender she'd talked to when she made the call to the bar a few days earlier.

Misti shook her head. "He quit too. Or at least I think he quit. He was a no-show last night. Same thing tonight. So he's either

180

found another job or left town too."

"What do you mean, 'too'?" Daniel asked.

"What?" Misti was looking over at the table next to them. It was easy to see the customers were eager for their drinks.

"Too — you said he left town too. Who else left town?" Daniel had to shout over the noise around them.

"Dorisanne left town. She told Darrell before he fired her. Look, I've got to work. I'll check on you in a while. If you find your sister, tell her to ask about her job again. At this rate, Darrell will be glad to have her back. Enjoy the cokes." And she walked over to the next table to give them their drinks.

Eve glanced around. Every table was full and it had gotten very loud. Several musicians had joined Hicks onstage and were tuning their instruments, getting ready to start the set. She shouted over to Daniel, "I guess there's no one else to ask anything." She took a sip of her coke.

"I guess," he shouted back.

The musicians began to play while the crowd cheered.

"You want to go?" Daniel asked.

Eve looked at Daniel and then at the stage where Hicks had started to sing the old Lynyrd Skynyrd tune "Sweet Home

Alabama." "Let's just finish our drinks," she said.

Daniel smiled. "Of course," he said. And like Eve, he turned to watch the singer onstage, neither of them spotting the two men at the end of the bar, dressed in dark suits, who were asking the bartender the very same questions they had just asked Misti.

TWENTY-FIVE

Eve couldn't sleep. Maybe it was the coke she'd had at the lounge or the coffee and the late dinner. A full stomach and caffeine were both culprits that often hindered her ability to fall asleep. Maybe it was seeing Taylor Hicks live and in person. Her first real concert, if you discounted the piano recitals and visiting chanting monks at the chapel in Pecos. She did get a bit more excited than she tried to let on, and she hoped Daniel hadn't noticed.

Or maybe the inability to fall asleep had to do with Dorisanne and the dead ends she and Daniel kept running into. Where else did they have to go? What would they do tomorrow? Who had any answers?

Where was her sister?

She turned over in her bed once again, noticing that the clock read 2:15 a.m. She sat up, turned on the light, and reached for her prayer book. She opened it and started searching for the appropriate daily readings. She had missed the day before, so she returned to the prescribed scriptures and tried to pay attention to the words. She was halfway through the order when she realized she hadn't remembered anything she had read or prayed.

"I am wide awake," she said out loud, as if the announcement might shake something loose or help her know what to do with the early morning hours that seemed to stretch before her.

She sat up. "Surely there's something I can do to move this investigation along." She closed her eyes and said a short prayer and then got out of bed. And although it surprised her, a thought surfaced that actually gave her some direction.

She dressed, combed her hair, brushed her teeth, grabbed her wallet and room key, and headed out. She stopped at the room beside hers, the room where Daniel was staying, and listened at the door. She thought that if she heard sounds from the television or some noise from inside, if she could tell that he was also awake, she would knock on the door and share her plans with him, invite him to join her. No sounds emerged. And so she tiptoed from the door, making her way to the elevator.

She pressed the elevator button to the lobby and wondered why she hadn't said anything to Daniel earlier about her discovery at the diner. Her silence about it hadn't been intentional — at least she didn't think it had been. When they left the diner they had simply started talking about something, she couldn't remember what, and then they were at the Rio and there was Misti and Taylor Hicks and the place was so noisy, she had just forgotten to tell him. And now, she thought, well, now it didn't seem right to wake him up and tell him that little bit of news. She'd just make the trip herself, see if she could find out anything on her own, and be back in her room, and hope-fully in her bed asleep, in a couple of hours.

The elevator stopped and the door opened. She was in the hotel lobby. She noticed the freshly painted walls and the small living room–like setting by the large floor-to-ceiling windows that looked out over the Strip. Unlike the Rio, this establish-ment had a bar but no casino. She assumed Daniel preferred it that way. She hadn't asked him too much about his activities while he came to Vegas, but she didn't think he spent a lot of time gambling. He had mentioned the pool and the buffet, both of which she had not yet experienced; and with all the efforts they were making to try to find Dorisanne or anything about her, she wasn't sure she'd have much of a chance to enjoy either of them while they were there. She wondered how long they would actually stay, realizing they hadn't really talked about a departure day.

She recalled that the Captain had not seemed to need a return date from Daniel, that he seemed perfectly content to be on his own. All he had mentioned earlier when they had spoken was that when she got back it was her job to talk to Caleb Alford and break the news about the marriage license.

She headed toward the front door of the lobby and thought about Caleb Alford, this new information about the young miner leaving North Carolina, traveling to New Mexico and getting married and, if it were true, wondered how he must have felt signing the license, taking the vows, agreeing to something he had to know was illegal and clearly a betrayal of his family back home. She thought about the two women, his two wives, and whether they ever had a feeling, some intuition that something was just not quite right.

Then she considered Dorisanne and her marriage and wondered what she knew for sure about her husband, if she had known about his debts before they married, what she might have just discovered that caused them to leave town in a hurry and what the knowledge had done to their relationship.

She walked past the hotel bar, catching a glimpse of the few employees standing around inside, counting tips and smoking cigarettes. One of them, a busboy, stared as she made her way toward the front of the lobby. She gave a smile and walked on, not quite sure where she was going. She headed toward the glass doors and was just about to push them open.

"You need a cab?"

The question surprised her, and she turned in the direction it had come from. Behind her a man was sitting at the front desk. He looked to be in his late fifties, wore glasses, a shirt, and tie, and held a stack of receipts in one hand and was working on a calculator with the other. Perhaps he was the night manager or auditor going over the day's profits.

"Yes, I guess I do," she answered, still standing where she had stopped.

He pressed a button somewhere behind the desk.

"It'll be a few minutes," he reported.

Eve nodded and glanced toward the front door.

"You'll see him when he drives up. I'd stay inside if I were you. It's a bit chilly out there."

Eve turned again in his direction and smiled. "Okay, thanks."

She felt odd being out that late, not so much afraid or conflicted about what she was doing, just odd. She had certainly been awake at two o'clock in the morning before. She often struggled with sleep, having battled insomnia since she was a teenager, but usually at the abbey she could go to the chapel or take a walk on the grounds. She sometimes even started breakfast for the community, baking bread or grinding coffee. She actually enjoyed the early morning hours, the time of being alone, unnoticed, uninterrupted.

Since she had been back at home in Madrid with the Captain, she sometimes just got up and sat in the kitchen, drank a cup of tea, and read mysteries or the stories of the saints. Occasionally, she would take a walk up the road that overlooked the sleepy town below, listen for coyotes, gaze at the stars. She was accustomed to being awake while the rest of the world slept.

Here, however, in a strange hotel in a strange city, being awake at this time of night didn't feel as natural to her. There were bright lights still beaming and traffic moving along the streets, and there were other people all around. She was unaccustomed to sharing the night hours with anyone. And even though none of what she was experiencing frightened her, it did make her feel out of sorts.

"There he is," the man behind the desk announced, and she looked out the front windows to see a yellow cab pulling into the hotel driveway.

"Thank you," she said as she opened the door.

"Be careful out there," the man added.

Eve felt a slight shiver at the man's caution but simply waved as she got into the cab. Precaution had never been advised on her many other sleepless nights, and she thought about how being careful had never been a need in the wee hours of the mornings in New Mexico. She thought more about the man's warning, giving her decision to leave Daniel and go out on her own a second thought.

The driver waited. She shook away the fearful thoughts, shut the door, and noticed the driver eyeing her in the rearview mirror.

"Where you go?" the man finally asked with a halting accent, breaking the silence.

"Oh." She realized that he was waiting for

her instructions. She recalled Pauline and the woman at the diner and the costumes they were both wearing, the way she had figured out her sister's neighbor worked on the casino floor, serving drinks to gamblers, the way she seemed to know she would be working at that time of night.

"Caesar's," she said, her voice clear, a sign of her resolve. "The casino at Caesar's."

He punched a button on the meter and they took off.

Twenty-Six

Eve emerged from the dank, stuffy cab as a man in a sharp gray suit opened the door for her. As one door opened, several more followed, and instantly Eve moved out of the dark night and into a grand palace lobby. It was bright inside Caesar's Palace, as if it were the middle of the day. *Bright and busy,* Eve thought, making her way around the card tables, blackjack tables, she thought, and slot machines. Several of the sections were closed, but the ones that were open had at least three, maybe four customers sitting together. The high-end poker room was full, she noticed, knowing what it was only because of the sign on the closed glass door. Six tables, all active with workers and gamblers playing their games.

There were several men in suits and ties standing near the tables, several employees attired in similar gold uniforms, dealing hands of cards, separating chips, and calling out numbers to gamblers at their stations. She saw a couple of women serving drinks, but neither of them were Pauline, and so she kept walking.

She ended up in a row of slots, one near the back of the casino, the only row without someone sitting in front of a machine and playing. She sat down in one of the seats to think about how she might get a waitress to serve her, wondering if they served only at the tables or in the private rooms, how she might find out if Pauline was around.

She figured if the woman had not yet gone to work when she and Daniel were at the apartments, and if she worked an eight-hour shift, she was probably still on the job. Eve just didn't know where that job took her. She shifted on the stool and faced the machine. A bell rang and sirens blared at a machine a few rows over. She stood up and tried to see what was happening, but the machines were too tall. She sat back down, assuming that someone had apparently won a big prize.

"It doesn't work unless you put money in, love."

Eve spun around at the sound of the low, scratchy voice. An older woman had taken a seat at a machine right behind her. There was a tank of oxygen at her feet and a cigarette hanging out of her mouth, a deadly combination. Fortunately, the cigarette was unlit.

"Oh, I wasn't going to play," Eve responded.

"Then you ain't going to win," the old woman pointed out.

Eve smiled. "I suppose that's right."

The woman barked a deep and ragged cough.

Eve watched as the woman slipped a card into a slot, pulled out a small wad of bills from a pocket in the front of her dress, and fed a five-dollar bill into the machine. A few whistles and bells announced that she was ready to play. She pushed a button and the images on the screen whizzed around. When they stopped, she pushed the button again.

"What do you look for?" Eve asked.

The woman wheezed a bit before answering. "You want the sevens to sit side by side right on that line, or if not the sevens, then the stars or the gold bars." She pointed to a narrow horizontal line situated in the middle of the moving images. She pushed the button and three different images came to a stop in front of her. There was one bar, one blue number seven, and one stem of cherries. "That's what you don't want," she explained.

Eve smiled.

"You waiting on your husband?" the woman asked.

"What? Oh, no," Eve answered.

"A lot of women sit here waiting on their husbands or boyfriends to finish their game of poker or jack. They look about as bored and useless as you do."

Eve had to laugh. She had never been told she looked useless before. "Do I appear that way?"

"Honey, you look about as comfortable sitting here as a nun in a whorehouse."

This really made Eve laugh. The woman turned around to see what had caused the big response, but Eve didn't explain. The woman turned back to the machine, pushed the button again. Still nothing.

"It's no use waiting on him," she continued. "He ain't coming for hours. You'd do better just to go on to bed without him."

"I'm not actually waiting on anybody," Eve said.

The woman coughed, pushed the button. "You looking for a party?"

Eve didn't answer. She didn't understand the question.

The woman turned around. "A party? You trying to make some money?"

Eve still didn't understand.

"Nah, never mind. If you was a hooker you wouldn't be dressed like that."

Eve glanced down at her clothes and finally understood what the woman was suggesting. "You think I'm a prostitute?"

"Not since I got a good look at you," she replied, turning back around.

"So, the women who sit here at two o'clock are either waiting on the men at the tables or are prostitutes?"

There was a pause. The images spun once more.

"Pretty much," came the answer.

"What about you then?" Eve wanted to know. "You're a woman sitting here at two o'clock, and you aren't waiting on a man at the tables, and I doubt you're a prostitute."

"Nah, I'm an old-timer. There's a few of us here too," she explained. She pushed the button again and nothing. She reached into her pocket and took out another five-dollar bill, stuck it in the machine, and waited.

"You staying here?" Eve asked.

The woman turned back around. She peered at Eve over the thick glasses she was wearing. "Do I look like I could afford to stay here?"

Eve shrugged. "I don't know. Yes."

The woman coughed and wheezed. "I stay

at the Gardens," she answered Eve. "It's an old folks' home downtown. My grandson drives a cab, and he drops me off at the start of his shift. I go to all the best places. Caesar's, Treasure Island, Mirage, Paris. I do like he does and sleep in the day and come out at night. I like it that way. It's quiet — I get the best machines. Don't have to fight with all the cowboys and teenyboppers. And the drinks are better."

Eve perked up. "You can drink here?"

The woman turned back again. "Can you drink here? Honey, what rock did you come out from under?"

Eve shrugged. "I thought you had to be at the tables or in a bar to be served," she answered. "I didn't know they served you if you were sitting at the machines."

The old woman laughed, then coughed, then laughed again. "Well, I think they prefer that you're actually playing a machine and not just sitting at it, but yeah, you can get a drink here." She pushed the button again and this time three cherries lined up side by side. Alarms started blaring and lights started flashing and the old woman reached down, turned off her oxygen, pulled the tubing out of her nose, pulled out a lighter, and lit the cigarette that was hanging out of her mouth. She blew out a long trail of smoke.

"Darling, you sat at the right machine tonight. We'll get us some drinks now for sure. Pauline will be here before you can shout hallelujah."

And as soon as she said the familiar name, a waitress turned the corner, an empty tray in her hands. She looked first at the old woman and smiled. "Clara, you lucky dog! I didn't know you were here tonight. I'll bring you a beer right away." And then she turned to look at Eve. "It's you," was all she said.

TWENTY-SEVEN

"Where's the cop?" Pauline asked when she returned with the old woman's drink. She set the plastic cup of frothy beer down next to the machine where Clara was still pushing buttons. She had finished her cigarette and reattached the oxygen.

"He's back at the hotel, sleeping, I imagine," Eve answered. She was still sitting at the machine behind Clara.

"I guess he doesn't know you're out here by yourself." Pauline took the five-dollar bill Clara had fished out of her wad of money. "Thanks, doll," she said. "I'll check back on you in a bit."

"Sure, Pauline," Clara replied.

Eve jumped up. "Pauline, can we go somewhere and talk?" she asked.

Pauline glanced around. "It's slow," she explained. "Sit down at the last machine near the back door. It's a penny slot. It's the one place where we can stand and not get in trouble." She looked at Eve. "But you got to play." And she turned and walked away.

Eve looked first one way and then the other, trying to figure out where the back door was located.

Clara watched. "It's that way." She gestured to the right with her head. "Play the Princess. She's the only loose one down there."

"Thanks," Eve responded, having no idea what a loose princess actually meant, and headed in the direction Clara had pointed out. She turned back. "Good luck, Clara," she added with a smile.

"Honey, I'll take all I can get." And she pushed the button once more, picked up her drink, and took a long swallow.

Eve walked through the rows of slot machines, passing a few gamblers, and found her way to a rear wall. There was, however, no door. She glanced around and noticed a sign designating the machines in that area as penny slots. She followed the row of empty machines until she saw a swinging door.

She smiled when she saw a machine with a princess on the front about midway down the row. There was a dragon on one side and a kind of Prince Charming soldier on the other. Eve sat down and tried to figure out how the game worked. She reached for her wallet, realizing that she didn't have change, but soon noticed that the machine didn't take coins. She pulled out a one-dollar bill and tried to insert it just as she had seen Clara do it. In a matter of seconds, the machine lit up and she could see that she was ready to play. She pushed the big button on the right side and whirling images filled the screen. When the images stopped, it didn't appear as if she had won. She pushed the button again.

"Okay, I got ten minutes for you," came a woman's voice from behind. "But keep playing so I don't get in trouble."

Eve turned to look at Pauline. She had done a good job with the makeup covering the bruise under her eye. It was hardly noticeable, Eve thought. "Thanks," she said, smiling.

"I don't really know anything to tell you about Dorisanne," she volunteered. "I told you what I knew at the apartment."

"Yeah, thanks for that," Eve responded. "So, you just said that Dorisanne and Robbie left last week and that it seemed like they were in a hurry, that Dorisanne told you that they were going on a trip and would be back soon."

"That's what she told me."

"When was that? What day?"

Pauline shrugged. She was studying her fingernails, holding her tray under her right arm.

"Maybe Monday or Tuesday." She looked at Eve. "I'm not sure. It may have even been the week before, now that I think about it."

Eve waited. "It would really help if you could remember exactly what day."

Pauline closed her eyes and seemed to be mouthing dates. It appeared as if she was trying to recall the day she spoke to Dorisanne based upon some schedule, some routine that Pauline kept.

"It was Friday, two weeks ago. I was coming back from pulling the graveyard. Kathy, the other slots waitress, wanted to go to some concert and I said I would cover for her, so I worked a double. I was exhausted. But I made good tips that night. There was some Vietnam Vets group from Madison, Wisconsin, staying here, and they were excellent tippers." She played with her nails. "The men always tip better than the women," she added.

"You went home, and what, you ran into Dorisanne and Robbie as they were leaving?" Eve asked.

Pauline shook her head. "No, I saw that

their door was open, so I thought I would just peek my head in and say hello." She smiled. "I like your sister. We've done some things together," she said and then seemed nervous about the comment.

Eve didn't ask what kind of things. She didn't really think it mattered. "And she was packing?"

Pauline nodded. "A small bag, throwing things in it, like she was in a hurry."

"Where was Robbie?"

"She said he had gone to get some gas and was on his way back."

"And then they were heading out?"

Another nod.

"And she didn't say where."

Pauline glanced up when a man started walking in their direction. "You got money in there?" she asked.

Eve looked back at the machine. "Yeah," she answered.

"Then you need to push the button," Pauline said. "It's the floor manager, and I'm taking your order."

Eve turned back to the machine and took another turn. Images of a palace and a princess, a gold chalice, and a white horse spun around.

"What do you drink?" Pauline asked.

"Just water," she replied.

"Okay, I'll be back. Keep playing."

And before Eve could reply, Pauline had headed through the swinging door at the end of the row of machines. She hit the button again.

The man Pauline had mentioned, a short guy wearing a dark suit and a silver tie, followed her through the swinging door, smiling at Eve as he passed.

She threw up her hand in greeting and glanced at her watch. It was almost 3:00 a.m.

TWENTY-EIGHT

Eve waited for ten minutes. The dollar was spent, and she looked in her wallet to discover that the next-smallest bill she had was a five. She hated using it — it was like paying to sit on a stool. But she pulled it out and inserted it into the princess machine anyway. She sat, watching the door where Pauline had exited. When it swung open and the manager walked out, she pushed the button for a spin. In a few minutes Pauline was back.

"Everything okay?" she asked the waitress.

Pauline placed a bottle of water next to Eve. "It's fine," she answered, not sounding very convincing.

Eve pushed the button again while Pauline glanced around and then leaned back against the machine beside Eve. "This job," Pauline said, blowing out a long breath. She shook her head.

"How long you been doing it?" Eve asked.

"What? Waitressing? Here?"

Eve nodded.

She hesitated, appeared to be counting up the years. "I'm coming up on my six-month anniversary here. They keep telling me I'll move into the poker rooms or over to the tables when there's an opening." She slid the tray beneath her arm. "But so far, it's just been the graveyard slots. There's not a lot of movement right now."

"What's that mean?" Eve asked.

"It means girls aren't leaving their jobs. It means it ain't so easy anymore to make a lot of money like it used to be."

"How long have you been in Vegas?" Eve swiveled in her chair to face the waitress.

Pauline shrugged. "I don't know. Nine or ten years. I came out here to dance." She looked at Eve. "Dorisanne and I had that in common. And neither one of us ever got much of a shot. We had that in common too."

"But you stayed," Eve said.

"Yeah, well, where else you going to go?" She sounded tired. Her voice was flat, defeated.

Eve studied her and wondered if Dorisanne sounded the same. She wondered if her sister was working the same kind of late-night shifts, still dreaming of making it as a showgirl. They spoke so seldom about life in Las Vegas. She didn't know whether her sister was happy or not.

"Did you and Dorisanne spend a lot of time together?"

Pauline looked at Eve. "Some, I guess," she replied. "We aren't best friends or anything like that. Steve doesn't like Robbie all that much, so he doesn't want me over there."

"Is Steve your husband?"

Pauline gave a short laugh. "Boyfriend," she answered.

Eve nodded.

"Steve's not the marrying kind," she added.

Eve didn't know what to say.

"But that's okay. I don't really want to be married again anyway."

Eve nodded, acting as if she understood.

"You ever miss dating or having a boyfriend?" Pauline asked. "I always wondered about that with nuns."

Eve thought about the question. "I don't think so," she replied. "I really never dated much in high school, and then in college I was trying to decide about the convent. I just never gave it much thought."

"Dorisanne said you had a boyfriend once."

That bit of news surprised Eve. She had
not talked about David in a long time. She
hadn't even known that Dorisanne
remembered their relationship.

"Once," she responded, hoping not to
have to say more. She turned back to the
machine and pushed the button.

There was a lull in the conversation, and
Eve suddenly remembered something. She
turned to Pauline. "You said that Dorisanne
told you something else when you saw her."

Pauline waited.

"You said that she told you not to let
anybody in her apartment." Eve was recalling the earlier conversation. "Why did she
say that?"

Pauline thought about the question. "I
don't know."

"Did she think somebody might try to get
into her place?" Somehow, this information
seemed important, Eve thought. This might
be a clue as to why Dorisanne had left so
abruptly.

"There were these two guys one time,"
Pauline recalled.

"What two guys?"

"I don't know. They weren't all that social,
if you know what I mean."

Eve nodded, even though she really didn't
know. "Do you think they were trying to

collect money?"

Pauline watched Eve. She paused. "You know about that?"

"I know Robbie had some debts, and I know he sometimes couldn't pay them. Is that who you think those two guys were?"

Pauline shrugged. "I try to stay out of people's business," she said. "Steve tells me that I'm too nosy."

"But you do, don't you?" Eve pushed. "You think those two guys were trying to get money from Robbie."

"Yeah, I think that's who they were."

"And is that who you think Dorisanne was talking about when she said not to let anybody in her place?"

"Maybe," Pauline responded. "Or maybe she was talking about Travis."

"Who's Travis?"

"The night manager at the apartment. We've caught him snooping around before."

"You and Steve?"

She shook her head.

"You and Dorisanne?"

She nodded.

"At her place?"

She nodded again. "She thought he was working for the men trying to get the money from Robbie."

Eve sighed. None of this was really help-

ing her figure out where her sister had disappeared to, but she did think that another
trip to the apartment was going to be necessary. Maybe Daniel could get something
from this Travis guy.

Pauline looked ahead and Eve followed
her glance. The manager was coming back
in their direction.

"Look, I got to get moving."

"Wait," Eve called out.

Pauline turned back toward her.

"If Dorisanne told you not to let anybody
into her apartment, that must mean you can
get in there."

There was no answer.

"Do you have a key?" Eve asked.

Pauline didn't respond.

"I just want to see if she left something, a
clue maybe that might help me know where
she is. You can go with me to make sure I
don't take anything."

Pauline pulled a tube of lipstick from the
front of her uniform and blotted her lips
with the bright red color. She looked in the
machine where she stood to see her reflection and placed the lipstick back in the front
of the tight one-piece costume. "Come over
tomorrow after lunch, about two, and I'll
let you in." She looked Eve squarely in the
eye. "But not before then. Steve works in

the afternoon, and he won't be gone until then."

Eve nodded.

Pauline turned and left before Eve could thank her. She pushed the button one last time, and, much to her surprise, the bells and whistles she had heard from other machines started blaring from her own. She watched as the screen in front of her lit up. "Well for heaven's sake," she said to no one in particular.

"I don't really think heaven has anything to do with it," came a voice from behind her. "But of course, you'd know more about that than I would."

TWENTY-NINE

"Daniel! You scared me to death!" Eve spun around and found her friend standing right behind her. "What are you doing here?"

"I think I ought to be asking you that question. Is there something you haven't told me?" He sat on the stool opposite her, his arms folded over his chest. "You need me to call Gamblers Anonymous? A priest?"

Eve rolled her eyes. "I couldn't sleep."

"So you decided to come all the way down the Strip to Caesar's and play the slots?"

She wasn't sure how to answer. She had to admit that sitting at a slot machine at three o'clock in the morning didn't look great for her. She also knew that leaving her hotel room in the middle of the night to follow a clue without informing Daniel wasn't going to go over that well either. She shrugged and gave a silly grin.

He glanced above her. "How much did you win?"

She spun back around. "I don't know," she replied. "It appears as if the princess and the prince with the blond hair and tight red leotard ended up on the same line. A dragon was apparently slain and the treasure box was opened, with all the gold and rubies and diamonds falling out. I think it's twenty-five cents."

"How do you know he's a prince?" he asked, studying the images on the screen in front of them.

"I don't know," she answered. "Just figured that's how it works. A princess ends up with a prince." She elbowed him in the side. "Maybe he's not her prince in shining armor; maybe he's a cop following her. You own a leotard?"

He shook his head. "Not a red one," he replied, dropping down on the stool beside her.

She turned to him. "How did you know where to find me?" she asked.

"I didn't know where to find you," he responded. "I thought you were sound asleep in your bed at the hotel, where you're supposed to be."

"Then what are you doing here?"

"Great drinks?" he answered.

She studied him, waiting for the truth.

"I recognized Pauline's uniform," he

confessed. "Figured she'd be working tonight and thought I'd come chat her up."

He waited. "Now, your turn?"

She shrugged. "Same thing," she answered.

"You knew she was wearing a Caesar's uniform?"

"I put it together when I was talking to that woman at the diner. She had on the same one and she told me where she worked."

"Two plus two," he responded.

"That's four," she played along.

"I should have known you'd be somewhere you're not supposed to be."

"Why should you have known that?"

"Have you forgotten that I worked with your father for almost twenty years?" he answered. "That Divine fruit doesn't fall far from the tree."

"Divine," she corrected him. "Don't call me that."

"Just as touchy about the name as he is too." He laughed. "Your dad used to hate when somebody mispronounced the name."

"We all hate it," Eve said.

"I would think it would be an asset in your line of work," he teased her.

She rolled her eyes but didn't respond.

"So, did you find Pauline?"

She nodded, reached for her bottle of water and took a sip. She held it out for Daniel to see. "She works the slots," she noted.

Daniel smiled. "You're a smart nun."

"Apparently not smart enough to figure out these machines. I still don't understand how I won, or what I won, for that matter." She was studying the screen again. "Where did the money go?"

He leaned over to take a closer look. "It's there." He pointed to a number on the screen. "It's points now. They don't spit out the money unless you ask for it. This keeps you playing a little longer. And it's twenty-five dollars not twenty-five cents."

Eve felt a bit of pride, but for what? She'd only pushed a button. There was no pride in that. It was such a strange business.

"Pauline?" he asked again.

"Oh, right," she said. "She has a key to Dorisanne's apartment. She's going to let me in tomorrow after Steve goes to work."

Daniel nodded.

"She says there were two men that came by once before, and she figures that is who Dorisanne and Robbie are hiding from."

"She get a look at them?" Daniel asked.

"I think so," Eve replied. "I didn't really ask about that." She wondered what other questions she had failed to ask.

Daniel stretched his back, raised his arms above his head, and yawned.

"Couldn't you sleep?" Eve asked.

"I did for a couple of hours and then when I woke up, I couldn't get back." He turned to her. "You?"

"Never could drop off," she answered.

"How did you get here?"

"Taxi," she replied. "The guy at the hotel called one for me."

She noticed him staring at her.

"What?" she asked.

He shrugged, took out a couple of dollar bills, and put them in the machine in front of him. "You're just more resourceful than I thought."

"I've been in a convent, Daniel, not a cave."

He laughed, pushed the button, and waited.

"Pauline also told me that the night manager at the apartments was snooping around Dorisanne's place. She thought he might be connected with the guys trying to find them." She pushed the button on the princess machine. It was another win. She raised her hands at Daniel, demonstrating that she didn't know how it was happening.

"Is it luck or are you invoking some

saint?" He pushed his button, using the last bit of his money. He spun around on his stool. "I got nothing."

"Maybe I should try it for you," Eve suggested.

"Let's get out of here," he said, watching as Eve pushed the button on her machine once again.

"Oh, look, I opened another treasure box!" She clapped her hands.

Daniel shook his head, waiting for Eve to close out of her machine. He stood up behind her as the two of them waited to grab the winning ticket. He followed her as she threaded her way through the slots, making her way to the old woman still sitting at one of the machines. Clara turned around as they approached. "Well, it looks like the princess was a winner." She grinned. "You hit the jackpot, sissy." She eyed Daniel. "Tall, dark, and following you like a puppy."

"Here." Eve handed the older woman her winning ticket. "It was loose, just like you said, although I still don't know what that means."

Clara looked at the ticket, then back at Eve, then over to Daniel. "Well, what it means is that it appears to be a lucky day for us both." She took the piece of paper and winked at Eve. "Glad it's worked out for you."

Eve patted the woman on the shoulder and started to walk away.

"Check his wallet before you name your price," Clara called out behind them. "He's true blue if I ever saw one."

Daniel laughed as they walked away. "I don't even want to know about that," he commented. "And how did she know I'm a cop?"

As they headed toward the front doors, laughing, Eve caught a glimpse of the man sitting at a high-end slot machine, the one with slicked-back hair and a dark mustache, waiting for the waitress to return with his drink.

THIRTY

When Eve woke up, the sun was full and shining through the window by her bed. She looked over at the clock, reading the time to be eleven o'clock, realizing that she had slept for almost seven hours straight. She rubbed her eyes and sat up, recalling coming in from Caesar's and falling into bed. She looked down and realized she hadn't even put on her pajamas. She was still in the clothes she had worn the previous night.

She wondered if Daniel was awake or if he had managed to sleep throughout the entire morning as well. She thought about banging on the wall behind her to get his attention, but then thought better of it. The red light on the bedside phone blinked insistently. She studied it for a few minutes and then understood that a message was waiting for her. Maybe Daniel had called, was up, and wanted to tell her where he was. She picked up the receiver and dialed the front desk and was told that a message had been left in a voice-mail box.

She followed the instructions given, waited for the message to begin, and was surprised to hear the Captain's voice:

"Evangeline, Daniel said you were up late last night and told me just to leave you a message. He's apparently gone out to talk to his friend on the force out there. He said you got a couple of leads yesterday and he thinks it's time to include Las Vegas's finest. He's probably right." He cleared his throat. "Look, I think your sister tried to call me again." There was a pause. "I don't recognize the number. It's not one I have for her, but it's a Las Vegas area code. I think it must be her. The call came this morning, about four. I think she's trying to get hold of us." Another clearing of the throat. "I didn't talk to her. It was a missed call," he repeated himself. "Just call me when you get this."

And he murmured something about stupid machines, coughed a few times, and was cut off. Eve put down the receiver and then picked it back up. She dialed his cell phone number. The Captain picked up on the third ring.

"I just got your message," she said after a gruff greeting.

"Where you been all morning?" he asked.

She waited. She wasn't sure she wanted to say she was still in bed.

"Never mind," he groused. "Daniel called and said you were out late, searching for clues, but he didn't fill me in." He coughed. "What have you found out?"

"Just that she's not in the apartment," she replied. "She and Robbie apparently left a few days ago. We've talked to the neighbor."

He coughed again.

"You think she tried to call you this morning?" Eve asked.

"It's a Las Vegas number on the screen. I didn't hear it when she called. I think I turned the phone off before I went to bed." He cleared his throat.

"Are you all right?" Eve thought his voice sounded ragged and harsh.

"Allergies," he informed her. "Junipers blooming everywhere."

She knew he fought allergies all year: pines in the fall, cottonwoods in the summer, and now, apparently, junipers in the spring. He made a loud hacking noise.

"Maybe you should try something to help clear out the congestion," she suggested.

"I don't need anything," he replied. "I

checked and there's no message in my mailbox," he added.

"What's the number?" Eve asked, swinging her legs over the side of the bed and reaching for a pen and paper.

He called out the number and Eve wrote it down but didn't recognize it. The Captain was right — it was the Vegas area code. "Did you dial the number?" she asked.

"Did I dial the number?" he repeated sarcastically. "Of course I dialed the number."

"And?" She chose not to react to the tone of his voice.

"And nobody answered," he replied.

He coughed.

Eve waited.

"You still there?" he asked.

"Yes," she replied.

"I don't figure it helps anything, but I just wanted you to know," he said, his voice a bit softer.

"Thanks, I'm glad you called."

There was a pause.

"What else is going on?" she asked.

"Been out to Salazar's place. He wants me to pick the spot to dig." More coughing.

Eve didn't respond.

"Oh, and that Alford fellow thinks he found a picture of his great-grandfather."

"Where?"

"He was looking around at the What Not Shop, found some old mining pictures. There was a shot of a man holding up a set of beads like the one he got in the mail a few years ago. He's certain it's his kin."

"Does he know about the marriage license?" She recalled the latest information on their client and that the Captain had wanted her to break the news when she returned.

"Nah, he doesn't know about that." The Captain blew his nose.

Eve thought about the man's find. The What Not Shop was on the main drag of Cerrillos and carried a lot of old paraphernalia from the mining days. She had gone through a stack of old photographs herself since she'd returned home from the convent. It had not occurred to her that information about the missing miner might be found at the local shop.

"Anyway, I don't know why I'm going on about that. I just wanted to tell you about the phone call this morning."

"Okay, thanks," she responded. "I'll keep calling the number and maybe she'll answer. It would be great to hear her voice and know that she's okay."

Eve could hear him breathing on the other

end of the phone. She waited to see what he wanted to say, wondered if he wanted to confess his fear or worry about his youngest daughter.

"I'm glad Daniel's going to the police," he finally said, breaking the silence.

"I think they'll help us a lot," she responded.

"Okay." He coughed. "Be careful," he said, clicking off before Eve could reply.

"Right," she said to the line gone dead. She put down the receiver and fell back on the bed.

Eve went over what she had just learned, naming the details out loud: "Dorisanne calls home at four o'clock in the morning. She has a Las Vegas number, not her old one, dials our father's cell phone, but doesn't leave a message and doesn't pick up when he calls her."

She ran her fingers through her hair.

"Dorisanne, where are you?"

THIRTY-ONE

By the time Eve had showered and gotten dressed for the day, Daniel had returned from his visit to the Las Vegas Police Department. They were both starving and decided to grab a bite of lunch before heading over to the apartment building. They found a Chinese restaurant close to the location where they were heading and ate quickly. It was 1:45 when they arrived at the building, and they both agreed they should wait until after two o'clock to make sure Steve had left and gone to work, keeping things as easy as possible for Pauline.

"So we can't file a missing person report because both Dorisanne and Robbie are missing, and there doesn't appear to be any trouble at their apartment." Eve was recounting what Daniel had already told her. "What did your friend at the department say about Robbie?" she asked as they sat in the parking lot. It was hot and she lowered the window. They had spoken about a few other events of the morning, but they had not discussed Dorisanne's husband and whether or not there was any suspicion from the police cast in his direction.

"Like I've told you before, he's had a little trouble in the past," Daniel answered.

Eve waited. This wasn't late-breaking news, she knew.

A few cars came and went from the parking lot. They both watched them, knowing that they wouldn't really be able to tell if Steve was in one of them or not since neither of them had seen him during their first visit.

"Possession of stolen property, a few forged checks." Daniel placed his hands on the steering wheel in front of him.

Eve could see he wasn't finished. She remained patient.

"There's talk," he finally said.

"Talk?" Eve asked.

"My friend James Drennan thinks he's involved in a credit card theft ring, stolen identities racket."

"But no arrests?"

Daniel shook his head. "They've never really caught him in the act. Not enough evidence."

"So when you told James who Robbie

was, he knew about him." She glanced ahead, watching the sights through the windshield.

"I told you I had him checked out when they first got married, so my friend was already alerted to Mr. Robert Miller."

Eve recalled Daniel's earlier trips to Vegas, the Captain's confession about the background checks on Robbie. She didn't realize, however, that one of them had talked to police officers about her brother-in-law.

"Was this credit card thing something from before they got married or is it recent?"

"A few months ago," he replied.

Eve sighed, leaned her head back against the car seat. She had been hoping the best about her sister's husband, hoping that this incident was only a bad debt that could be quickly remedied. But things were sounding a bit more complicated.

"James thinks Robbie was on the ground floor, a Dumpster diver, somebody who finds the numbers and passes them along to the smarter guys."

"So he sorts through trash for credit card vouchers?"

"Maybe."

"I thought most of that kind of theft happened because of computer transactions. I

226

was going to do the banking online for the office, but the Captain was convinced the account could be hacked. He doesn't trust computers."

Daniel laughed. "A lot of folks don't. But it's actually not as risky as it was once thought to be. Most of the banking stuff is pretty secure. The truth is that the top methods identity thieves use to steal personal data are still pretty low-tech. These guys simply steal mail and try to get information from phone conversations. Stolen wallets, checkbooks, and credit and debit cards make up almost half of the reported incidents of identity theft."

"Robbie was going around stealing from mailboxes?" Eve asked. "That doesn't sound very lucrative, and it seems pretty stupid, actually."

"Yeah, well, that's why it's the ground floor. But he was most likely not going around looking in mailboxes. He was probably going into hotels and casinos, hanging out around ATMs. There are usually a lot of drunks getting cash to gamble, and they tend to be a little sloppy with how they do things."

"Easy targets," Eve added, with a new understanding of credit card theft and her brother-in-law's possible extracurricular activities.

They were quiet for a bit. Eve glanced at the clock on the dashboard. It was now fifteen minutes after two. She tried to push a thought out of her mind but finally had to ask Daniel's opinion.

"Do you think that's the trouble Dorisanne had gotten into at the lounge, why she was fired? Do you think she's involved somehow with Robbie?"

Daniel turned to Eve. "I don't want to think that about Dorisanne." He turned back to look ahead. "But Robbie may have told her they didn't have any options, told her she only needed to do a few hits, watch the ATM near the lounge, get a few numbers, and then they'd be out." He drew in a breath. "You never know." He shook his head. "There's nothing predictable about your sister."

Eve watched a motorcycle make an exit from the parking lot, wondered if the driver was Steve, Pauline's boyfriend, but she had no way to know. She leaned back again and closed her eyes. Could Dorisanne actually be deep into this mess too? Could she be involved in a theft ring? These were thoughts Eve didn't want to consider.

"Look, James said they had no record on Dorisanne. She's not wanted for anything.

She's not been targeted by her boss. Let's not jump to conclusions about her involvement yet, okay? Let's just focus on finding her."

Eve nodded. She knew Daniel was trying to make things easier for her.

"Did you notice your dad's cough?"

"He said it was allergies," Eve answered.

"Right, yeah, that makes sense," he responded.

The conversation paused while they both watched the minutes tick away. When it was finally two thirty and they both agreed they had waited long enough, Daniel started the engine to move closer to Pauline's apartment. He pulled into a spot just below the unit and parked. They were just about to exit the car when they heard the sirens blaring, coming in their direction. They watched as three police cars and two ambulances pulled into the parking lot complex and stopped right in front of them. Neither of them moved.

THIRTY-TWO

"What the . . . ?" Daniel appeared just as alarmed as Eve while the squad cars and emergency vehicles rushed into the lot.

They both watched from the car as the officers jumped out of their cars and headed up the steps and gathered outside Pauline's door.

Someone from the apartments arrived at the landing and opened the door with a key. They all rushed in.

"Something's happened to Pauline," Eve said, reaching over to open the door.

Daniel grabbed her by the hand, pulling her back.

She turned to him quickly, surprised at his response, feeling slightly annoyed.

"Let's just wait here," he instructed her. "We can see what's going on."

Eve sat back.

Six police officers barreled through the front door while the paramedics stood out on the landing. All Eve could make out was the group of uniformed men and women standing at the door.

"What do you think has happened?" she asked Daniel, who still had his hand on hers.

He shook his head. "I don't know, but it doesn't look good."

"Can you call your friend?" she asked, wondering if the police officer he knew could tell him about the call to Pauline's apartment.

"Looks like I don't have to call." He raised his chin at another officer who had just pulled up and was hurrying up the stairs to join the others. "That's James," he added.

Eve watched as the man, a large guy, African American, dressed in a dark suit, headed up to the landing where everyone else was waiting. He flashed a badge and entered the apartment. "I don't think this is good news," Eve said. She turned to Daniel. "Do you think Steve beat her up?"

Daniel didn't answer.

"What if he found out she was helping us?" She pulled her hand away from Daniel's. "I think we should go up and find out what's happened. Maybe we can do something."

"Just wait, Eve," Daniel instructed her. "Just give it a few more minutes. We'll find out something soon enough. We would just be in the way up there."

As soon as Daniel's words were uttered, the paramedics hurried into the apartment. Eve pulled down her rosary from the rearview mirror and began to pray.

When she finished her prayer and looked up, Daniel was opening his car door. "There's James, let me talk to him." And he exited.

Eve watched as Daniel hurried to the Las Vegas detective's side. She could see him filling in details. They would both look at each other and then up to the apartment. James, Daniel's friend, kept shaking his head, making Eve fear the worst.

She fingered the rosary and said more prayers for Pauline and for the first responders at her side. In just a few minutes, Daniel returned.

She waited until he had gotten in and closed the driver's-side door.

"Domestic violence," he reported. "A neighbor called it in."

"Is she okay?" Eve asked.

"She's alive," he answered. "Apparently she was beaten pretty bad. The guy used a baseball bat."

"Is he still in there?" she asked, referring to Steve, Pauline's boyfriend.

Daniel shook his head. "But it doesn't look like he's been gone long. The 911 call just came in about twenty minutes ago. The neighbor said she heard the fight start about an hour earlier and then the screaming came later. The officers think he beat her up and then left, and she started yelling for help when she knew he was gone."

"So we've been sitting down here while . . ." Eve didn't finish the sentence.

Daniel reached over and took Eve's hand again, this time trying to console her. "We don't know the timetable; James was just guessing."

Eve leaned her head against the window of her door. She closed her eyes and could see Pauline, smiling, inviting her over to the apartment, warning her not to come too early. She wondered if Steve had seen Daniel's car and figured out that they had returned, that Pauline was going to let them into Dorisanne's apartment, that she had somehow disobeyed his instructions, and had then paid the price.

She knew from the women who came to the abbey that an abuser could choose anything as a reason for violence, that she and Daniel weren't to blame for Steve's apparent outburst, but she still felt somehow responsible and wished she had not made the trip the night before to track down her sister's neighbor or that she had said something during their conversation at the casino, something that might have kept her from coming back to the apartment.

"Did you tell him why we were here?" she asked Daniel, wondering if his friend knew why they were parked near the crime scene, knew that they were there to talk to Pauline.

"He didn't get that far with his questions, but I'm sure he'll want to know the answer to that." Daniel pulled his hand away from Eve's.

They looked up when they saw some more commotion at the top of the landing at Pauline's door. A gurney was being wheeled out with someone, apparently Pauline, strapped in. There were two paramedics holding IV bags over the victim's head, and two police officers moving the long, narrow stretcher. They headed toward the end of the building where Eve assumed there was an elevator. In a few minutes they were walking out from below, heading in the direction of the ambulance. Eve could see Pauline's blond hair, loose and spilling over the end of the gurney. She had on an oxygen mask, and there was no movement that Eve could see from the patient. The paramedics and policemen loaded her into the back, and soon the ambulance was speeding away.

"Do you know where they'll take her?" Eve asked.

Daniel shook his head. "No, but we'll find out."

They waited and continued to watch as the police officers walked around the apartment complex. A couple of them stayed with the man who had opened the door. One went to the neighbor who had been standing in front of her door watching the entire event. Eve heard the knock on Daniel's window before she saw his friend James standing beside the car.

Daniel opened the door and got out. Eve could overhear the conversation and listened as Daniel explained about the prearranged meeting scheduled with the victim and that they planned to use the spare key that she had to get into Dorisanne's apartment. She heard him tell James who she was — he peeked in the window at her at that point — and then how she had met Pauline the day before and spoken to her again later that night.

"No," she heard him say, "there was no evidence that Pauline seemed afraid to come home. No evidence that her boyfriend had known about their conversation or that

Eve knew anything more about what could have happened."

"It looks textbook," she heard James say, but she was not so sure. "We've been called out a few times before. But this time it's a felony. She's knocked unconscious, lost a lot of blood."

"You know where the perp is?" Daniel asked.

"We've sent a unit to his place of employment. These guys usually go right on about their business as if beating up their girlfriends is just a part of their routines. It amazes me how stupid they are."

She heard a few more bits and pieces of their conversation, and then, while reaching up and hanging her rosary back on the rearview mirror, she glanced behind her to see a man sitting on a motorcycle outside a fence at the rear of the parking lot. She instantly recognized it as the same bike that had exited the area only a few minutes earlier, and then, with his helmet removed, his dark hair slicked back, and the mustache, she also knew the driver's face was familiar.

Thinking he might be Steve, she leaned forward to get Daniel's attention.

THIRTY-THREE

"Does Steve drive a motorcycle?" she asked, stepping out of the car, directing her question to the Las Vegas police officer.

"I don't know," James answered. He was writing down notes.

When Eve glanced back, the man on the motorcycle was pulling away. "I've seen that guy before."

Daniel and James both looked behind them, hearing the engine as the driver circled around and exited the area.

"Yeah, me too," Daniel replied. "He pulled out of here about half an hour ago. I recognize the bike. I guess you would too," he added, smiling at Eve, knowing her love for Harley-Davidsons. "What is it? Low Rider?"

"No. I don't mean just now. And I don't just mean the bike; I saw him last night," Eve noted. "He was sitting at the slots when we left Pauline. He was at Caesar's. And it's a Dyna Super Glide, probably a '97."

Daniel watched as the motorcycle sped away. He shook his head.

"Do you think it's Steve?" Eve asked. "Do you think he came back to see about her? That he was at the casino last night and saw us talking to her?"

James pulled out his cell phone, apparently taking an incoming call. Daniel and Eve waited for him to finish.

"It's not the boyfriend on the bike," he said. "They just picked him up at the construction site where he works. His boss said he arrived there less than an hour ago, but he claims he hasn't been home since last night." James shook his head. "Says he's innocent."

"That's original," Daniel responded.

Eve didn't comment, but something didn't quite fit for her. If that wasn't Steve on the bike, she wondered, who was this guy watching Pauline's apartment, and why did he leave and come back? Why was he at Caesar's last night? Could he have been the one who beat her up? She decided to keep her questions to herself for the time being, but when she looked up at Daniel, he was watching her as if he was considering the same thing, both of them thinking like cops.

"Look, if you want to get into your sister's

apartment, I can get the key from the super," James said, slipping his phone back into his pocket. "I mean, since we're all here and everything."

At first Eve didn't respond.

"That's why you're here, right?" He turned to Eve. "You were going to take a look around?" He waited for her answer, eyeing her as if he was suddenly suspicious.

Eve nodded. "Right," she said.

"Then I'll let you in. I don't think the manager is going to care, and even though I can't see how this domestic violence call is related at all to your missing sister, he's not going to know the difference. I need to hang around a little longer anyway, so you can do your business while I'm still here."

Eve looked at Daniel.

"I'll find out where they took Pauline, what hospital," he noted. "We can head over there after we look around." Daniel closed the car door and waited for Eve to join him.

The three of them headed up the stairs and waited outside Pauline's apartment as James went in and found the manager, who was being interviewed by another police officer. The two of them came out in a few minutes.

"I don't see what you think you're going to find in there," the manager said as he

239

pulled out his set of keys and stuck one into the lock on Dorisanne's door.

"Yeah, I'm sure you're right; there's probably nothing, but we just want to make sure there's no one else been hurt up here," James commented, standing behind the manager.

"Well, I know that these guys have been gone a week, so they aren't a part of this." He pushed open the door and stood aside for James. Daniel and Eve waited.

"Robert Miller and Dorisanne Divine," he said, "that's who lives here."

"It's Divine," Eve said, correcting the mispronunciation.

The manager turned, noticing her and Daniel for the first time.

"And you say they've been gone a week?" James asked.

"Yeah," he replied. He seemed to be studying Daniel. "I've seen you," he finally noted. "You've been here checking up on them before. I remember."

Daniel smiled, held out his hand. "Detective Daniel Hively," he said.

"You aren't with the Las Vegas PD," the manager commented.

"No," Daniel responded.

The manager seemed to be deciding whether or not he was going to let the three of them enter when James pushed past and walked in. "Thank you, Mr. . . ."

"Stanley," the manager gave his name. "Stanley Whitehorse."

"Thank you, Mr. Whitehorse, we'll take it from here."

Daniel and Eve followed James inside, leaving the manager out on the landing with a confused look on his face.

"I'd say we have about five minutes before he decides we shouldn't be in here, so you might want to hurry," James told Eve.

Eve glanced around her sister's apartment.

"Anything look out of place?" James asked.

Eve studied the furniture, the belongings in the open living area. There were a few things that looked familiar, wedding pictures on the wall, pieces of their mother's pottery, an old blanket that Eve knew had come from their home in New Mexico. Most of the things, however, Eve didn't recognize, including a basket of yarn. *Does Dorisanne knit?* she wondered. And copies of *Conde Naste Traveler* and *Coastal Living,* aspirational magazines that made Eve wonder if Dorisanne intended to move again or just longed to visit new places. And seeing such things caused her to realize once more how little she knew about her sister's life, the things that brought her comfort, the furnishings of her home. She shook her head.

"I've actually not ever visited her here," she confessed. She turned to her friend. "Daniel, you've been in here before. What do you think?"

He shrugged, glancing around from wall to wall, corner to corner. "I don't see anything that seems suspicious or out of place."

Eve headed into the bedroom. The bed was unmade, which for some reason made Eve smile. Something finally felt familiar to her. At least this room felt like a place she was able to recognize as Dorisanne's. A couple of the dresser drawers were open and articles of clothing were hanging out. A few clothes were piled in the corner. The closet doors were also open, but Eve could see that blouses and dresses were hanging there. Not too much looked to be missing. Shoes lined the floor underneath the clothes, and Eve studied the pairs of high heels, remembering how her sister loved to play dress-up when they were little, how she loved wearing their mother's dressy shoes.

She glanced around, noticing newspapers stacked in the corner, a couple of books by the bed, and beside her on the nightstand there were a couple of empty cups, a clock, a hairbrush, and a framed picture of the Divines. Eve picked it up. There were the Captain, their mother, and the two girls, both awkward teenagers, all posing for a family shot, a birthday, Eve recalled. Perhaps their mother's. Eve studied the photo, remembering the celebration, how she had come home from college for the weekend, how she told them later on that occasion that she was contemplating entering the convent, how Dorisanne and the Captain remained in their never-ending power struggle. She hadn't remembered the picture being taken, though, and couldn't recall who had been the photographer. She knew it was her mother's idea to have the four of them in a shot together; it was always her mother trying to get family pictures.

Eve put the picture back down and could see that the small drawer in the stand was slightly ajar. She reached over and pulled the handle. She turned on the lamp and discovered a few pieces of paper, letters in envelopes written in their mother's hand, some ChapStick, lotion, a couple of photographs with Dorisanne in her waitress uniform, and a small address book. Without knowing why, Eve took the book out, along with the loose photographs, and slid them into her back pocket. She didn't think those things could shed any light on where her sister had gone, but she just wanted something to make her feel closer to Dorisanne.

When she could find nothing to give a clue as to where Dorisanne had gone and why, she turned off the lamp, and headed back into the living room where Daniel and James were waiting.

"Anything?" Daniel asked.

Eve simply shook her head.

THIRTY-FOUR

By the time Eve and Daniel made it to the hospital, Pauline had been taken to a room in the Intensive Care Unit. There had been no need for surgery, just blood transfusions, X-rays, IV fluids, fifty stitches on the top of her head, and close observation. No bones were broken; her skull had not been fractured, but there had been a large gash, bruising, and a substantial concussion. She was heavily sedated, and they were told by the attending doctor that she was not to be roused for conversation. She needed this time to rest and to make sure there had not been any brain damage. She was in and out of consciousness anyway and hardly able to answer questions, but the doctor made it clear she was not to be disturbed. Once he found out Eve was a nun and a friend, however, he allowed her to stay at Pauline's bedside.

Since he knew the man had been picked

up by the police, Daniel planned to go to the jail and interview Steve, find out what he could as to whether or not he was in fact the perpetrator. He told Eve he would use his best interview skills and was confident that he would be able to tell if Steve had been the one who had done this to Pauline and even find out why. He also planned to find out if he had any knowledge about the guy they had seen earlier on the motorcycle.

He agreed that later he would return to the apartments and have a lengthier conversation with the manager, Stanley Whitehorse, just to see if he had any more information about when and why Dorisanne and Robbie had left. They both thought that he seemed to know something about their departure, and Daniel thought it might be beneficial to try to talk to him a little longer and without the presence of the Las Vegas police.

As Eve sat praying next to Pauline's bed, her thoughts turned to the time she had spent in the hospital with the Captain after his amputation surgery and during his recovery, which had led to her decision to take a leave from the convent and care for him. She thought about those days at St. Vincent's, the ongoing conversations with nurses and therapists, the conferences with the medical staff about her father's prognosis. She recalled Dorisanne's phone calls and her decision to stay away, how her sister confessed she hated hospitals, hated the sounds and the smells, had all she could take of that during their mother's illness and would not return to New Mexico while her father remained a hospital patient.

She sat, listening to the quiet hum of the IV machines, the low talk from people in the hallway, and remembered all the family members she'd met in the waiting rooms, the friendship that was forged between herself and Megan Flint, the Captain's client and a Hollywood star. Eve thought about all the extra time she had while caring for her father in the hospital, time to think, to reflect, to consider her vocation and her decision to live in community as a Benedictine nun. It had been a very important and introspective time in her life, and she wondered if she would have taken all of that time for reflection had she not had so many hours in the hospital to wait and think. She had not enjoyed the required caregiving for the Captain; he had been a difficult patient, but it had certainly given her the space to reflect upon her life and her call.

"And here I am again," she said softly,

"sitting at a bedside in a hospital room, still not any further along in my process than I was then." She reached out and took Pauline's limp hand in her own. "Only this time I'm with a cocktail waitress from Vegas instead of Captain Jackson."

She squeezed Pauline's hand. "And still, just like before, Dorisanne is nowhere to be found."

Eve tucked the patient's hand under the sheet, patted it, and sat back in her chair. When she did, she felt the small book she had found earlier at her sister's apartment, the one she had stuck into her pants pocket. She reached around and pulled it out and began flipping through the pages. She pulled out the photos, flipped through them as well, stopped at one and ran her finger across Dorisanne's face, smiling at her goofy grin. She placed it back between the pages in the book.

She looked at the cover of the book and then opened it up again. It was a small address book, apparently an old one, as she could see that there were dark lines drawn through most of the names and numbers. She figured Dorisanne was transcribing them to another book or to her cell phone, and she wondered how far along she had gotten. She found her parents' home address and various phone numbers from over the years, all with a line crossed through them, along with Daniel's number and contact information for a few friends Dorisanne and Eve shared in Madrid. There were casinos and managers' names sprinkled throughout the book and names that Eve didn't recognize. Some were not crossed out.

She found Pauline's and Steve's names, both listed under P, and there were two numbers written there. Eve assumed they were cell numbers, and she wondered if one of them was Steve's or if they were both Pauline's, and she wondered what her sister knew about the domestic violence that apparently went on next door to her. She had not asked Pauline how long they had been neighbors and how much of their lives they actually shared.

She looked at the young woman in the bed, her face swollen and bruised, and wondered if Dorisanne had given up her hospital phobia to sit with Pauline on any previous occasions, if she had been a friend to Pauline during times like this one. She glanced down at the book, at the written name, a star next to the number, a thin line drawn through it, and immediately understood that she had. She knew that loyalty was one of her sister's best qualities, and if a friend was in need, no matter how uncomfortable it made her, she was always there. Dorisanne had been that way from the time she was very young. The other girls in Madrid used to say if you were friends with Dorisanne, you were friends for life. And with all the names in the address book, names and numbers from years and years of her life, it certainly seemed like that was still so.

She closed the book, thinking that maybe later she would study it more closely, maybe even call some of the listed numbers to ask if they knew of Dorisanne's whereabouts, but as she started to put it back in her pocket, a small piece of paper fell out of the book. Eve bent down and picked it up. It was a receipt of some kind, with a four-digit number written off to the side. Eve didn't know for sure, but it appeared to be a credit card receipt, and she could tell it was from the Rio. She thought about her conversation with Daniel, about Dorisanne's possible involvement with the identity theft ring, and she folded up the piece of paper and stuck it back in the little book.

"Dorisanne," Pauline was speaking. She turned to face Eve, who was startled by the name and the sudden movement.

"Dorisanne," she called out again, reaching for her hand.

"It's Eve," she said, leaning forward and sitting closer to Pauline. "It's her sister," she explained. "I'm Dorisanne's sister."

Pauline looked closer at Eve, clamping on more tightly to her hand. Suddenly an alarm began to beep from the machine next to the bed, the numbers showing that Pauline's heart rate was increasing and her blood pressure was rising.

"What is it?" Eve asked. "What's wrong, Pauline?"

The patient closed her eyes, began to breathe harder, and said something that Eve couldn't make out.

"What?" Eve asked, leaning in closer.

Pauline became restless, began yanking at her IV lines, squirmed and fidgeted in the bed.

"Pauline, calm down!" Eve called out. And before she could get Pauline to explain what she was saying, what she meant, a nurse had rushed into the room and was pushing her out the door.

Eve stood in the hallway outside the room and watched as several members of the medical staff ran in to join the nurse at Pauline's bedside. They quickly lowered her bed and appeared to be adding medications to her IV line. She heard one of them call for the doctor. Eve felt completely helpless; it appeared that Pauline's condition was quickly deteriorating. She wanted to call Daniel but was too afraid to take out her cell phone and dial the number. She waited and prayed, watching through the window to the room.

After a few minutes a nurse, the first one who ran in, came out.

"Is she okay?" Eve asked.

The nurse nodded. "Her pressure shot up and she's still very agitated." She seemed to be looking for someone. She pulled out her phone to read the screen. "And she's calling for Dorisanne." She looked at Eve. "Is that you?"

Eve shook her head. "That's my sister. She thought I was my sister."

The nurse appeared to study her. "Is your sister okay?"

"I don't know," Eve confessed. "Why? Did Pauline say something? Did she say something about Dorisanne?"

The nurse looked up and Eve followed her glance and noticed the doctor coming in their direction. She turned her focus back to the nurse standing in front of her.

"What?" Eve asked as the doctor dashed past them into the room.

"Nurse, get in here!" the doctor shouted, and the nurse quickly turned to head back to Pauline's side. "She said he knows it's you," she called out. "He knows." And she hurried into the room, shutting the door behind her.

THIRTY-FIVE

"She's okay now?" Daniel wanted to know. He had returned to the hospital, and he and Eve were driving back to the hotel.

"They got her stabilized, but she was really upset." Eve pulled on the strap of her seat belt. She turned to Daniel. "She thought I was Dorisanne," she explained. "She got all hysterical because she thought I was in trouble, that somebody, a *he,* that was all she'd say, knew it was me and was looking for me. It was like she was trying to warn me against something or somebody."

Daniel seemed to consider Eve's report. "Do you think she was talking about Steve? Do you think she's worried that her boyfriend will come after you, I mean, Dorisanne, next?"

Eve shrugged. She hadn't figured out Pauline's warning. When she was allowed back into the hospital room, her sister's neighbor was even more heavily sedated than she had been earlier.

"I don't know. I guess that makes sense. If Steve was mad at Pauline for helping out Dorisanne, he'd be mad at Dorisanne for getting her involved." She blew out a breath. "But what would Dorisanne have gotten Pauline involved in? Why would Steve be mad about that?" She shook her head. "I don't know what to think. I just know Pauline was beaten really badly and that she was truly frightened that something was going to happen to Dorisanne next."

There was a pause in the conversation as Daniel headed out across the intersection, moving away from the hospital and back toward the Strip.

"What about you? What did you find out? Were you able to get in and see Steve?"

Daniel took one hand off the steering wheel and propped his arm on the door. "James got me in. I talked to the boyfriend for a little while. It's no surprise that he claims he didn't do it."

Eve waited for more. She watched as Daniel moved in and out of traffic. She was starting to recognize points of interest, the casino with the dancing fountains and the one with the pirate ship.

"He says he got drunk and stayed at a friend's house last night, fell asleep there,

255

and didn't go home today. He says he hasn't seen Pauline since yesterday morning when she got home from the previous night's shift."

"Has anybody checked out his story?"

Daniel shrugged. "It turns out that nobody is in a real hurry to let this guy out. He has a couple of outstanding warrants for past grievances, and they're not really interested in proving his innocence. They want to let him stew a while." He glanced over at Eve. "The Las Vegas police like to prioritize their assignments, and this one is at the bottom of the pile." He turned back to the road. "But James has promised to call me if he finds out anything."

"Do you think he's telling the truth?"

Daniel stopped at a light and turned back to Eve. "I do," he said softly. He waited for the green light and moved ahead. "He said he and Pauline have had fights in the past, that he's hit her and he feels bad about that, but he swears he didn't do this. And he seems really upset about what's happened. He kept asking me to call the hospital and see if she was okay."

"But that's not that unheard of," Eve noted. "The women who come to the abbey say there's nothing like the concern they get after the husband or boyfriend realizes how badly they've hurt them. Flowers, candy, jewelry, they call them guilt gifts. Some of the women laughed about it."

"I know," Daniel agreed. "But he didn't seem guilty. He acted more jumpy than anything. It's almost like he wanted to get out of jail to protect her, not to keep her from talking or try to make amends."

"Well, if his alibi proves solid, then I suppose he didn't do it." She didn't think it would be that difficult to find out the truth. "You can't be at two places at once."

"He admits he has a bit of a problem with that."

Eve waited for the explanation.

"He said his friend left his house early this morning. He doesn't really have anybody to back up his story."

"What about the apartment manager, Mr. Whitehorse? Did you get back to the complex to talk to him?"

Daniel nodded. "He says he didn't see any strangers around the place this morning."

"He doesn't remember the motorcycle coming in or going out?" Eve was still bothered by the familiar mustached man she had seen earlier and wondered if he had anything to do with what had happened.

"He claims there are a couple of tenants who ride bikes. Both Harleys, he says.

Didn't recall hearing one before the police arrived, and even if he had, he wouldn't have thought anything about it because he's used to hearing one leave every day after lunch. Guy goes to work about the time we were there."

"And would he give you the names of these Harley owners?"

Daniel turned again to Eve.

"What?" she wanted to know.

He shook his head. "You," he answered.

"What about me?"

"You just have the instinct for this kind of thing," he replied.

Eve couldn't help herself, she smiled. It pleased her to hear her father's former partner giving her such praise.

"And no, Mr. Whitehorse didn't care to share the names of his tenants. He's pretty protective of the place."

"A little too protective, if you ask me," Eve commented, remembering how he didn't want to let them into Dorisanne's apartment, how he questioned who they were and why they wanted to get in there. "He seems a bit hypervigilant for an apartment manager."

"Yeah, well, maybe he loves his work." Daniel made the turn into the hotel parking lot. "You want to get something to eat?" he asked.

Eve glanced at the clock on the dashboard. It was well after seven. She was pretty hungry. "Let's go back to that diner," she suggested.

"You hoping to find that Caesar's waitress again?" Daniel asked. "Talk to her, see if she knows anything?"

Eve glanced over at her friend. She shook her head and grinned. "No, it's not anything like that. I just enjoyed the meat loaf."

THIRTY-SIX

After supper it was too late to go back to the hospital. Eve called the Intensive Care Unit, and after being unable to attain any information because she was not family, Daniel called, gave his title as Detective, his rank and badge number, and claimed he needed to know the victim's condition for the ongoing investigation, never mentioning, of course, that he wasn't actually involved in the ongoing investigation, that he wasn't even an officer in Las Vegas.

He was told that Pauline was stable, that though she remained in critical condition, they planned to upgrade that status to satisfactory if her vital signs continued to stay normal. She was still sedated, but there had not proved to be any neurological damage from the head injury that she had sustained. She was not, however, the nurse reported, awake and talking.

He closed his phone and told Eve

everything he had just heard as they sat in the parking lot. "Are you going up to your room?"

Eve studied him. "You keeping tabs on me?"

Daniel smiled. "Well, you have been known to take off in the middle of the night."

She nodded in agreement. "That is true."

They got out of the car and Daniel glanced behind him, seeming to study the cars around them. Eve looked at the SUVs and sedans and didn't think anything appeared suspicious or familiar. He turned toward her, and they walked into the hotel lobby and started toward the elevators.

"You want to stop in the bar before we go up?" Eve asked.

He glanced in the direction of the hotel lounge ahead of them. "I don't think there's any American Idols in there." He grinned, nudging Eve in the side.

"I think I can manage to sit in a lounge without entertainment," she replied.

They walked into the bar, found an empty table in the corner, and took a seat. There were only a few other customers in the establishment — a man and a woman at the bar and two men at a table near the front. They all seemed to be watching a ball game that was being shown on a large screen over the bar.

"Baseball and a beer," Daniel said. "My favorite way to spend a weekend evening."

"Wow, it's already Saturday night, isn't it?" Eve had lost track of the hours. She turned to Daniel. "Don't you need to get back by tomorrow?" She realized that they hadn't actually discussed how long they were going to stay in Vegas. Originally, she thought they would be heading back by Sunday, but since they had made no discoveries concerning the whereabouts of Dorisanne, she had less of a feel for their plans.

"I got PTO," he answered.

Eve didn't know what he meant and he read her expression.

"Paid time off," he explained, glancing around, stopping at the table with the two men.

She nodded.

"Don't you have to request that in advance?" The Captain and her mother would make yearly plans of the dates they wanted him to take off. They would decide at the beginning of every year the times and places of the family vacations based on his approved requisitions.

He shrugged. "I can call tomorrow. It's

not a problem." He went back to watching the game.

The waitress, a young woman with long black hair pulled back into a braid and a butterfly tattoo on her bare right shoulder, came over and took their orders. Eve requested a cup of coffee while Daniel chose a draft beer. She thought about the Captain and wondered if he was watching the same game. He liked baseball, and she often heard the games on Saturday nights through her bedroom door while she read or enjoyed a bit of solitude. He would usually choose any sport over Saturday evening Mass.

Eve turned her attention to the waitress, noticing her braided hair swishing as she talked to the other customers, watching her as she rang up the sale and then brought over the drinks. Eve agreed to let Daniel pay and noticed how the server took his credit card and headed back to the bar. In a few minutes she had returned with the drinks and the question about running a tab. He agreed and she left without giving him a receipt or returning his card.

"How do you run a tab?" Eve asked, thinking about the process of purchasing drinks and meals using a credit card. She was used to dealing primarily with cash at restaurants. The sisters and monks at the monestery used a credit card only for large items.

"They just don't cash out the card," Daniel explained, taking a sip of his beer. "They swipe your card, but they just keep adding drinks as you order, and they don't tally up the costs until you're ready to go."

Eve nodded. It made sense to her, and as she thought about the transaction just carried out, she recalled their earlier conversation about Dorisanne and the possibility of her involvement in credit card fraud at her place of employment, at the bar at the Rio. She realized, watching the waitress who was serving them, how easy it was to get credit card numbers in that profession. She also realized that cocktail waitresses were generally serving a vulnerable population by the end of a night. Drunks were less likely to pay attention to who had their cards or for how long.

"What's wrong?" Daniel asked. He had been watching Eve.

She shook her head. "I was just thinking about Dorisanne, hoping she's okay."

He reached over and placed his hand on top of Eve's. "She's okay," he said, sounding as reassuring as he possibly could.

"What if this guy on the motorcycle, the one I saw at the casino last night, what if he is after her? What if Pauline knows where she is and told him? What if that's why she was beaten? And it's not Steve. It's that guy and he's after my sister."

Daniel squeezed her hand.

"If he knew where she was, he wouldn't have come back to the apartment. He would have gone right to where she was." He sat back in his chair. "No, she didn't tell him anything like that."

Eve nodded. What Daniel was saying did make sense to her. If Pauline had given him Dorisanne and Robbie's location, he would have left the scene and not come back. She wanted to believe that was true, but it still bothered her that Pauline was so afraid for Dorisanne, that she was trying so desperately to warn her that "he" knew it was her. She thought again about Pauline's words that the nurse had relayed: "He knows it's you."

"What could she have meant?" she asked, not explaining her thoughts.

Daniel shook his head. "I'm not following you."

"He knows it's you," she repeated. "What does that mean?"

Daniel seemed to think about Eve's question. He'd been told what Pauline said when she'd gotten so upset and caused the nurse to make Eve leave the room. "That he knows Dorisanne has done something, that she's the one who committed some act that obviously angered him." He looked up at Eve. "But we don't know who she's talking about. She could be talking about Steve, that it's Steve who knows that Dorisanne was the one who got Pauline involved in something."

Eve shook her head. "I don't think it's Steve. I want it to be him. I want it to be that simple, and I want them to keep him locked up for good and away from Pauline and away from my sister, but I don't think he did this. I think the guy from Caesar's, the one who was at the apartments. I think it was him. And I think he's after Dorisanne and Robbie. And I think Dorisanne has done something to make him angry enough to beat poor Pauline to get information from her. But what?" Eve wanted to know. "What could she have done?"

The butterfly-tattooed waitress walked up to their table. "Here, I forgot to give you the card," she said, handing the credit card back to Daniel. She smiled and glanced over to Eve. "More coffee?" she asked, and Eve stared at the credit card placed next to Daniel's mug of beer.

"She's involved in the theft ring," Eve announced.

The waitress stepped back. "What?"

Eve looked at her and shook her head. "No, no, not you. It's fine. And no, no more coffee, thanks," she responded, waiting for the young woman to leave.

Daniel had leaned forward. "How do you know?" he asked.

She reached into her back pocket, pulled out the small address book, and took out the small piece of paper that had fallen out earlier. She placed it on the table in front of him. It was a bar receipt. "She kept receipts. She got the numbers," Eve said. "At the Rio, she kept the cards and copied the numbers."

THIRTY-SEVEN

"If what you're saying is true," Daniel noted, "then her boss could have found out about it. That could be the reason she was fired."

"And that's easy enough to confirm," Eve said. "All we have to do is call him up tonight and ask him."

Daniel shook his head.

"What?" she wanted to know.

"The manager is gone, right?"

Eve suddenly remembered the conversation they'd had at the Rio. The waitress had told them that the manager was away for a few days. "Well, we could call human resources," she suggested.

"That will have to wait until Monday."

Eve tried to think of another way to confirm her suspicions. "We could go back to the Rio and try asking around again."

Daniel took the receipt still on the table

between them and appeared to be studying it.

"This doesn't really tell us anything." He laid it back down. "There's not a full card number on it, no personal information other than a name. I don't see that this proves anything. I don't see that this confirms she was stealing numbers."

Eve glanced down at the receipt again. Daniel was right, she knew. But she still couldn't understand why her sister would have kept a bill from a customer. It had to be something important; it had to be a clue, she told herself.

She drank her coffee and noticed that Daniel was once again eyeing the two men sitting at the table near the front of the bar.

"Do you recognize those guys?" she asked.

Daniel turned to her and smiled. "I'm not sure," he replied. "I've seen them somewhere before."

Eve glanced once again in their direction. One of the men was young, looked to be barely thirty, the other was older, mid-forties, she thought. They were dressed in shirts and ties, no sport coats, and they seemed interested in only the baseball game playing on the television. They were drinking beers, and as far as she knew, they had not looked at or appeared interested in

Daniel or Eve since they walked into the bar. She wondered if she and Daniel were both starting to see things that weren't there.

"Okay, let's go over what we have," she said, drinking the last of her coffee.

Daniel leaned back in his chair, waiting for her to start.

She nodded. "Dorisanne is missing."

"Yes." Daniel rested his arms on the table and clasped his hands together.

"We believe she left with Robbie, and Pauline and the manager of the apartments both seem to know when they left." She closed her eyes, wanting to get the details straight. "She was fired from the Rio."

"But for what, we don't know," Daniel interjected.

Eve opened her eyes. "Right. It could be that she missed too many shifts because of hurting her ankle or she could be stealing credit card numbers from customers."

Daniel blew out a breath.

"Robbie is very likely involved in some sort of theft ring. The police knew that he had some connections with guys who are known for credit card theft. They assume he's an active participant." She looked at Daniel. "That is right, isn't it?"

Daniel didn't remark but finally nodded.

"So either Dorisanne knew about her husband's activities, perhaps even participating in them with him, stealing names and numbers from her customers, and they both left town because they've done something to cause trouble, or she's not involved, and she just ran away with him because he's in trouble and told her that if he was in trouble then she was in trouble and needed to leave town as well."

Daniel dropped his head into his hand and rubbed his brow. Eve thought he looked tired. Had he actually had any sleep since they'd arrived in Las Vegas? She looked at her watch. It was after ten o'clock. They ought to call it a night, just go to bed and work on things again in the morning. But first she wanted to make sure she was clear about everything they both knew or were guessing.

She glanced back down once more at the receipt she had found in Dorisanne's belongings. "Okay, let's try and see if she's involved." She studied every line on the bill but could see nothing that indicated Dorisanne was stealing.

"What would implicate her in this theft ring? How would she get the numbers? It doesn't show up on the customer's receipt."

"Most of the thieves have a skimmer."

"A skimmer?" Eve waited for an explanation.

Daniel placed his hands back together on the table. "It's about the size of an ice cube and it stores information."

An ice cube. Eve tried to think if she had seen anything like that in Dorisanne's nightstand drawer.

Daniel continued. "They attach the skimmer to any credit card reader and it stores the numbers." He reached over for his mug and took a drink of beer. "I've seen them attached to gas pumps, ATMs, even vending machines, anywhere people use cards."

They both turned to the couple at the bar who had suddenly cheered loudly. Apparently one of the teams playing on television had just scored. Eve watched as they gave each other a high five. She then noticed that the men at the front table still seemed to be glued to the same game, but they were not enthusiastic about what had just occurred. She looked again at Daniel. "What do they do with the numbers then? What good are they once the person notices that the card is being charged for purchases they didn't make?"

"There's a couple of ways to make money. One is that these ringleaders gather more information from the card owners, open up

272

new accounts, and create fraudulent cards using the stolen card owners' information. You really only need an address, a phone number, maybe a date of birth. Or they sell the numbers to somebody who makes a lot of purchases real fast and then turns around to sell those items — all done before the theft is discovered." He shrugged. "If Dorisanne was just gathering numbers, I would guess that somebody else was taking the numbers and buying and selling the merchandise."

Eve nodded. It was making sense to her, but she still couldn't understand why Dorisanne would keep the receipt of a customer. She studied the name but did not call it out. Marcus Winters, it looked like, but she wasn't sure. And yet it was exactly as Daniel had said. There was no complete credit number listed and no personal information written about the customer. She suddenly had a thought and pulled out the small address book, turned to the back, and began searching the names that started with a W.

"What are you looking for?" Daniel wanted to know. "And what is that book, anyway?"

Eve glanced up, her finger pointing to a line. "I got it at Dorisanne's," she confessed.

"When we were looking around."

"You took something from the apartment?" he asked.

"It's in here," she said.

Daniel waited. He shook his head.

"The man who signed the receipt — his phone number is in here."

THIRTY-EIGHT

"So she has a receipt from a man, a customer at the Rio, whose address and phone number she kept in her address book?" Daniel asked, but he sounded more alert than he had a few minutes earlier. "Is there a credit card number also written in there?"

Eve studied the listing and looked up. She shook her head. "Just a couple of phone numbers," she answered.

"I guess that's good news," he responded.

"I guess. Or it could just mean that she keeps those numbers somewhere else, that it's like you said and she uses a skimmer and has it with her."

Daniel nodded. He was once again watching the men at the front table.

"Do you think they're following us?" Eve asked when she noticed where he was looking.

Daniel turned back to face her. "I don't

know," he replied. "I don't even know if I actually saw them before." He glanced in their direction, leaned in closer, trying to get a better look. "They just seem familiar somehow." And then he shook his head and drank the last swallow of his beer.

Eve studied them as well, tried to imagine if she had seen them somewhere since arriving in Vegas, but it was of no use. Even though she was certain she had recognized the guy on the motorcycle, with these two guys she was simply drawing a blank. "Maybe they're just staying here and you saw them in the lobby or on the elevator or something."

Daniel nodded. "Could be," he responded. "But I don't think that's it. I've seen them somewhere else."

"Maybe they're cops; maybe they're familiar because they look like you look when you're following somebody."

Daniel didn't respond at first, then he just shook his head.

Eve turned her attention back to Dorisanne's address book. As she studied the cover, a pink-and-purple paisley design, she thought she remembered seeing her sister with it before. She must have brought it home to New Mexico sometime in the last few months or years. She checked out

276

the front inside cover to see if there was a year written somewhere. There was none, but she did find her own address written under the E's: *Eve, Our Lady of Guadalupe Abbey and Convent,* and both the Pecos address and the phone number were listed.

With a different color of ink she had added Eve's cell number, and seeing it made Eve think about the phone call a few nights before that had gotten the Captain so upset. It made her wonder once again if it had been a real phone call and, if so, why Dorisanne made the call to the Captain and not to her. Clearly, she had her sister's number.

She recalled what had happened the night of Dorisanne's contact and realized that the call in the middle of the night was the main reason she was in Vegas at all, and she thought about the sequence of events that led to her trip. She looked for the Captain's number, but she could not find a listing. She searched under Divine, Captain, even Mom and Dad. There were no numbers listed. Of course, it wasn't that odd, she thought; the address and the landline number were the same from when they had both been children. Surely, Dorisanne, like Eve, had all of those details memorized.

Neither of them would need to write them down.

However, Dorisanne had contacted the Captain using his new cell phone number; she hadn't called him on the landline. And even though Eve didn't recall giving her sister that number, she assumed Dorisanne had gotten it somehow. And yet it was not listed anywhere in this address book.

"You look puzzled," Daniel noted.

"Just trying to find a number in here," Eve responded.

"Pauline's?" he asked.

Eve shook her head. "No, the Captain's."

"Why would she need the home number in there? Wouldn't she know that by heart?"

"His new cell number," Eve answered. "That was the number he says she called the other night. But it's not in here."

Daniel didn't respond right away.

"I guess she could have that already added to her new contact list in her phone," Eve said.

"I guess," Daniel agreed.

There was a pause.

"Why wouldn't she take the book with her?" Eve wanted to know. "If it has all these contacts, why wouldn't she want that with her?"

Daniel considered the question. "Didn't

you say that there are lines through most of the names? Could be that she was marking them off."

"Maybe recording them somewhere else," she said, as she had guessed back in the apartment when she first found the book.

"Most people keep all that information in their phones nowadays. Maybe she was adding them to her digital contact list and didn't need the book anymore." Daniel seemed to think this was the answer for what Eve had found.

"That makes some sense," she said, flipping through the pages. "But not all of the names and numbers have a line through them. I guess that could just mean she didn't want to keep them all."

"Could be," Daniel agreed.

She kept looking through all the names. There were a few that she recognized, but most of them were names she didn't know. About half of them had a line drawn through them.

"Your guy, the customer?" Daniel asked.

She looked up, understood that he was asking if she had drawn a line through his name. She found the listing, glanced up again, and shook her head.

"So either she didn't record it or didn't need it," Daniel noted.

Eve shrugged. "Maybe we should call him?"

Daniel looked at his watch. "Sort of late," he said.

Eve nodded. She studied the numbers and noticed that they were both Las Vegas exchanges. She had become familiar with the 702 area code.

"Let's wait until the morning," he suggested. "I think we've done all the damage we can do today." He hesitated. "But we could go back to the Rio tonight if you want and see if the manager is working."

"No, you're right. Misti, the waitress, said he'd be gone until next week," Eve remembered. "Besides, I think we could both use a good night's sleep. Maybe Pauline will be up and able to answer questions in the morning, and if so, we'll know a lot more about everything."

Daniel nodded. "Okay," he agreed. "Plus we can call the customer and see if he knows Dorisanne."

Eve stifled a yawn and rubbed her eyes.

"Late hours for a nun?" Daniel smiled.

"Late hours for anybody," she answered. "You don't look so bright-eyed and bushy-tailed yourself."

He stretched his arms above his head and gave a big yawn as well. "You're right. Even police officers need their beauty rest. Speaking of, did you call your father today?"

"I called him back this morning before we left for the apartments. He had left a voicemail message for me to call him after he talked to you." She remembered the conversation and how he was on his way to check out Mr. Salazar's claim about gold on his property and how Caleb Alford had called the office but he had not talked to him.

"I only talked to him for a minute when I was on my way to talk to James. Had he heard from anybody?"

"You mean Dorisanne? Had she called again?"

"Yeah," he replied.

Eve shook her head. "There was a call," she answered. "From here, but if it was Dorisanne, she didn't leave a message."

Daniel nodded.

They watched as the young couple sitting at the bar drank the last of their drinks, paid the bill, and headed out. The two men at the front table each had another beer served to them, and Eve thought about Daniel's uneasy feeling that he had seen them before. She glanced over and he was still watching them intently.

Thirty-Nine

Once again, sleep did not come easily. Eve tossed and turned, trying first to find a comfortable position on one side and then switching to the other, then flat on her back. She tried fluffing up her pillow, using one and then two and then one again, yanking on and off the covers, pulling them over her head, folding them under her arms, but nothing seemed to help.

Finally, she got up, went to the bathroom, and poured a glass of water, and then walked over to the window. She pulled open the curtains and gazed out at the lights and the cars parked below her in the hotel lot. There was not much going on. A taxi waited at the front entrance. His lights were off, and sitting as he was under the lighted awning, she could see the driver slumped in his seat, looking as if he was trying to take a nap.

A few cars passed on the road in front of

the place. She could hear sirens in the background but could see no indication of any activity around the hotel. She discovered that if she looked as far to the left as she could, pressing her forehead against the window and focusing very hard, she could just see the Strip with its blinking lights and hustling, bustling traffic. She pulled away.

She almost wished they were closer to all the action. Staying at the hotel Daniel had chosen kept her from being able to walk to the Rio or to Caesar's and perhaps find ways to make better use of the long night hours. At the very least, she could look for Clara again and learn more tips about gambling or about Vegas nightlife. She could people-watch or maybe find a chapel. Something other than just standing at a tall window that overlooked a parking lot. She looked again and noticed a dark sedan sitting under a light, two men sitting inside. They looked like the two men she and Daniel had noticed in the bar. She wondered about them, why they might be sitting in the car in the middle of the night, but then realized that people visiting this city kept very different hours. She told herself it meant nothing and headed back to bed.

She thought about the day, Pauline's attack, going through Dorisanne's things, finding the address book, sitting at the hospital. It had been long and emotionally draining, and she still had found no sign of her sister, no clues about where she had gone or why. Eve sat down on the bed and closed her eyes. *There has to be something in all of these conversations, all of this searching,* she thought, *that can give me some idea as to where Dorisanne has gone.* She thought about Pauline's outburst, the obvious fear she had for Dorisanne. She thought about Misti explaining how Dorisanne had been fired, how the bartender was also gone, and even the manager, which she didn't think was related, but still interesting. And once again she thought about the address book.

She found it sitting on the nightstand and she picked it up, leaned back against the pillows, and flipped through the pages, this time studying every name, every address, just to see if something jumped out at her, if something might offer a clue about her sister's activities or whereabouts. *The Captain would tell me to look closer,* she thought.

"There's always something to be missed. Read everything slowly and more than once," she said out loud, remembering her father's instructions when they were going over the files regarding the missing miner's case.

She took in a breath and started searching from the beginning. The first page had her name and the address at the apartment where they had been twice. *So she's had this book only since she's been married and living in the complex with Robbie,* Eve thought. That would make this book and its recordings at least six years old. There was a little heart drawn by her last name, something Eve remembered that Dorisanne had done since she was a child, and a small Rio sticker placed in the upper right-hand corner. She studied the heart, ran her fingers over the drawing, and then turned the page.

There were names of four people and one business that started with an A, all listed under that letter: Claire Anderson, Dwight Aldridge, Dr. Adelman, Annie, and Applebee's. There were phone numbers and a couple of addresses. These were all local, and none of them had lines drawn through them.

She moved to the B's. John Beadles, Best-Buy, Nancy Beech, Baker's Dozen, Betty Lou, and some place listed as Busybody. There were lines through a couple of these, Nancy Beech and John Beadles. The businesses were not marked. There was an address without a name, some place in Sparks, Nevada. Eve thought she had seen this town name before, but she wasn't sure she knew where it was. She kept looking, and that was when she noticed there was just the letter *B,* listed within the group, under the Busybody listing but a few lines above the Sparks address, and beside it was a local Las Vegas number.

Nothing any more exciting in the C's or D's. Then Eve looked at the E's. There was her name and information, plus Every Woman's Shoes, Tom Ely, and somebody named Esther. She moved to the next letter, *F:* Foxy Mama's, Dolores Fulbright, a few more. And then, just like what she had seen under the letter *B,* there was a letter *F,* and a number that had a different area code, one Eve didn't recognize.

She kept searching, through G, H, and then she turned the page to the I's. There were only a couple of listings. Indigo's — Eve had no idea what that could be; Philip Isley, a guy Eve remembered from Madrid, an old boyfriend of Dorisanne's, she thought, and then wondered why she would still be in contact with a high school sweetheart; and then there was another listing like the ones she had seen under the two other letters. It, too, was just the one letter, an *l*. There was no person's name or establishment. Just that, one letter *l* and another number with a different area code.

She flipped through the pages: J, K, L, M, N, several pages of people and places, some Eve recognized and some she did not. Then O, P, Q, R, which included lots of Rio numbers, the lounge, human resources, management, security, and then there were the other letters and listings. She quickly found the W's once more, with Mr. Marcus Winters, the name on the credit card receipt, the one name and number she wanted to call but knew she had to wait until a decent hour.

X, Y, and Z had a few names but nothing that seemed interesting. On the last page there was a group of numbers, Eve thought, that she should probably study and try to decipher, but nothing that offered any clues right now. There was another address without a name attached, some business or residence in Reno. And then the last page, the inside cover, had another sticker, this one from a carwash place somewhere in town.

She closed the book, leaned back against the pillows, and thought about the addresses and listings. Doctors, stores, friends, restaurants, bars, work, there was certainly nothing significant about any of them. Eve probably had a similar list herself in her little black book that she had started keeping at the private detective office. Names and numbers of clients and business offices that they had contacted over the past year — an address book from the Divine Private Detective Agency would look very similar to a cocktail waitress's address book in Las Vegas.

"Think, Eve," she said out loud. "There has to be something you're missing." She opened her eyes and shook her head. There was nothing. She put the book down, took a drink of water, and turned off the lamp beside her, deciding to try once again to go to sleep.

Reciting the familiar prayer might help: "Hail Mary, full —" But she stopped at that word, sat back up, turned on the light, and opened the address book once again. Something caused her to stop — something was there. Dorisanne was giving her a clue in that book, she knew it.

She reached for the pad and pen that had been placed on the nightstand and flipped the pages to the B's. She wrote down the letter *B* and the phone number.

She turned the page and copied down the

letter *F* and the number listed, and then she did the same with the other one-letter listing she had found: B F I. She shook her head.

"Dorisanne, you are one smart sister," she said.

Eve found her cell phone and walked over to the window. She pulled back the curtain and stood waiting for just a minute before dialing the first number she had seen, the local one.

"It's just too good to be true," she said, and then she couldn't help herself, she practically laughed out loud when she saw the man sitting on the passenger's side in the dark sedan parked below her pull out his phone. She moved away from the window, letting the curtains fall together, and quickly ended the call as he said hello.

FORTY

Eve tapped lightly on Daniel's door. She waited. She tapped again. "Daniel," she whispered. "Daniel, are you awake?" She leaned into the door. She tapped once again. "Daniel . . ."

There was nothing.

She knocked a little louder this time. "Daniel," she called out and then stopped, hoping she wasn't disturbing the other guests on the floor.

She glanced at her watch. It was three in the morning. She stood at the door a bit longer, placed her ear to listen for any noises coming from inside. There was nothing.

She pulled out her phone and dialed the hotel and asked for his room. She heard the phone ring. Once, twice, three times, a fourth, he didn't pick up.

"He's not in there," she said to herself and went back to her room.

Eve sat down on the edge of the bed to

think. *Where could he be? And why did he leave without telling me?* She was disappointed that she wouldn't be able to tell him the news, explain to him who the two men were that he had seen in the bar. She wanted to be with him so that together they could try to figure out why Dorisanne might have FBI phone numbers in her address book and why the feds were following the two of them. She wanted Daniel with her because he might have some answers.

"Well," she said to no one in particular, "I could try to go back to sleep, and we could just talk about this tomorrow." She thought about the idea, realizing she was way too wide awake to try sleeping again.

"I could call him on his cell phone," she said, still talking out loud to herself. She considered this. But then she thought, *Maybe he's out in the parking lot watching those FBI agents, and a ringing phone might blow his cover.* She watched that scenario play out in her mind. She shook her head. "Not a good idea." She dropped her elbows onto her knees.

"I could just go downstairs to see if he's there."

She decided this was her best idea, realizing that even if he wasn't in the lobby, the night manager or some staff person might have remembered seeing him and would be able to give her some information about what time he had left and even might be able to tell her if he had mentioned where he was going.

She stood up, gathered her room key, her wallet, her phone, and, for some reason, Dorisanne's address book, and headed out. When she got to the elevators, she looked out the window to check out the parking spot where the dark sedan with the two men following them had been parked earlier.

The car was gone. From where she was standing, she could also see the spot where she remembered Daniel had parked earlier, an area of the lot that she couldn't see from her room window. His car was missing as well. She felt her pulse quicken.

Daniel had driven somewhere, and these men, these men she now knew to be FBI agents who had some connection to Dorisanne, whose phone numbers were in her book, had followed him. She considered the idea that maybe Daniel had figured out who they were and had confronted them. Maybe they all went out for a cup of coffee, she decided. But somehow that didn't make any sense. How would Daniel have known they were agents?

She waited for the elevator, and when it

arrived at her floor she got in and pushed the button for the lobby. When she got to the first floor, she noticed that the other elevator was heading to the floor she had just come from and wondered if it could be Daniel returning from somewhere. She stopped, thinking she should make a quick call to his cell. She dialed his number but then decided once again against the idea.

She found her way to the lobby and discovered that it was the same night manager from the night before, the one who had called her a taxi when she went to Caesar's.

"You keep late hours," he said when she was near the front desk.

"As do you," she responded.

He smiled. "Yep, but I get paid for mine," he said, and then seemed to consider what he had said and cleared his throat.

Eve could see he was embarrassed for some reason but couldn't understand what about his comment could make him blush.

"Do you need another taxi?" he asked, changing the tone of the conversation.

Eve thought about his question. *Do I?* she wondered.

"Do you remember the guy I came in with about ten o'clock this evening? The tall guy, dark, he drives a BMW?" She waited. "We checked in together a couple of nights ago." She knew this man hadn't registered them but hoped he might remember Daniel.

"Detective Hively," he said, nodding. "Sure, I remember Daniel," he added. "Nice guy, comes here a few times every year."

Eve smiled, remembering that the staff did seem to know who Daniel was. "That's him," she responded. "Did you by any chance see him come by here tonight?"

The man didn't answer right away. Eve thought it was a simple enough question and waited. She didn't understand the hesitation. Either he had seen him or he hadn't.

"You know, I've never seen you come with him before," the man noted.

"No, this is my first time," Eve explained.

He nodded, still seemed to be deep in thought about the question that had been asked.

"We're friends," Eve volunteered, not sure why she needed to add this bit of information to the stranger.

He nodded again.

"We're here trying to locate my sister," she added. "She lives here and we haven't heard from her in a while. We came from New Mexico to try and find her." Now Eve was telling everything. It was all just flying out of her mouth and couldn't be stopped.

"We think she's in trouble and her neighbor was beaten up earlier today and is in the hospital. And there's some guy —"

"He left about an hour ago. He didn't say where he was going," the man said.

"Oh." Eve was stunned to hear the answer and stunned to be stopped midway through her story.

"Do you want a cab?" he asked again.

"Did he say where he was going?" She thought that was a long shot.

The night manager shook his head. "Just said he couldn't sleep."

She thought about the exchange Daniel might have had with the hotel manager and the fact that they knew each other.

"Does he do that a lot when he stays here?"

The night manager seemed to be studying Eve. There was a long pause before making his reply.

"Sometimes," he finally answered.

Eve waited.

"He likes to go to the Rio," he said.

She smiled and nodded. "Yeah, he likes to go there," she said softly. "That's where my sister works . . . worked," she corrected herself.

"So, maybe you could find them both at the Rio," the man suggested.

"Yeah, maybe." The thought of something so easy, so perfect almost made her want to try it.

"So, you need a taxi?"

Eve glanced out the lobby doors and saw the cab sitting at the entrance. "I think I see one waiting," she responded. "Good night," she said and headed out the door.

She jumped into the back of the cab and looked at the man in the rearview mirror. It was not the same driver from the night before.

"Alta Bates Hospital," she said, thinking that sitting with Pauline made as much sense as anything at the moment.

And the driver took off, whipping them out of the driveway and onto the street. Eve was looking out the windshield, watching as they pulled away. She heard the whine of a motorcycle close behind them, but she gave the sound no thought and simply placed her attention on the road ahead.

FORTY-ONE

"I think I've changed my mind," Eve said to the cabdriver.

He glanced at her in the rearview mirror as he slowed down.

He waited for new instructions as Eve suddenly thought about going to the Rio to see if that was where Daniel had gone. Her mind was a jumble. Maybe he was talking to someone in the lounge, she thought, and if she found him, she could tell him about her discovery, about the FBI.

She shook her head. "No, never mind, I still want to go to the hospital." She wanted to let Daniel know what she had found out, but she also wanted to visit Pauline again, to see Dorisanne's friend and see if she might be able to answer a few questions.

She felt the car speed back up and decided to close her eyes for a second. She was tired and thought she might rest.

She was surprised when she felt the car

come to a stop. "Here," was all he said, waking Eve from her brief nap. She glanced around, noticing that the cabdriver had stopped at the hospital emergency entrance.

"After hours, you have to enter in through there," he explained.

Eve looked at the double doors where she was being dropped off. She hadn't considered that it might be difficult to go up to the floors this late at night, so she wiped her eyes and tried to straighten her hair, wanting to make herself look as presentable as she could. She paid the fare and made her way into the hospital. She was greeted by an older woman, dressed in blue scrubs and a gray sweater, a pair of reading glasses perched on the end of her nose, who was sitting at the front desk, busy typing on a keyboard. "What's the emergency?" she asked without glancing up from the computer screen in front of her.

Eve waited, unsure of exactly how to answer.

The woman glanced up. "What's wrong with you?"

Eve shook her head. "Nothing's wrong with me," she answered. "I'm here to visit someone who is a patient in the Intensive Care Unit." Eve knew she was there after the visiting hours for that floor, but she hoped the woman would still allow her through.

"Are you family?" the attendant asked, having returned to her computer work. She was not watching Eve for an answer.

Eve nodded, somehow thinking that the nonverbal lie was not as damaging as a verbal one.

The woman looked up.

Eve was still nodding, a stupid grin plastered on her face.

The attendant seemed to be studying her. She eyed Eve from above the top of her reading glasses. "Visits to patients in Intensive Care are for family members only, and not even they get in at this hour," she reported. "You can visit at seven in the morning. They're real strict about letting the patients get their rest at night."

Eve took in a breath. There was a bit of commotion in the waiting room beside the desk. A child started to cry and Eve watched as a young man, probably the father, picked the little boy up and held him. The child whimpered and then quieted.

"I couldn't sleep," she said, turning back to the woman at the desk, not sure why this was anything she needed to be sharing, not sure why this information might help her get to Pauline's room.

"So take a pill, drink some hot tea, count sheep." She went back to the computer data entry she was working on.

Eve remained at the desk. She thought about telling the woman that she was a nun, thinking that perhaps playing the religious order card might have some leverage with hospital desk clerks. She waited. "My cab just left," she explained, deciding to try for pity.

There was a long, drawn-out sigh from the woman at the desk. "What's the name?" she asked while she typed a few commands on the keyboard.

"Pauline," Eve answered, and then realized she didn't even know her last name. She suddenly felt as if she had surely blown her chances at that point to be allowed into the hospital. "She came in yesterday, through the emergency room. Pauline . . ."

"You got an address?" the woman asked, not waiting for the last name.

Eve thought. "Desert Home Place," she answered, recalling the name of the complex.

"Pauline Evans?"

"Yes, that's her, exactly. Pauline Evans," she answered, relieved to hear the last name.

The woman looked again at Eve. "She's not in Intensive Care," she reported. "They moved her to a regular bed a couple of hours ago."

"Oh, then where is she?" Eve asked eagerly, glad to hear she was no longer in critical condition.

"Room 515," the woman replied. "Bed B." She paused for a second and then leaned over and picked up a small sheet of paper and wrote the room number down. She handed it to Eve. "You'll need to tell the security guard at the elevator where you're going and that I let you through."

Eve took the small piece of paper. "Thank you so much," she said.

"Don't go making any noise up there," the woman responded. "They hate it when people come in the middle of the night and make noise. I'm not even supposed to let you in, but since you're family and all . . ." She smiled slightly at Eve and went back to her computer work.

Eve walked around the desk and made her way to the bank of elevators, passing several doors marking various departments. When she got to the elevators, she noticed that there was no security guard around, so she hit the button, and when the elevator door opened in front of her, she walked in. She pressed the number 5 and felt the elevator start to rise.

The door opened and she was standing in front of a long, narrow desk filled with files and computer screens, several chairs pushed beneath the flat top. The station seemed deserted, so she waited a few minutes, thinking she should probably let somebody know she was on the floor. She finally decided to find the room on her own and followed a sign on the wall pointing her in the right direction. She turned the corner, hearing the elevator door close behind her.

When she arrived at number 515, she tapped lightly on the door and then pushed it open. In the bed by the door, a patient was tucked under blankets and clearly asleep. Eve didn't think it was Pauline, but she wasn't certain. She stared at the back of the patient's head, could make out it was a woman, but her hair was short and black, not Pauline's long blond tresses. The woman was snoring, and Eve thought of the Captain and how she could hear him making the same kind of noises through the walls and two closed doors. She wondered if Pauline was able to sleep with such a noisy room-mate.

She stood at the door for a few minutes, concerned that she might wake the patient in bed A and noticed that there was a pulled curtain separating the room. She walked in as quietly as she could, assuming that bed B was behind the curtain and that would be where she would find Pauline sleeping.

Eve headed through the door and to the other side of the curtain. She stood at the edge of the bed, surprised to find it empty.

She looked around. The sheets on the bed were tangled and strewn about, and Eve suddenly wondered if she had entered the right room, if she was at the right bed. She wondered if Pauline had been taken down for some test or, worse, returned to the Intensive Care Unit. She checked the bathroom behind her and saw that the door was cracked and no one was in there. She walked past the sleeping patient in bed A and back out into the hallway.

As she glanced down the hall, she saw Pauline being helped through the exit door of a stairway by another woman who was just about the same size. Eve's eyes grew wide, and she had a hard time believing what she was seeing.

"Dorisanne," Eve called out, but before she could make her way to the exit, a nurse had rounded the corner and was standing right in front of her.

FORTY-TWO

"What are you doing here?" The nurse stood between Eve and the direction she needed to go to chase after her sister and the patient she was helping to escape.

"I have to follow . . ." Eve was trying to step aside and head for the stairs, but the heavyset nurse stood in her way.

"How did you get up here, anyway?" the nurse asked before she could finish her sentence. She had a cell phone in her hand as if she intended to place a call. "Nobody is supposed to be visiting at this time of night."

"I came in through the emergency department. The attendant let me come up," she explained. Eve tried to see around the nurse, but she was too big. She heard the exit door close and assumed that Pauline and Dorisanne were already moving down the stairs.

"I never heard from security that a visitor

was coming up here; the guard always alerts me so I'll know who to look for." She seemed to be watching Eve's every move. "Peter never called, and I've had the phone with me the whole time." She held up the cell phone she had in her hand.

"Because Peter wasn't there! Nobody was there. There was no security guard at the elevators. I came up on my own. Now, I really have to —"

The nurse moved closer to Eve, acting as if she was trying to smell her breath or check out her pupils. "Who are you looking for? Who is it you're trying to see?"

"Pauline," Eve answered, stepping back. "Pauline Evans. She was moved from Intensive Care sometime this evening. I was told she was in this room." She pointed at the door behind her. "Bed B, but she's not there!"

"What?" the nurse asked, stepping into the room, yanking Eve by the arm. "You're not going anywhere," she announced, closing the door behind her, pulling Eve with her as she walked around the curtain. "She's gone!"

"That's what I'm trying to tell you!" Eve responded, unable to break away.

"Where is she?" the nurse asked. "Where did she go?"

"I don't know. I only just got here, but I think I saw her heading down the stairs. I need to follow her. I think she's in trouble and my sister is with her."

Still holding Eve by the sleeve of her shirt. The nurse held the phone closer to her and dialed a number. She placed it to her mouth. "I need some help up here," she said to whoever answered her call. "It's Patsy from the fifth floor, room 515," she added and then clicked the phone off.

"Do you think you could take this somewhere else?" The patient in bed A had awakened. She sat up. "I'm trying to sleep. Isn't that what you tell me I need to do? Get some sleep?" She paused. "What is going on?"

The nurse looked over at the patient. "I'm sorry, Mrs. White. We just have an after-hours visitor situation that I'm trying to handle." And she pulled Eve back out into the hall and closed the door to the room.

"Are you the patient's family?"

Eve shook her head. "I'm a friend," she answered. "I was worried about her and came to check on her."

"Why were you worried about her?" she asked.

The elevator bell sounded, indicating it was stopping on that floor, and Patsy, still holding on to Eve, glanced in that direction. "Now I can get some help," she said, but then she seemed surprised when the door opened and it apparently wasn't the person she'd expected. "Wait a minute." She let go of Eve's sleeve. "That's not Peter."

Eve looked down the hall and saw the person coming off the elevator. He was no security guard. He was the man on the motorcycle she had seen at the apartments earlier that day, the same man she had seen at Caesar's the night before. He looked taller standing than he did sitting, but he wore his hair in the same slicked-back fashion and was still sporting the dark mustache.

She wanted to say something, but she couldn't find the words.

"Who are you?" the nurse asked as the man headed in their direction.

He grinned. "Not who you thought," he said, then he reached up and quickly and calmly placed a cloth over the nurse's mouth and nose. She dropped to her knees before she could respond. The phone fell beside her.

Eve watched in shock as the nurse slumped to the floor.

"Hey, who's out there?" Mrs. White called from inside room 515, and as the man turned to see where the voice asking the question had come from, Eve took off in the direction of the exit stairs.

She could hear the footsteps following her as she hurried through the door and down the steps. She jumped down two stairs at a time, as fast as she could, but she could hear the motorcycle man gaining on her, and she suddenly became concerned that he would catch up with a frail Pauline and Dorisanne, who she assumed couldn't be that far ahead of her.

She made a quick decision and opened the next door she came to, the one to the third floor, and sped down the hall. As she moved away from the stairwell, she tried several of the doors on her left and on her right, pushing and pulling, but soon stopped when she saw that there was a keypad next to every set of doors. She knew that she was going to have to keep running down the hall until she could find either an unlocked door that led to someone who could help or another stairwell or bank of elevators so she could get to another floor.

She heard the exit door open and close behind her. Two more sets of double doors were on her left, and as she hurried past them she pushed. One of the doors opened, and she ran inside and slid down behind it, landing on her heels. She looked above her head, saw the lock, and turned it, just before she felt the door being pushed from the other side. She sat for a moment, her heart pounding. And as she closed her eyes and waited, she smelled a dank and familiar smell.

The door was struck and kicked a few times, and then the attempts to gain entry stopped. She could hear voices from farther down the hallway.

"I must have taken a wrong turn," she heard the man just on the other side of the door saying.

She waited.

"The cafeteria," she heard him say in answer to a question.

And then there was silence. She heard what sounded like a muffled conversation, then silence again. She suddenly worried that another hospital employee might have been harmed, rendered unconscious like Patsy on the fifth floor, but then she could make out some more conversation, directions being given to the cafeteria, she thought, and then footsteps leading away from where she was hiding.

She stayed where she was, sliding all the way down until she was sitting, her back against the door, her legs stretched out in front of her. She held her hands to her chest, thinking that might somehow slow her heart rate, heard nothing else, and finally looked around at the room where she was hiding. Suddenly, she remembered that smell from being in the hospital in Santa Fe when she was looking for the girlfriend of the dead Hollywood director.

Eve had landed in the morgue.

FORTY-THREE

Eve closed her eyes and remembered her unexpected visit to a hospital morgue when she was following Megan Flint, the Captain's client and Hollywood star, and the hospital security guards as they hurried along the hospital corridors and down the exit stairs. She had been nosy and meddlesome then and gotten into a bit of trouble for her curiosity, and here she was again. Maybe not as nosy and meddlesome as concerned and involved — it was her sister's well-being, after all, she told herself — but still, once again she was stuck in the room of the dead. She glanced around. There was a dim light that gave her some sense of what was around her. She could see a wall of small doors to her left, and in front of her and to her right a steel table, on which two folded sheets had been placed. It felt cold, even though she was sure the room was no cooler than the other places in the hospital.

She shook her head.

"That was Dorisanne," she whispered to herself, recalling what she had just witnessed, whom she had seen, and she dropped her elbows to her knees and her chin into her hands. She found herself completely grateful that even though a man was chasing her and also very likely chasing her sister and Pauline, and even though she still didn't understand what kind of trouble Dorisanne was in and wanted desperately to talk to her, she had seen her, laid eyes on her, and at least from the distance that was between them and by the way she was assisting Pauline, she seemed okay. She was unharmed, at least for that second.

Eve said a prayer of thanks, offered another petition for divine assistance for her sister, and then began to reassess where she was and what she needed to do. She could stay hidden for a while longer. She could try to find another way out of the room. She could take her chances and step out through the door she had entered, the one that was locked and secure behind her. Or . . .

She reached into the pocket of her pants and pulled out her cell phone. Why hadn't she thought of that in the first place? She dialed Daniel's number. There was no answer. She left a message: "I'm at the hospital. I need your help. Call me when you get this." And she hit the End button. And suddenly without giving her action much thought, she punched in another number, the number she was most familiar with. There was just one ring.

"Hello," came the response. His voice sounded startled and sleepy.

And suddenly, Eve felt the tears forming in her eyes. "It's me," was what she said.

There was a hesitation and then a barrage of questions. "Are you okay? Where are you? Did you find your sister? What time is it?"

Eve cleared her throat and looked down at her watch. She could barely make out the time. "It's five in the morning here." She thought for a second. "Six there." She paused. "I'm sorry I woke you."

"I was awake."

She knew he was lying.

"Where are you? What's wrong?"

"I saw her. I saw Dorisanne. I'm at a hospital here in Vegas."

"A hospital? Is she hurt? What's happening?"

"No, no, she's not a patient here. Her neighbor is . . . was a patient . . . and I got here and saw Dorisanne helping her leave. I couldn't get to them because some man is chasing me or maybe them. I don't know."

"Evangeline, where is Daniel?"

She shook her head, then realized he could not see her response. "I don't know."

She heard labored breathing and figured he was trying to get out of bed. "Are you safe right now?" he asked. "Are you in a secure place?"

"Yes, I think so," she replied. "I think I'm in the morgue. The door is locked and I think he left."

"Okay, I want you to hang up, call 911, tell them exactly where you are and what has happened. And then you wait until somebody comes, a police officer or a hospital employee. Don't leave that room until you are sure you're not in jeopardy."

Eve nodded.

"Evangeline, do you hear me? Are you able to do that?"

There was a ragged cough from his end.

"Are you okay?" she asked.

"Allergies," he said. "Just allergies." He coughed again. "Did you hear what I said, Eve? Can you do what I said?"

"Yes. I will hang up and call 911 and tell them where I am and what has happened."

"And then you'll call me right back and let me know you're safe."

It was not a question. Eve nodded.

"I'm sorry I called and worried you," she said. "I know it's late . . . or . . . early, and I know it's not helpful when you're so far away. I shouldn't have called. I'm fine now."

"Evangeline, I'm your father. Who else should you call?"

"I know," she said softly.

"Before you hang up and call the police, tell me about the man who is chasing you. Have you seen him before?"

"He's been in a couple of places where Daniel and I have been. He was at the hotel where Dorisanne's neighbor works. That was last night. And then this morning he was at the apartments when we were there to meet with her, to get a key and search Dorisanne's place."

"Did he speak to you? Did you meet him?"

"No," Eve replied. "I just saw him."

There was a pause.

"You still there?" the Captain asked.

"Yes," she answered. "I think he's the one Dorisanne is hiding from. I think she and Robbie stole from him or turned him into the police." She recalled what she had discovered earlier. "I think Dorisanne is working with the FBI," she said. "There are two men who have been following me and Daniel, and I think they're agents."

"What makes you think that?"

Eve stopped. There was a noise outside in the hallway.

"Evangeline, are you still there? Is everything okay?"

"I hear someone," she whispered. She felt the door behind her slightly pushed.

"Okay, stay calm. Hang up and call 911," he instructed her.

She waited. There was no more noise, no more pushing on the door.

"It's okay," she told him. "I think whoever it was is gone."

"Why do you think Dorisanne is working with FBI agents?"

She heard the cough again.

"She had a kind of code in her address book. I called one of the numbers and a guy, one of the two following us, picked up. It was his phone. And I think that's where Daniel is now. Both cars were gone out of the parking lot. I think they must be together. Maybe they're figuring this whole thing out."

Eve stopped. There were more sounds coming from the hallway. Voices, several people shouting, heavy footsteps. She froze.

"Evangeline . . . what's going on?"

She hit the End button on her phone and jumped to her feet.

FORTY-FOUR

"Who's in there?"

She could hear a voice just behind her.

"Give me the key!"

Eve looked around, trying to find a spot to hide or another exit, but there were no other doors and there was no good place that she could see and there was no time to keep searching. She jumped onto the steel table by the door and pulled both of the sheets over the top of her. She had no idea who was on their way into the morgue, and she only hoped they weren't going to look where she had landed.

The door flew open. The overhead lights came on.

"What makes you think somebody's in here?" It was a man's voice, sounding to Eve like a person in charge, strong and commanding.

"It was locked. I checked all the doors on this floor when I came down a few minutes ago. The morgue doors aren't ever locked. So I came to get you before entering on my own."

"You want me to check the coolers?" somebody asked from behind them.

Eve thought there were three men standing somewhere very close to her. She didn't know what the coolers were, but she assumed that's what the small doors on the side and back walls must lead to. She hadn't gotten a very good look at the room because the light was very dim when she entered and because she had been concentrating on her phone calls. At just that moment, she felt her cell phone vibrate and she was glad she had muted it. She knew it was the Captain calling back, and she only hoped the men at the door couldn't hear the buzzing sound beneath her.

"You sure you want to do that?"

"Why?"

"Aren't you a little scared of dead people?" There was a tiny bit of nervous laughter.

Eve realized that the men were very likely hospital employees and that she should make herself known, but somehow she just couldn't move from her hiding place.

"Nah, there's nobody in here. I think Anne was right and the guy left through the emergency department. Let's get downstairs before the police arrive and make everybody nervous. Mr. Jansen is not going to be happy about this chain of events. I guess the manager on duty already called him?"

"Yep. He's on his way. Him and that PR woman he's always with."

"Debbie."

"As in *Debbie Does Dallas*?"

"As in Debbie Does a Full Nelson."

"What are you saying?"

"I'm saying Debbie from PR is actually Debbie Double D from WOW."

"Debbie D from Women of Wrestling is our PR person?"

"The very one."

"Dawg, I knew she was hiding some guns under those two-piece suits."

"Guns you better not mess with."

"She's hot."

"She can also take you down."

"Not that I would mind that count."

"Could you two shut up for a minute?" It was the first man's voice, obviously the boss.

"Sorry."

"Does Patsy seem okay now?"

"Yeah, it was just chloroform. She was fine as soon as the guy ran and the handkerchief fell off of her face. Lucky she called before he did any more damage."

"So this guy showed up before you did?"

"Right," came the answer.

"She get a good look at him?"

"Patsy?"

"Yes, Patsy."

"Doesn't she get a good look at everybody? She can tell me the height and weight of every person she meets."

"Just tell me what she said."

"Caucasian, six foot two, about 180, dark hair, mustache, black leather jacket, hazel eyes."

There was a pause. "She says she remembers the color of his eyes because they were the last thing she saw before she fainted."

"Patsy's tough."

"What about the woman?"

"She thinks they're together. And somebody got to the patient before they did — what's her name?"

There was a pause.

"Pauline Evans."

"Right, she thinks somebody got the patient out of the bed and off the floor before these two showed up."

"So we got a man . . ."

"With hazel eyes."

"Right, a man with hazel eyes and a woman . . ."

There was another pause.

"Five foot five inches, weight around 145 . . ."

Eve almost sat up. She wasn't 145 pounds, couldn't be. She wanted to tell them Patsy wasn't as good as they thought she was. She bit her tongue.

"Short dark hair, dark clothes, a black jacket, biker boots, about forty or so."

"A man and a woman trying to get to a patient who was beat up earlier today, who has now left the hospital AMA."

"AMA?"

"Against medical advice," came the reply. "Didn't you study your manual?"

"I studied the parts I needed to know to pass the test. I can tell you about a Code Blue, a Code Pink, and a Code Red. I didn't learn about AMAs."

"Well, you need to. We get a lot of them."

"Right."

"Do you want to take a look around this area, or have we been down here long enough?"

Eve lay very still, eyes closed, holding her breath. She knew she hadn't really done anything wrong, but she also knew she didn't want to spend a couple of hours trying to explain to these security guards, and the police who were on their way, why she was at the hospital at three o'clock in the morning, lying on a table in the morgue. She didn't want to have to give some detailed report of what she saw and who she thought was chasing her. She just needed to get out of that hospital and find Daniel. He could help her make sense of all of this.

"Let's go. And Peter, check the other suites on this floor. Make sure all the doors are locked and the codes are set. There shouldn't be anybody down here."

Eve heard the door close and footsteps moving away from the morgue. She waited a few minutes and sat up. Her phone was still ringing.

FORTY-FIVE

"EVANGELINE LOUISE DIVINE, WHERE ARE YOU AND WHAT IS GO-ING ON?" It was Daniel. She had to hold the phone away from her ear because he was screaming so loudly.

"I'm fine," she whispered, hoping the security guards had left the area. She was sure anybody within fifty feet of her could hear him yelling.

"I'm on my way to the hospital. How on earth did you get there? Why didn't you tell me you were going over there? And why is the Captain calling me all the way from New Mexico and yelling at me for not knowing where you were?"

"I tried to call you before I called him," she said, still whispering and quietly sliding off the table.

"I never got a . . . hold on a minute . . ."

She pulled the sheets away and placed them back where they had been.

"Oh, okay, I see you called. Well, why didn't you leave a message?"

"I left a message. I told you where I was and to come and find me."

"Oh." She heard some things being said under his breath. She guessed that the language was probably more than just a little blue.

"This phone is so lame."

"It's okay," she said, trying to reassure him.

"It's not okay," he responded.

"Where did you go, anyway? I tried to find you before I left the hotel. You weren't in your room because I checked."

"I left not long after we got back. I sat down for a few minutes, thought through some things, made a few calls, and finally figured out who the two men were. They're with the —"

"FBI," she interrupted him.

"Right . . . Wait . . . How did you know that?"

"From Dorisanne's address book. I found a code. I couldn't sleep either, so I started going through the book, page by page —" She stopped, thinking she heard a voice down the hall.

When she was sure it was nothing, she continued. "That was why I came looking for you. I wanted to tell you."

"You found out after we got back to our rooms too?"

"Uh-huh." Eve walked over to the door and listened. She couldn't hear anything. She thought it was probably a good time to try to get out of there.

"A code? You found a code in the address book?"

"I'll tell you about it later." She slowly opened the door and peeked out. "Hold on just a second."

She looked left and then right; there was nothing. She closed the door again, thinking she would finish the phone call and then make her exit.

"You really need to let this nun thing go and use your gifts, girl."

"So why is the FBI following us?" She wasn't going to take that bait. She knew she didn't need to talk about her vocational decision at that particular moment.

"Why are you whispering?"

"I'll tell you about that too."

"Dorisanne made a deal. She's been feeding them information on members of the ring. They found her and pulled her into the sting."

"That's why she went into hiding?"

"Seems so. They lost contact with her a

couple of weeks ago. They figured either the bad guys got wind of her association with them or Robbie got scared and yanked her out of town. They don't know."

"Are they worried about her? Do they know about Pauline?"

"They think she's okay. And yes, they know about Pauline."

"So why were they following us?"

"Because when we showed up, they thought they'd see what we found out."

"We've been doing their dirty work for them."

"Something like that."

There was a pause.

"I'm almost there," he said. "Just a couple of miles away. Where do I meet you?"

Eve thought about the best place to exit the hospital without being seen. She knew the woman at the emergency entrance desk, apparently named Anne, and Patsy from the fifth floor, and probably the security guards would stop her if she got anywhere near them. "Just get to the hospital. I'll figure that out in a minute."

"Is Pauline okay?"

"Pauline is with Dorisanne."

"What?"

"Yeah, I saw Dorisanne. She was here. I guess she must have found out about what happened to Pauline, and she came to get her out of the hospital. It was just in the nick of time too."

"How's that?"

"The motorcycle guy. He was here. That's who I'm hiding from. He got here right after I did. In fact, he may have come to the hotel. I'm not sure, but I had a funny feeling about somebody on the other elevator when I was leaving. Anyway, I didn't see him there, but he must have known where Pauline was, and he almost got to her."

She heard Daniel blow out a breath.

"You talked to the Captain," she said, stating the obvious.

"Yeah, he's more than a little worried."

"You should call him and let him know you're coming for me," she told Daniel.

"Holy cow, there must be ten or fifteen units out here."

"Are you out front?"

"At the emergency entrance."

"Don't stop there."

"Where else can I go?"

Eve thought for a second and remembered the stairwell she had just been in, the one she had seen Dorisanne and Pauline exit into. She opened the door once again and stepped out of the morgue into the hallway. No one appeared to be around.

She moved back in the direction she had first come from, saw the stairwell door. She walked quickly and carefully. There was a window by the door, and she could see that she was on the back side of the hospital. The sun was rising and she got her bearings.

"Drive to the east end," she instructed Daniel. "The one on the opposite side from the emergency department."

"Okay," came the response.

"There should be an exit there. I'll be coming out that door in about one minute."

"Right, I see it."

Eve walked into the stairwell and down two flights of stairs. "Daniel?" she called out.

"Daniel?" She glanced down at her phone and could see that she had lost her signal. She stood at the door leading outside, closed her eyes, hoping he had arrived, and pulled on the handle. The beams of light from the waiting car blinded her for only a second.

FORTY-SIX

"Hurry up and get in."

Eve jumped into the passenger's side and Daniel took off. They headed in the direction of the rear of the hospital. She pulled on her safety belt and dropped her head back against the seat. "What a night!"

"There's a security guard waiting at the end of the parking lot," he informed Eve.

She looked up and saw a man standing a few hundred yards ahead of them. He appeared to be checking everyone exiting the lot. "They have a description of me," she told Daniel, sliding down in her seat.

Daniel slowed the car. He reached behind him and pulled a blanket from the backseat. "Here, put this over you."

Eve took it, wondered how many more times she was going to have to hide, and pulled the blanket around her shoulders and back, forming a sort of concealing hood out of the loose edge, and slumped over in the seat. She felt the car come to a stop and could suddenly feel a blast of cold air rush in and assumed Daniel had rolled down the window.

"Hello, Officer," Daniel said, his voice polite and cheerful.

"Hello," the man called out.

Eve recognized the voice as one of those she had heard inside the morgue. She knew that those men had not seen her, but she also remembered that they did have a description of her from the nurse on the fifth floor. Although once she thought about that again, she remembered being labeled as 145 pounds, and she almost sat up just to prove she was right and Patsy was wrong.

"Something going on?" Daniel asked. "Seems like a lot of excitement for a Sunday morning."

"We had an incident."

There was a pause.

"You taking someone home?" he asked, and Eve knew the guard had noticed that someone was sitting on the passenger side wrapped in the blanket.

"My wife," Daniel answered.

The lie surprised Eve. What would she do if the guard asked to see her face? She hoped Daniel could talk himself out of this one.

"We've been in the emergency room all night." His voice quieted. "Migraine headache, she gets them all the time. Usually we can handle them at home, but she needed a shot. Lost the feeling in her face, vomiting. She's finally stopped, but if she sits up and has that morning sun in her eyes, it'll start all over again. I think she's asleep." He reached over and touched Eve. She didn't respond.

"Oh yeah, I had a migraine once," the guard replied. "It's okay, no need to wake her. Sounds like she's had a pretty awful night."

"Yeah, nothing like a weekend in the ER!"

The guard gave a slight laugh. "You don't even know the half of it."

Eve thought it sounded like he was about to tell Daniel the whole story of the escaped patient, the man who chloroformed a nurse, a woman on the run. She hoped he would think better of that.

"Okay." She heard a tap on the side of the car. "Be careful going home. I'm glad she's better."

"Thanks," Daniel said, and she could tell he had rolled up the window and felt the car moving forward.

She waited.

"You can get up now," he said. "The coast

is clear."

Eve pulled the blanket hood from her head and face and sat up a bit. "Your wife?" she said.

"What, you don't think you look like a wife?"

She sat up fully and shrugged. She kept the blanket wrapped around her shoulders. "I don't know. I guess I never thought about it before."

"Well, it was better than saying you were my sister," he responded with a grin. "We might have some 'splaining to do about that, Lucy. I'm not sure we could have pulled that one off. We do look a little different."

Eve glanced over at Daniel. "Yeah, that probably would have stumped the guard a bit more than wife."

Daniel sped out of the parking lot and onto a side street.

"Speaking of 'splaining, you got some to do," he said.

"I've got some explaining to do?" she replied. "You're the one who doesn't seem to know how to work his phone."

He shook his head. "Okay, you got me on that one."

She turned back to look at the hospital parking lot as they passed, just to see if the motorcycle she had seen before might be parked somewhere nearby. There was one near the side of the hospital, but it was not the Harley she remembered.

"Did you call him and tell him you found me?" she was asking about the Captain. After hanging up on him, she was concerned he might have gotten upset. She knew stress was not good for a diabetic.

"He called me again before I could dial his number. He was pretty anxious, said your call got disconnected and then you didn't pick up when he tried to call you back. He was worried about you."

Daniel stopped at a light and looked at Eve.

"Are you all right?" He seemed to be studying her.

She nodded. "Just a close call," she replied. She thought about the events of the evening and realized how lucky she was to be out of the hospital and in Daniel's car. She leaned back against her seat.

"I can't believe Dorisanne was there," he said.

"I know. I was so close to her."

"Did she ever see you?"

Eve shook her head, recalling how the stairwell exit door had closed before she shouted out her sister's name. She thought about her assisting Pauline down the stairs and wondered where the two of them had gone. She turned to Daniel, who seemed to be thinking the same thing.

"We can stop and check out the apartment, but that seems way too easy." He glanced in his rearview mirror.

"I know. I can't imagine them going back there either, but I don't know where else they could have gone."

"Back to the hiding place where she's been, I guess. Must be a good one."

The light turned green and Daniel hit the gas. Eve could see he was heading in the direction of Dorisanne's apartment. She closed her eyes, feeling the lack of sleep and coffee.

Daniel had noticed. "You know, why don't we go back to the hotel and you can get a nap? I'll check out the apartments myself. There's no need for both of us to go over there. Look at you, you're exhausted."

She turned to him. "Last I heard, you hadn't gotten any sleep last night either." She could see that he appeared to be as tired as she felt.

"I'm used to this," he said with a wink. "Police officers are built to run without sleep."

"Well, so are nuns," she responded with a

wink of her own.

"Yeah, but sometimes praying can look a whole lot like nodding off." He leaned over and elbowed Eve in the side.

"Yeah, well, sometimes so can police work." She grinned.

He made a turn, and Eve recognized the street as the one where Dorisanne's apartment was located. They quit talking as he made his way into the parking lot.

FORTY-SEVEN

It turned out that no one was at the complex. Both Dorisanne's and Pauline's apartments were without tenants present. The manager, a different guy from the one they had met earlier, let Eve and Daniel into both places after Daniel flashed his badge. Once they got in, they both saw that nothing had changed since they were last there. Neither of the women had returned.

While Daniel took a look around the back of the building, Eve called the Captain to explain what had happened. He sounded relieved, and when he asked when she was getting home, she didn't have an answer. "Soon," was all she could tell him, and she hung up after she promised to call later in the day.

Daniel returned to the car shaking his head. "Nothing," he said as he got in and started the engine. "I don't think they came back here," he added. He sat back and scratched his chin. "I didn't expect that we'd find anything, but I don't know . . ."

Eve waited. "What?"

"I just hoped I would walk up there and she'd answer the door. It sure would make things a lot easier." He gripped the steering wheel.

"We could go to the Rio," Eve suggested. "See if anybody there might know a friend she has or where she might go to get away."

She felt like they were starting back at ground zero, and there was a heaviness inside her. They'd figured out that Dorisanne was working with the FBI, and Eve had even seen her and knew that she was okay at that moment, but she was still missing, and because the guy on the motorcycle was still out there, she was still in danger.

Daniel looked at his watch and shook his head. "Too early," he said. "There wouldn't be anything going on there now. The night crew, the people she worked with, are all likely to be gone and won't be back until later."

Eve didn't respond. She knew he was right. They sat in the car in silence.

"Doesn't the FBI know anything?" she asked. She suddenly realized she hadn't had a chance to hear what Daniel's conversation had been about the previous night. He hadn't reported much about what the FBI told him.

"No," he replied as he put the engine in Drive and headed toward the exit out of the lot. "They were waiting to see what we found out."

"They have no idea of a place she might hide?" She was surprised that the law enforcement team placed on Dorisanne's case wouldn't have any clue as to where she might go with Robbie.

He shook his head. "Her departure was as big a surprise to them as it was to us," he answered.

"What about the motorcycle guy?" she asked.

"What about him?"

"Do they know who he is?"

Daniel thought about the question. "He didn't come up," he replied. "But I'm sure he's with the theft ring. That only makes sense."

Eve nodded. That's what she thought too. She watched as Daniel stopped at the apartment exit. He seemed unsure of what direction to take.

"Are they worried about her?" She had to ask. She wasn't sure she wanted to know everything they knew, all the details of her brother-in-law's involvement in illegal activities, all of Dorisanne's engagements, but she at least wanted to know if they were as concerned about where her sister was as she and Daniel were.

Daniel didn't answer, and after a few moments she understood that his silence meant they probably weren't worried. It seemed likely that her sister was just an informant to them and that was all. Any danger Dorisanne found herself in was danger she was likely going to have to get herself out of, without any help from the FBI.

Even though Eve knew now that Dorisanne was not a fugitive and was not involved in the theft ring, the search for her was just as urgent as it had been when they first arrived in Las Vegas.

"What else is in the book?" Daniel wanted to know, breaking the silence.

For a moment, Eve didn't follow.

"The address book, the one you found the FBI code in, is there any other clue in there? We have the customer's name, right?" He turned with the traffic onto the Strip.

Eve pulled the book from her back pocket and flipped through the pages again. Nothing stood out to her. She dropped it in her lap and shrugged. "Yeah, we have that one, and now that we know she was leaving

clues, we could just go through every listing," she said, thinking that might be the
best option.

"Call and just ask if Dorisanne is there?"

She paused. "It's all I can think of to do."

"I could go back and see Pauline's
boyfriend," Daniel suggested. "I'm pretty
sure that he's still in the same place. Maybe
he knows more than he has let on."

Eve considered the idea of Daniel going
back to the jail and interviewing Steve
again. "It doesn't look like he's the bad guy
after all," she noted.

"He'll probably find out from one of the
officers that she's out of the hospital," Daniel noted. "Not that I guess that matters,"
he added.

"You think they'll keep him in much
longer?" Eve wanted to know. She wasn't
sure what evidence would be necessary to
keep him locked up.

"I don't know," Daniel replied. "If they
figure out what happened at the hospital,
that somebody was looking for her and she
escaped, somebody on the force might put
two and two together and decide he might
be innocent and let him out. But I don't
expect that to be the case," he said. He
turned to Eve. "We sort of like to keep abus-
ers behind bars for as long as we can."

"Well, then I think we should go and talk to him. Maybe you can make him a deal. Maybe he'll give you something new."

Daniel acted surprised. "I'm in no position to make a deal. If you recall, I don't have any power in the state of Nevada."

"No, but he doesn't really know that. If you use your persuasion powers, he might truly see that you are likely the only official person who believes he didn't do this to Pauline. I would imagine that counts for something. You can promise that you will at least plead his case to someone who can make a deal."

Daniel seemed to be thinking it through. "I guess it's worth a try." He made a quick turn. "But I don't want you in there," he said. "I'll drop you off at the hotel and then I'll go. You can take a nap."

"I'll just take a taxi and meet you there," Eve replied. "I'm not sleepy, and I'm starting to learn my way around the city."

Daniel shook his head. "You can stay out in the car and start making some calls from that address book."

Eve smiled. "Yes, sir," she replied.

Daniel headed away from the Strip and onto Highway 10 toward the city jail. He was just making the exit off the thoroughfare when an ambulance came flying up

341

behind him. He quickly pulled the car off to the shoulder of the road and they both watched it pass.

FORTY-EIGHT

The new inmate had been stabbed while standing in line for breakfast. He did not survive. This information was given to Daniel by one of the guards who had been called to the cafeteria after the stabbing occurred. The officers had separated all the other inmates and were still trying to find out who had killed Steven Albright and how a weapon had gotten inside the jail. The interviews were expected to last all day. So far, no one was saying anything, and the video recording of the incident had just been witnessed by the jail staff. There were so many men in the breakfast line and standing around the victim that the perpetrator couldn't be identified.

Eve stayed in the car and watched as they wheeled the victim out on a gurney and placed him in the back of the ambulance. Even before Daniel came out and confirmed it, she knew it was Steve. She didn't really know what Pauline's boyfriend looked like, and she never even got a clear look at the victim's face, but she just knew. She had just finishing saying her prayers when Daniel returned. The look on his face told her everything she wanted to know about the man's identity and his condition.

"It went straight through his carotid," Daniel explained as he took his seat and shut the car door. "His neck," he added, not sure Eve knew where the carotid artery was. He just shook his head.

"Was it a fight?" she asked.

"No one's talking," he answered. "But I don't think this was the result of a common disagreement between cell mates."

"Why? What makes you say that?"

"It happened too quickly, too methodically, and the guard said the guy has been in lockdown since he got here. He wasn't on his best behavior when he arrived, so they kept him in isolation. He's not had time to make enemies. This was his first time actually out in an area with the other inmates."

There was a pause in the conversation.

"You think it had to do with Pauline?" Eve asked, trying to understand what had just happened.

He nodded. "I think so."

"But what makes you think that? What happened exactly?"

Daniel turned to Eve. "Whoever did this knew what he was doing."

Eve closed her eyes and said another prayer. She was praying for Steve and Dorisanne and Pauline and for herself; she wasn't even sure who or what she should be praying for anymore. When she finished, Daniel was looking at her. "What?" she asked.

He shook his head, and she knew the news was not good.

"Daniel, what is it?"

"The guard said he had a visitor this morning, about an hour ago."

Eve wanted to stop him from telling her anything else, but she also wanted to hear the truth.

"The man stayed just a few minutes and then took off. The guy I talked to said Steve seemed pretty upset after he left, wanted to make a phone call, kept saying his girlfriend was in trouble."

"Did the guard let him make the call?"

Daniel shook his head. "He just thought it was a ploy for Steve to call and threaten his victim, and he had already made his calls last night." He waited. "He was right to think that. Lots of guys do anything they can to call their wives or girlfriends and try to talk them out of making a statement or going through with the charges."

"So what happened?" Eve asked.

"He sent him to the cafeteria for breakfast, told him he couldn't make any calls. That was the last time he saw him."

Eve ran through everything Daniel was telling her.

"This guy that came to visit him, did the guard have a description?" She had a very sick feeling she knew who the visitor was.

"Better than that, he had a photo." Daniel handed the picture to Eve.

She didn't have to study it for long. She recognized the man in only a second. She had already gotten more chances than she needed to retain that image in her memory. He was the same guy from the casino, the guy on the motorcycle, and the guy she had just encountered at the hospital who had chloroformed the nurse and chased her. It was as if she and Daniel were on the exact same path as he was, only in regard to Steve and getting to the jail, they had arrived too late.

"Do you think Steve told him something about where Pauline and Dorisanne might be?" She dreaded hearing Daniel's answer.

"I do," came more quickly than she was

prepared.

She felt the tears gather. She reached up to wipe them away and Daniel took her by the arm.

"But I don't think he's gotten to Dorisanne and Pauline. I think they're safe."

"Yeah, but for how long?"

Daniel didn't have an answer to that question. "Where's the book?" he asked, pulling his hand away. "That's all we have, and we need to pay attention to it. If Dorisanne kept a code in there for how to reach the FBI, she must have information in there about where she and Robbie might hide."

Eve dried her tears and handed the address book to Daniel. "There's nothing in there," she said. "I looked at all of the listings while you were in the jail. It's just names of friends and business places she would go."

"But that's all we need, one name, one place," Daniel reminded her. "Let's go through them again. Maybe if I read them aloud to you, something will jump out."

Eve didn't respond, but she saw little hope in figuring out a clue that way. She had gone over every contact. Nothing stood out, and she knew that to try to call every number would take way too long. The man on the motorcycle would have gotten to her sister well before they could get through the first couple of letters.

"A," Daniel began.

Eve shook her head. "Don't start there," she said. "Start at the back."

"Okay."

Eve waited.

"How about the W's?"

She nodded, and just as he was calling out the listings, she remembered something very important. "Marcus Winters," she shouted, remembering the name of the man whose receipt she'd kept. "Call Marcus Winters."

The look on Daniel's face told her that it was a name he recognized. "Who did you say?" he asked.

She repeated it, and before she could say anything else, he had his phone out and was placing a call.

FORTY-NINE

Daniel dialed the number while Eve leaned in to listen. She could hear the phone ringing. After the fourth ring, a sleepy voice answered.

"Hello."

"Is this Mr. Winters?"

There wasn't an answer.

"My name is Daniel Hively. I'm a friend of Dorisanne Divine."

Eve could hear the man clearing his throat.

"Divine," he said, pronouncing it correctly, just as Daniel had done. "Not Divine."

"Yes," Daniel responded.

"It's 2245 Lone Star Place," was what he said next.

"I'm sorry," Daniel replied.

"It's 2245 Lone Star Place," he said, repeating himself, "89048."

There was a brief pause where neither of

them spoke, and then Mr. Marcus Winters ended the call.

Daniel hit Redial three times, but the man whose name and number were listed in Dorisanne's address and phone book never picked up again.

Daniel and Eve turned to each other.

Eve spoke first. "Could it be that easy?" she asked.

Daniel didn't answer, but he seemed convinced. He reached into a small drawer hidden under a drink holder and pulled out a small electronic device. Eve recognized it from earlier in their trip. It was a GPS. She watched as he plugged it in, turned on the engine, and typed in the address that had just been given to them. Immediately, a map was displayed.

"Okay, 2245 Lone Star Place," Daniel said as directions started to be given. He looked at Eve. "We're going to find her." He put the engine in Drive and left the city jail parking lot. He followed the instructions and headed south out of the city.

Eve pulled away from Daniel and glanced out the window. She couldn't believe it might be so easy. She couldn't believe Dorisanne would just give out an address to a man Eve had never heard of. And how did he know to give it to Daniel? Had

Dorisanne expected the family friend to show up and look for her? It just didn't make sense, and she was worried that this was actually some setup, some trap that she and Daniel were about to walk, or drive, right straight into. She reached over and touched Daniel on the arm.

"I don't know if this is the right thing," she said.

He slowed a bit but kept driving as the directions were leading him.

"It's the right thing," he responded, without an explanation for his confidence.

Eve closed her eyes. She wanted to believe him, but she knew that the man on the motorcycle had already tried to kill Pauline, was after Eve at the hospital, and had apparently found Steve and had him murdered at the jail. If this was a trap set by him or the people he worked with, she and Daniel could be making a fatal mistake by going to this location.

"I think she must have known we'd come searching for her," Daniel finally explained.

"How could she have known such a thing?"

"She knows the Captain. She knows you."

Eve looked at Daniel. "And you," she added. "You're the one who's been coming out here all the time, checking up on her.

I'm so grateful for you, Daniel."

He turned away. And there was something about the way he moved so quickly, the way he had looked since she had told him that she saw Dorisanne at the hospital, the way he had gotten so worried since leaving the hospital. Suddenly, things began to come together. She thought about how earlier he seemed not to want to talk about his many trips to Vegas, the way he so quickly and easily changed everything at his work to come with her, the way people recognized him in the town. Eve knew then that there was something more going on with her friend and his relationship with her sister.

The voice from the GPS gave another instruction about a turn Daniel would need to make.

"You're in love with Dorisanne," Eve blurted out.

Daniel quickly faced her. "What?"

"I said, you're in love with Dorisanne."

"That's crazy," was his reply. And he rolled down his window a bit.

And just like that, several things were clear to Eve. "Your coming out here all those times, that wasn't for the Captain. You came out here for yourself."

Daniel shook his head. "She's young enough to be my daughter," he answered.

"And Mama was young enough to be the Captain's. I don't think age has anything to do with falling in love."

"And you're such an expert on this?"

"I'm not an expert on anything," she replied. "I think we both know that."

The GPS reported they had about fifteen more miles to travel. Lone Star Place was not in Las Vegas, it was in the neighboring town of Pahrump.

"When did this happen?" she asked.

Daniel didn't answer at first.

She waited.

"A while ago," he answered. "After my divorce."

Eve leaned back into her seat.

"It was before Dorisanne got married. I came out here, and I don't know — things just happened."

"What things happened?" Eve wanted to know.

Daniel turned to her and smiled. "Just things," he answered.

"But why did she marry Robbie? Why didn't we find out about this? How long did it go on?" She knew she was already asking way too many questions, and there were way too many more rattling around in her mind.

"I broke it off," he answered. "I just couldn't see this as something that would work. I'm your father's best friend."

Eve thought about what he was saying. "So?" It was all she could think to say.

He made a kind of laugh. "So?" He shook his head. "Are we talking about the same man? Do you remember the Captain?"

"I remember him just fine. And I know you. And I know Dorisanne. If you two fell in love after knowing each other your whole lives, then so what? Don't you think he would much rather it be you with Dorisanne than Robbie the credit card thief?"

Daniel didn't answer for a few seconds, and then he blew out a breath. "It doesn't matter. It was wrong. And I value your father's friendship. I didn't want to lose that."

"I don't think you'd have to," Eve responded. "He's a bear, we both know that. But he also loves you both. You're both adults and have been for a long time. I don't think he'd be as against the relationship as you think."

He nodded but didn't appear to be convinced.

"What did Dorisanne say?" she wanted to know.

"She said that the two of them never got along anyway. It wasn't such a big issue for her."

"How did she take the breakup?"

He shook his head. "She got married in three months."

Eve didn't know what to say. She was remembering the wedding, how Daniel had not come, saying he was out of town for that weekend. She recalled her sister's demeanor and how Eve had even questioned her about the quick timing of the event. Dorisanne had never let on what had happened between her and Daniel. No one in the family, at least as far as Eve knew, had had a clue.

She wanted to know so much more, but before she could ask another question, Daniel made the announcement.

"This is it." He turned the car into a short driveway and came to a stop.

Fifty

Eve looked around at the place. There were no cars or motorcycles in the driveway. The curtains were closed on the front windows. The yard was untended. There were a few rolled newspapers by the front door. The small dwelling, an old wood-framed house with flaking paint and bars on the outside of all the windows, was situated at the end of a short street in what appeared to be a zoned business area. There were a few warehouses at one end, and two other houses on the street, which both appeared to be empty, were surrounded by chain-link fences. If you didn't know there was a house at this address, you would never have known to look.

Daniel turned off the engine, and they both reached to open their doors. Eve suddenly felt his hand on her arm. She turned to him.

"You gotta stay here," he instructed her.

"And I mean it this time," he added. "I can't have you in there with me."

She started to object.

"I have my gun." And he slid aside his jacket to reveal a pistol attached to his belt. Eve had not recalled seeing it the entire time they had been in Vegas. She wondered if he had kept it hidden from her in an attempt to reduce any anxiety she might have had or if he hadn't worn it until her call from the hospital.

"Do you think you'll need that?" she asked.

"I don't know," he answered, pulling his jacket back over it.

Eve could still see the outline of the Glock pistol under his coat, the same model of gun she recalled her father having when he worked on the police force.

"I do know that I'm prepared if I do need it. I can handle whatever happens in there, but I have to be fully attentive when I get inside. I can't be worried about you." He took her hand. "You'll only be a hindrance to me and to Dorisanne if she's in there and in trouble."

She glanced down and then back at him. "Maybe we should call the police here. Maybe we should have some sort of backup."

"And tell them what? That we got this address and we think someone is hiding here?" He shook his head. "That doesn't really warrant a police officer coming to this address. Besides, we don't know what this is. There may just be someone here who can tell us something. We don't want to get anybody into trouble."

Eve nodded, even though she still thought having someone else present, having some other law enforcement officers involved, would be a better idea than Daniel going into the house alone.

"Please, I'm asking you, just stay in the car. If she's in there, I'll come and get you right away. And if she's not, I'll be right back to tell you what I find out. But just stay here. Keep your phone out and call 911 if you hear anything . . ." He didn't finish the sentence.

Eve held her tongue. She wasn't sure why, but she wasn't as defiant or as argumentative with Daniel as she was with the Captain. Maybe it was because she knew this was an argument she would not win. And she also knew that what he was saying was true. If she walked in with him and there was some kind of danger, she would be of no help to him. She could help more by doing exactly what he said. She would stay outside and make a call if something happened.

She nodded and removed her hand from the door handle and pulled out her phone. He squeezed her hand, and she watched as Daniel exited the car and made his way to the front of the house. As he walked away, Eve noticed again the hardscrabble yard, the weeds around the front porch, the peeling paint on the front of the house, and the iron bars on the windows. The house looked neglected, and she wondered what Daniel would find when he went inside. He turned back once and looked in her direction, nodded, and then turned back and knocked on the door.

It was just a few moments before the door opened. Eve couldn't see who let him in, and she strained to find any opening in the door or window coverings that she could peer through from her seat in the car. Then, just like that, he walked inside and the front door closed behind him.

Eve sat, doing anything she could to stop herself from jumping out and following Daniel into the house. She started saying a prayer, the Our Father. She finished it quickly and started over again. She recited the rosary, reaching for the chain hanging on the mirror, the one she had been using throughout the entire trip to Vegas, and then she stopped, dropping her hands into her lap.

What if there was some sort of scuffle or shouting? She wouldn't be able to hear from her location. At the very least, she needed to open the car window. She thought about starting the engine so that she could do that, but then, worried about the noise it would make, she decided against that idea. So, without specifically defying Daniel's instructions about going to the door, she decided she would simply step out of the car and get closer to the house so that she could make sure she would hear anything that might signal danger.

She stepped out slowly, not noticing as her phone slid from her lap to the floor of the car. Just planning to get closer to the house, she pressed the door closed and glanced around. She could feel her heart race and she took in a deep breath. She was scared, but she was also determined to find out what was happening. Not hearing anything, she crept toward the house, deciding to stand near the front window. She thought she saw a car turning in their direction, and she wondered if she should run and dive back into the car and hide. She watched, relieved, as the vehicle kept going past the warehouses and the street she and

Daniel had turned onto.

She continued and got as close as she could to the front of the house, trying to hear if there was any sound coming from inside, but there was nothing. She tried standing on her toes to peek inside, but she could not see under or around the curtains. Without any way to see or hear anything from inside, she decided she might have a better shot of finding out what was happening if she moved around to the back of the house. Maybe there was a kitchen or some room in the rear of the house that she would have a better chance at seeing into or hearing whatever might be going on.

She slowly and quietly walked around to the back, noticing the short fence around a small square yard and the empty lot behind it. Beyond that, a long ways from where she stood, there was another street and houses situated on both sides of it. All around the house was just scrubby desert terrain, an area that she guessed was being groomed for other places of business, other warehouses like the ones at the end of this street.

Still, there was very little movement anywhere around, and Eve saw nothing out of the ordinary. She continued to move closer to the back door, noticing an unobstructed window that gave a full view of what appeared to be the kitchen. Eve stopped and looked in, and that's when she saw her sister and Daniel standing at the kitchen table, Dorisanne crying and Daniel holding her in his arms.

The sight of such a thing both surprised and calmed her, and thinking that everything must be all right for the two of them, she was reaching up to knock on the window, to make herself known, when she noticed that Dorisanne and Daniel were not alone. She dropped down out of sight, but only after she had seen the man she'd run from at the hospital standing in front of them, a gun pulled and pointed straight at Daniel's chest.

FIFTY-ONE

Eve held her breath and crept back around the house. She was trying to make her way to the car when she heard the front door of the house open, and she quickly slid back to a hiding place under the kitchen window. She leaned over and peeked around the corner. The man with the gun was walking toward the driver's side of Daniel's car, Dorisanne stumbling in front of him, held close to him, his arm wrapped around her waist, the gun pointed at her side.

Eve dropped back to where she was hiding and heard the car door open and close, peeked again, and watched then as both of them hurried away from the car, going back in the direction of the front door. She heard the beep signaling that the man had taken the keys from the ignition and locked the car.

It appeared that he had come outside and was checking to make sure that Daniel was alone. She was glad she had made an exit when she did, happy that her instincts had been right. He must have opened the door to take the keys, though, and, she realized as she felt around in her empty pockets, her phone not there, that he had probably also taken that or, at the very least, locked it inside the car. She realized that she had no way to get back into the car and no way to make a call. She slumped down, her back against the side of the house, and tried to figure out what her next move should be.

She looked to her left and saw the row of warehouses, with no vehicles anywhere around. The closest business, she recalled, was a diner about a mile away from the house. She looked to her right and in front of where she sat, the view from the back of the house, and noted that the street with the closest houses was also more than a mile away. The thought of heading toward the diner seemed like a good plan, but she worried that if she made a run for it in that direction, the man would see her from the rear window, and that would only make things worse for Daniel and Dorisanne.

Eve was unsure of what move she should make, knowing that going for help in either direction was going to involve almost twenty minutes of walking. Feeling anxious, she leaned back against the side of the house, closed her eyes, and prayed. It was just one simple word, the prayer she prayed more than any other: "Help."

She took in a breath and then glanced back again to her left and then to her right. She couldn't believe her eyes. She smiled as she noticed that just around the corner of the back side of the house was what she knew to be the tip of the rear tire of a Harley-Davidson, Dyna Super Glide, more than likely from the year 1997.

She dropped to her knees and headed for the bike, crawling and staying well below the windows of the house. She couldn't hear anything from inside, and she hoped that was good news, that the man holding her sister and friend hostage had not yet started shooting, that perhaps Daniel was trying to talk their way out of there or that there was something, anything, keeping the man from killing his prisoners.

She reached the corner, stood up, and walked around to the front of the Harley. She glanced around, still not seeing anyone in the vicinity. She reached around the handle bars and felt for a key but quickly discovered it was not there. But of course, who left a key in the ignition of their ride?

Knowing that the noise of the engine

would be loud enough to reveal her presence and likely cause more trouble for everyone, she turned the bike around and walked it away from the house, into the empty lot to the east and well behind 2245 Lone Star Place.

She crossed herself as she usually did when she was about to do something questionable like hot-wire a bike and then reached for the ignition cap and removed it. She found the wires, leaned down, and yanked them apart. She figured out which one was the hot one, crossed it, and made her leap onto the seat just as the engine started. She slid the motorcycle into first gear and took off, heading away from the house and hoping that the man didn't hear his Harley being stolen right out from under his nose.

Eve drove as fast as she could through the empty desert lot until she finally hit the row of houses behind the one on Lone Star Place. She thought about stopping at the first house she came to and asking if she could use their phone, but she worried that time was too valuable. She knew that having to explain who she was and what she needed and why she was riding a motorcycle through backyards without a key in the ignition might create more trouble than it would alleviate.

She drove through the first yard in her path, watching in her rearview mirrors as a man ran out the front door, screaming at her, and then she sped up, making her way to the paved street and heading toward the main drag that she and Daniel had been on before making the turn onto Lone Star Place. She was speeding toward the diner when, out of nowhere it seemed, a police car came flying up behind her. She had not seen it anywhere previously, but it didn't matter, she knew it would provide the assistance she needed. She quickly pulled off to the side of the road, dropped the kickstand, leaving the engine running, and jumped off the bike.

She was running in the cruiser's direction when she suddenly saw the driver's door open and a gun being raised and pointed at her.

"GET DOWN!" the police officer shouted from behind the door. "GET DOWN RIGHT NOW!"

Eve stopped and dropped to her knees. She raised her hands in front of her.

"Turn around. Hands behind your head!"

Eve did as she was instructed, spinning around on her knees, turning away from the officer, and placing her hands behind her head.

"Now, drop facedown to the pavement."

Eve started to turn around and speak, try to explain what had happened, what was going on at the house just a few miles away from them, but she soon felt a heavy hand on her neck, pushing her face to the ground. She was in a bowed position, one of submission and obedience, a position that she knew all too well.

"I'm trying to get help," she said to the man standing behind her. "My sister —"

"Just shut up!" the officer responded. "It seems a lot of people are looking for you. I saw the APB on this bike about an hour ago. Of course, they think you're in Vegas, and the description they have of you is all wrong since the report is that they are looking for a man, but they definitely got the bike right." He was trying to pull out a pair of handcuffs while he held on to Eve's neck, but he seemed to be having some trouble doing it with only one hand.

"I stole the bike," Eve said, her face pressed against the street.

"Well, that's just another charge we'll get to bring against you."

"No, I'm trying to explain that I stole the bike from the man you're looking for. He's got my sister. He's going to kill her."

The police officer was still trying to put the cuffs on her, getting one around her left wrist and starting to put the other one on her right. It appeared to Eve as if this wasn't something he was very used to doing, and she wondered just how much crime there was in Pahrump, Nevada, and if the officer had ever even made an arrest.

"Well, that's a nice story. I'm sure the Las Vegas officers will love to hear that. How did you learn to steal a bike anyway?" He continued to struggle with the cuffs, and Eve was tempted to assist.

It was then that she heard a vehicle heading in their direction. She turned to look and saw Daniel's car careening toward them. She jumped up and fell against the officer before the car made a turn, barely missing them both. She could see that the man with the gun was driving, but she was unable to see anyone else in the car.

"That's him!" she yelled at the officer. "That's the man you're looking for!"

FIFTY-TWO

The police officer immediately pushed her aside and reached for the receiver attached to his shoulder to make the call. "Base, this is officer 17 requesting backup at the intersection of Sage Brush and Lone Star." He released the call button and yelled at Eve, "You stay here!" He jumped up and ran to his vehicle, leaving Eve by the curb, between the bike and the squad car, trying to decide what to do.

"Hey, wait!" she called out, but he had already gotten into his vehicle and was giving more information to the dispatcher.

Eve did as she was told and remained at the curb.

She swept off the dirt and dust from her pants from where she had both knelt and then fallen. The questions swirled around in her mind: Did the man have Dorisanne and Daniel in the car with him? Where was he taking them? Were they back at the house?

Had they been harmed? She looked in the direction of the house on Lone Star and in the direction of where the stolen car had headed and then at the squad car still parked behind her.

She desperately wanted the police officer to return so she could send him either after the man in the vehicle or back to the house where Daniel and Dorisanne had been held at gunpoint. Every passing moment was critical to their well-being.

She considered running over to the officer in the squad car and begging him to follow them, but she knew that was not such a great idea since it seemed that he was convinced she was a dangerous suspect. And he still had the gun strapped to his belt, even as she still had his handcuffs attached and hanging from her left wrist.

Eve took in a breath, closed her eyes, and tried to be patient, tried to wait for the officer to return or at the very least drive after the man in the car who had only barely missed hitting them. She tried to pray, tried to recite familiar words. In the end, she could think of nothing meaningful to think or pray. She only knew to act.

She lifted up a quick Hail Mary before she finally bolted to the bike, whose engine was still running, a pair of handcuffs dangling from her arm, and took off. She was glad that she was unable to hear the officer's shouts behind her and just hoped he wouldn't take a shot, her back an easy target. She chose not to look in her rearview mirror to see how he was responding.

Considering the direction the car was headed, there was only one route the man could be taking, which was the same way she and Daniel had come earlier. Eve followed the road until she thought she saw the car speeding ahead of her. She leaned forward and hit the gas.

He made a turn and she made a turn. He sped forward and she did the same until she was almost close enough to . . . and she finally had that thought: *Close enough to do what?* She had no weapon. She didn't even have a phone. The motorcycle, although fast and a machine she could easily manage, was no match for Daniel's heavy sedan. All the driver would have to do if she did manage to pull up beside him was take a shot at her, since it was clear he had a gun, or even simply swerve a bit and knock her off the bike. She had no cause to stop him or even slow him down. And that was when she had another thought.

A rider loves his ride.

She glanced to her right and, recalling

how the street curved and turned toward the town of Pahrump, noticed a field that could provide her with the necessary shortcut. She headed off the road, driving as fast as the bike would go, until she figured out the way to beat the car that was still speeding ahead of and away from her.

She hit bumps and swerved to avoid the bottles and cardboard boxes, narrowly missing a set of old tires littering the barren area. She used every maneuver she had ever learned when she raced before she headed over a ditch, finally making it to the place she thought would be exactly where the car would arrive. She spun and stopped dead center in the middle of the street, and before she could second-guess her decision, she saw the car speeding in her direction. She didn't even have time to get off the bike. She closed her eyes, made the sign of the cross, gripped the handles, and prepared for the worst.

A horn blared. Brakes squealed. And when Eve opened her eyes, the car had come very close to her before veering off to the right and plowing into the ditch she had just jumped. She was right. The man could not bear to run into his Harley.

She drove over to the passenger's side of the car at the same time she heard the sirens heading toward her. When she looked inside the vehicle, there was only the driver, still dazed and slumped over from the hard hit. She leaned down and cupped her hands as she peered into the window. Dorisanne and Daniel were not in the car. She sat upright on the motorcycle seat, trying to determine her next move.

Eve knew she would be in trouble for not waiting for the police to arrive, but she also knew that getting arrested was now the least of her problems. She revved up the engine and headed back toward the house on Lone Star, passing a number of squad cars that were speeding to the location she had just left. She knew that no matter what she found at the house where Daniel and Dorisanne had been, the driver of the stolen car, the owner of the bike, would be apprehended and hopefully arrested.

Straight ahead on the street where she had been stopped by the first officer and then right at the warehouses and down to the end of Lone Star Place, Eve drove as fast as she ever remembered having driven a motorcycle. She stopped and jumped off the bike, throwing it down as she hurried to the front door.

"Daniel! Dorisanne!" She shouted and banged on the door, but there was nothing, no sound coming from inside. No one came to the door.

She ran around to the back of the house and at the same time she was trying to look in the window, she was pounding on it, calling out their names, trying to get their attention, hoping that nothing bad had happened but feeling more and more desperate as she continued to shout and pound.

Finally, she couldn't stand not knowing, not hearing anything, any longer. She looked around, found a large rock near the fence, picked it up, and hurled it through the window. When it landed inside, she hurried back and yelled through the broken glass.

"Daniel! Dorisanne! Are you in here?"

She thought she heard noises from a room off to her right, and she took off her jacket, rolled it around her hands, and knocked away the jagged edges of glass from the window. Then she pulled herself up and over and fell inside.

"Dorisanne!" she called out again, standing up, looking around and seeing a refrigerator, counters, a sink, and recognizing that she was in the kitchen, near the table where she had seen her sister and Daniel earlier. She grabbed a large piece of glass and, unsure of what or who might be there, crept toward the front of the house.

There was no one in the front room, but now the sounds from a room down the hall were even louder. Eve hurried past a bathroom and another door before she stopped at the room the noise was coming from. She held the piece of glass high in one hand while she slowly turned the knob.

FIFTY-THREE

"Thank God!" These words of relief came from Dorisanne, who was tied, roped back-to-back to Daniel, who faced away from the door and who was slumped over and appeared to be bleeding.

Eve ran to the two of them and immediately checked to see if Daniel was alive. She felt a pulse and gave her own simple prayer of gratitude. She worked on the ropes and was able finally to free them both.

"How did you get here?" Dorisanne asked as she rubbed her wrists, trying to restore the circulation. And then she immediately asked, "Is he okay?"

They both turned their attention to their friend, who was not participating in the grand reunion. As Dorisanne moved away from him, he collapsed to the floor. Eve knelt to his side, watched his chest move up and down, saw the wound on the side of his head, which was the cause of the dried blood smeared across his face.

"He hit him with his pistol," Dorisanne explained. Her voice sounded frantic. "He's been out since it happened. I kept trying to keep him talking, but he lost consciousness after he was hit."

Eve ran into the kitchen, found a towel, wet it, and brought it back and began cleaning off Daniel's wound. There was a gash, but it didn't seem very deep. She wiped away all of the blood, rolled the towel up, laid it beneath him, and gently placed his head on it. Then she pulled out the phone from his pocket where she knew he had put it and dialed 911. Calmly, she told the operator that there was one injured person, an apparent concussion, and gave the address.

When she finished the call she clicked off the phone and studied her sister. "Are you okay?" she asked, taking in the sight of her, taking in the realization that Dorisanne was sitting there in front of her. She had finally been found, and to Eve, she seemed to be unharmed.

Dorisanne nodded and then fell into Eve's arms. She began to cry. "I thought we were going to die," she sobbed into her sister's shoulder. "I just knew when I heard you outside the door that it was him, that he had found Robbie and now was coming back to kill us."

"Where is Robbie?" Eve wanted to know, pulling Dorisanne away from her.

"He drove to L.A.," she answered. "This morning he decided to get out of town. We found out about Pauline, and we got her out of the hospital and over to her mother's house." She looked at Eve and wiped away the tears. And then she turned back around and took Daniel by the hand.

"She was able to tell me about you and Daniel being here, but we couldn't come out of hiding because we knew they were onto us. We knew that if they got to Pauline or to Steve, they would find out where we were. I was lucky to get Pauline out before that guy found her." She tried calling out Daniel's name, patting him on the hand, trying to wake him.

Eve quickly glanced away, the name of Steve reminding her of what had happened earlier in the day.

"What?" Dorisanne asked, turning back to her sister after noticing Eve's reaction. "What's happened?"

Eve shook her head.

Dorisanne moved closer to Eve. "What? Tell me."

"It's Steve," was all she had to say.

"They got to him, didn't they?" Dorisanne began to cry again. "This was never supposed to get this messed up. There were never supposed to be other people involved. They promised me." She turned to Daniel, taking his limp hand once more. "Pauline, Steve, Daniel, you . . ." She looked at Eve. "So many people have been hurt." She dropped Daniel's hand and sat down with her back against the wall, pulling her knees up to her chest and dropping her face into her hands.

"Dorisanne, tell me what all this is about. Tell me what you're involved in."

Dorisanne stopped crying enough to be able to tell Eve about how Robbie got behind on his gambling debts and that he had borrowed money from loan sharks. He couldn't pay them back right away, so at first they charged a street tax and made him pay double. Soon he had no money, and that was when he told Dorisanne what had happened. Then they were both forced to go to work for the men Robbie owed money to.

It was exactly what Daniel and Eve had thought it was: a credit card theft ring. Robbie was getting card numbers from casinos and cash machines and from Dorisanne at the lounge where she worked. She was caught by the FBI the first time she skimmed numbers and was then set up by the feds to catch the guys who were the real leaders of the theft ring. First she was brought in by the feds and then Robbie.

Dorisanne supplied Robbie with phony numbers and fake receipts, and that was how the loan sharks finally figured out the couple had been turned by the FBI. They would try to make purchases from the cards and they kept getting turned down. The guys put two and two together and realized that Robbie and Dorisanne were working with law enforcement. It was the risk the couple knew they were taking but thought the FBI would protect them.

Once they found out they had been discovered, that the men they were working for were after them and that the FBI wasn't providing the protection they had hoped for, the couple went into hiding. They had been on the run for three weeks. Pauline had found them the house on Lone Star Place, and that was where they had been hiding ever since. They had tried to ask for help from the FBI, but because they hadn't gotten enough evidence for them to make an arrest, the agents had told them they were on their own.

"I'm sorry," Dorisanne said.

"Why are you sorry?" Eve asked. "You did what anybody would have done. You didn't have a choice. This isn't your fault."

"I knew Robbie had a gambling problem. I knew I shouldn't marry him, but I did it anyway." She shook her head. "The Captain gave me his full background report when I told him about the engagement. He had the entire history, but I still didn't listen. I still married him even though . . ." Her voice trailed off.

"Even though you were in love with somebody else?" Eve reached over and touched her arm.

"How did you find out about that?" Dorisanne asked.

Eve shrugged. "We've been together looking for you for three straight days. Something that important eventually just comes out."

Dorisanne nodded slowly and both women turned their attention to Daniel, who still had not awakened.

"You think he's going to be okay?" she asked Eve.

Eve nodded. "I do," she answered. "He's almost as hardheaded as you are."

Dorisanne smiled. She reached over and rubbed Daniel's arm. "He said it could never work for the two of us because of the

Captain."

"I know," Eve responded. "He told me the same thing."

Dorisanne looked up at her sister. "Do you think that too?"

"No," Eve replied. "But if he couldn't bring himself to tell him, then you would never really get the chance to give the relationship a try. So, I guess in a way, if Daniel thought it was too big of an obstacle to overcome, it was."

Dorisanne nodded.

There was a pause as they both heard the sirens heading in their direction.

"By the way, how did Daniel know that Mr. Winters would give us the clue to where you were? Who is Mark Winters?"

Dorisanne smiled. "Winners, not Winters," she explained. "It was something Daniel used to say to me when I first moved here."

Eve waited.

"He said that he knew I would do well in Vegas because I was marked as a winner, that I was lucky, special." She shrugged. "So, we just started calling the guy our guardian angel, Mark Us Winners. It was just a silly thing we shared, so I wrote the name on the receipt, hoping Daniel would find it." She looked away. "Find me," she added.

Daniel started to stir at that moment, and as Dorisanne rushed to his side, Eve headed to the front door to let in the paramedics, who, by the sound of the approaching sirens, she knew were just around the corner.

FIFTY-FOUR

Daniel was admitted to the same hospital where Pauline had been a patient. Eve found herself hiding her face every time she saw a security guard or a nurse. She was worried that Patsy from the fifth floor might recognize her or that there was still some search going on for her and she would be dragged away to jail.

"What are you doing?" Dorisanne finally asked after seeing her sister quickly turn away or jump up from her chair and face the wall or run into the bathroom every time a health-care worker came near them.

"She thinks they're after her," Daniel said, answering the question put to Eve.

The sisters glanced over at Daniel, who hadn't been very responsive since he'd been admitted. He had regained consciousness just as he was being placed in the back of the ambulance, but he had not been able to stay awake. He was diagnosed as having a concussion; luckily, tests revealed that there was no brain damage and no severe consequences. The doctors had been a bit concerned that he was unable to stay awake, but they also said that everything else appeared to be normal.

"Well, look who's joined the party!" Eve said, not addressing Dorisanne's query. She didn't really want to have to explain about her early morning mad dash through the hospital halls or about hiding in the morgue.

"You found her," he said softly.

"We found her," Eve responded. She reached over and squeezed Daniel's hand. "You had us pretty worried," she added.

He started to sit up but then seemed to think better of it. He winced as he raised his head off the pillow.

"Whoa there, Detective," Dorisanne said, stepping near him. "I think you may have quite the headache for a while. He hit you pretty hard."

Eve watched as the two looked at each other. She stepped back, giving Dorisanne a bit more room and the two of them a little more privacy.

"You had me really worried," Dorisanne said. She had leaned down and was stroking Daniel's cheek.

"Aw, you should know the best place for

me to get hit is the side of the head."

She laughed. "I think you used to tell me that."

He reached up and touched Dorisanne on the arm. There was a smile spread across his face. "You okay?"

She nodded. "I am now," she responded.

"I guess we owe all of this to your big sister over there," he noted, turning his attention in Eve's direction.

"I think we owe it to Mr. Marcus Winners." She moved closer. "How come you didn't say anything when I told you that name? How come you didn't let on that you knew it was a clue?"

He shrugged gingerly. "I wasn't sure about it," he answered. "It's been a long time since I heard that name being used."

Dorisanne squeezed his hand. "I didn't know who might find the book," she noted. "But I thought if it was you, you'd know to call."

"Who was the guy?" he asked, recalling that a man had answered the phone and given the address that had helped them find Dorisanne.

"It was Jason, the former bartender over at the Rio," Eve blurted, answering the question for her sister.

Both Dorisanne and Daniel glanced over at her.

"How did you know that?" Dorisanne asked.

Eve smiled. "I recognized his voice." She stuffed her hands into her pockets. "I didn't know it at the time," she explained. "I thought it sounded familiar, but I wasn't completely sure. But afterward, I thought about it, and I remembered that I had talked to him before. I knew it was Jason. He said to tell you hello, by the way. I called him back and told him you were all right."

Daniel shook his head. "She thinks she's a nun."

Dorisanne made a face. "I know. Crazy, right? She's always been good at this kind of thing."

"What?" Eve asked. "What kind of thing?"

"Solving mysteries, remembering familiar voices, knowing things," she answered. "You were always more like him and I was always more like Mom."

This way her sister had of telling family history surprised Eve. She had never heard her sister make a positive comparison between her and the Captain. The thought of such a thing made her feel proud.

"Speaking of," Daniel piped in. "Did you call him?"

Dorisanne waited for her sister to answer. She seemed to notice that Eve was waiting for her to answer. "Well, don't look at me. I haven't talked to him. I thought you were making that call."

Eve shook her head. "Yes, I called him. He's very relieved that you weren't hurt any worse than you were," she said to Daniel. "He said he owes you a very big thank-you for saving his daughter."

Dorisanne didn't respond.

"You talk to Rob?" Daniel asked.

She backed away just a step from the bed, slid her hands up and down her shoulders. "He left for Los Angeles this morning. He's supposed to call me when he's safe."

"You didn't call him to tell him the guys have been arrested, that the metro police rounded them all up?" Eve asked.

Dorisanne had a sheepish look on her face. "I left the phone at the house in Pahrump. I don't know how to call him."

Eve looked at Daniel, who was staring at Dorisanne. Neither of them said anything further.

"Don't you think he might be worried about you?" Eve asked, breaking the awkward silence.

Daniel closed his eyes.

"I told Pauline what happened. He'll call

her when he can't reach me, and she can tell him that we're fine." She kept a close watch on Daniel.

"Did she hear the news about Steve?" Eve asked, wondering if Dorisanne's neighbor had been informed about her boyfriend's murder.

Dorisanne nodded.

"How did she take it?"

"She's pretty upset about it, but she's also a little . . . I don't know . . . relieved, I think."

Eve nodded. "She seemed pretty scared of him."

"She was," Dorisanne agreed. She was still looking at Daniel, who kept his eyes closed.

"Maybe I'll go downstairs to the cafeteria and get a cup of coffee," Eve said, leaving the bedside and moving toward the door. She figured her sister and Daniel could use a little time alone.

"Don't get lost," Daniel commented, showing a slight grin.

"Morgue's on the third floor," Eve said, making her exit. "Cafeteria's on the first."

She glanced over at Dorisanne and winked, hoping her sister understood she had the time and space to talk.

FIFTY-FIVE

Eve watched him in the rearview mirror. He was resting in the back, able to stretch out a bit more than if he had taken the passenger's seat beside her. Since his car had been crashed, stolen by the guy who had kidnapped Dorisanne and caused his concussion, he had to rent a car. He chose a brand-new Lincoln Town Car, and Eve felt like a limousine driver behind the wheel, teasing him that she should be wearing a little black cap and serving him beverages and snacks throughout the trip. It had brought a tiny bit of laughter from him. Once they started the drive home, he dropped his head down on the pillow and had been sound asleep for four hours. She had gotten them across the state line from Nevada to Arizona, and they were already heading east on Interstate 40. It was about lunchtime, and they were almost halfway to Madrid, having made very good time since traffic had been light and she was driving slightly above the speed limit. Eve preferred her Harley on the open road, but she found she was enjoying handling the rented long sedan almost as much. And the view was still the same: the wide blue sky, the barren hills and mesas. Eve had always loved a western road trip.

She watched the highway in front of her and thought about their departure earlier that day. She had assumed all the way up to the last minute that Dorisanne would be going with them. She had even told the Captain when she called him first thing that morning to expect them both at home in time for dinner that day. She thought this had pleased their father, and she dreaded seeing his reaction when she arrived home alone. She wanted answers from Daniel or from Dorisanne, but she had left Vegas without knowing if anything had been resolved between her sister and their father's former partner.

She looked in the rearview mirror again; he was still asleep. Even though she was sad that her sister wasn't going home with her, she was glad for a few things. All the loose ends were tied up, and there was not going to be any federal or local charges against Dorisanne. No report had been filed about what happened between Eve and the Pah-rump officer. She never even heard anything about her little motorcycle theft or her fleeing from the police.

When it came time to leave, there were no charges made against either of the Divine sisters; however, the same thing couldn't be said about Dorisanne's husband. The FBI was still not completely forthcoming about whether or not he would be implicated in the credit card theft ring. Immunity was offered only to Dorisanne, not to Robbie, and because of the possible pending charges, he was not allowed to leave the state.

Eve blew out a breath and suddenly noticed Daniel stirring. She watched him as he moved around a bit and then finally sat up and opened his eyes. He yawned and stretched.

"You okay?" she asked.

He just nodded. He stretched out his arms again and then reached up and touched the big knot on his head. He winced and then leaned back.

"You tired of driving?" he asked. "I can drive some."

Eve shook her head. "No, I believe the doctor was very clear when he released you earlier than he wanted to: 'You can go, but you cannot drive.' Besides, I think those pain pills might make you a bit loopy."

He closed his eyes without giving a response.

Eve waited, kept looking back at her passenger, and then couldn't help herself. She had to ask the obvious question: "So, you okay?"

"You asked that already," he answered. "It's a headache, that's all."

She watched as he sat up a bit more. He leaned down and retrieved a drink from the cooler on the floor.

"I'm not talking about your head," she replied. "I'm talking about your heart. I'm talking about Dorisanne and you."

There was a long pause, no response, and then she saw him open the drink, take a swallow, and then turn his attention out the window.

"We talked a long time," he finally noted. "All night, in fact."

Eve nodded. She had seen her sister earlier at breakfast, her eyes swollen and red. There had not been much said, only that she wasn't coming with them. And then, just like that, she was gone.

"It just doesn't seem that it's meant to be," he said.

Eve hoped for more details. She kept looking at him and waiting, but he seemed to have nothing more to say on the subject of her sister.

She turned her attention back to the highway.

"You talk to your dad?" he asked, breaking the silence and changing the subject.

"It's not allergies," she told him, understanding that he was asking about the cough. "It's an infection. I'll take him to the clinic when I get back."

"You figured out how to tell that Caleb guy about his great-grandfather?"

"I have," she answered. "I want to check out the family of the woman he married first, just to see if they know anything, but yes, I think I know how to break the bad news."

"Yeah, I guess you Divine sisters know how to do that pretty well."

Eve did not respond. She simply watched him from the rearview mirror and continued in the direction of home.

FIFTY-SIX

"Are you Ms. Gallegos?" Eve asked. She was standing on the porch of a home just outside Madrid, off Highway 14 heading south toward Albuquerque. She had found the address in the county records. After hearing the Divines' investigative report, Caleb Alford had asked to join her.

"I'd like to go and meet my other family," he had told her when he got the news, and Eve agreed to take him.

"Elizabeth," the older woman answered, standing behind the screen door separating the homeowner from her visitors. "Elizabeth Gallegos."

"Hello, Ms. Gallegos, I'm Evangeline Divine. I live in Madrid. This is my friend, Caleb, who is trying to find some information about his great-grandfather. We're here because we think he may have married someone in your family."

The woman didn't respond at first, and

Eve waited, uncertain if Ms. Gallegos was going to let them in.

"It's nice to meet you, Ms. Gallegos," Caleb said.

There was a pause as a car passed behind them on the road. Eve watched as the old woman eyed the passing vehicle.

"Tourists," was all she said as she opened the door to let the two inside her home. "Drive up and down around here looking for turquoise like it's lying around everywhere."

Eve smiled at the woman. She knew not all of the locals were very happy about the popularity the little town and the road going through Madrid and Cerrillos known as the Turquoise Trail had attained.

Eve looked around as the door closed behind her. It was a small adobe home, typical of many of the residences in northern New Mexico. There were stacks of newspapers along one side of the room and the furniture was old and sparse. Ms. Gallegos picked up some magazines and brushed off a place on the sofa, then pointed to Eve and Caleb to sit.

"Don't get much company out here," the old woman noted, taking a seat across from the two of them.

"You live here a long time?" Eve asked.

"All my life," she answered. "If I live another two months, I'll be eighty-five."

Eve smiled. "How wonderful."

"Nah, it ain't all wonderful," Ms. Gallegos commented. "Some days I would be happy not to make it to nightfall." She shifted in her seat. "Old knees, old hips . . . hard to get around."

Eve nodded.

"You from around here?"

"I'm from Madrid. My parents are the Divines."

The old woman smiled, showing more than a few missing teeth. "You're one of Mary Divine's daughters?" She leaned closer to Eve to get a better look. "You're the oldest," she surmised. "Well, I'll be. I used to watch you barrel race at the rodeo."

"That's me," Eve replied.

"I thought you became a missionary or something." She sat back in her seat.

"A nun," Eve answered. "I joined the Benedictine Order in Pecos."

"That right?" the old woman responded. "I thought they made all the women leave," she added. "Wasn't that what the papers said? That the nuns had to leave?"

Eve never enjoyed talking about the politics of the abbey where she had been in community for almost twenty years. "We

398

just had to move out of the main building. They separated us from the monks," she noted.

The old woman laughed and slapped her knee. "Too risky even for the celibates, huh?"

Eve simply nodded in response. She turned to Caleb, who was not participating in the conversation.

"What are you two here about?" Ms. Gallegos asked. "You looking for some information about family?"

Eve answered for Caleb. "I'm doing some work for this gentleman, who has come to New Mexico looking for information regarding his great-grandfather."

"Why did he ask a nun to help him find his kin?"

Eve hesitated. Caleb didn't answer.

The older woman asked another question before either of them could reply: "Wait, your daddy does that kind of work, doesn't he?"

"Yes, he's a private investigator."

"And he's got you helping him?"

"Yes," she answered.

"Hmm . . . seems kinda strange, but okay."

"It turns out," Eve said, getting back to the purpose of her visit, "that in searching the records for my client's great-grandfather, he was reported to have married someone in your family." She stopped for a second, letting the older woman catch up. "A Katherine Gallegos."

"Katherine Alford," she replied, surprising Eve.

"My great-aunt Katherine married a miner. His last name was Alford." She sat forward a bit. "Didn't last long, but, wait a minute, where are my manners? Would the two of you like a cup of coffee?" She started to get up.

"No, no, that's fine," Eve replied, waving away the offer.

"So you do have a family member who has the last name Alford?" Finally, Caleb spoke up.

"Sure," Elizabeth Gallegos replied. "It was Katherine's first marriage. She married again, had four sons. They mostly moved over to Albuquerque and down south." She looked at Caleb. "What did you say your name is again?"

He cleared his throat. "Caleb," he responded. "My name is Caleb."

She paused. "You're kin to Caleb Alford?"

"He was my great-grandfather," he answered.

Ms. Gallegos studied the man. "Well, I wouldn't go around these parts making that claim," she responded. "He married Katherine, took all of her money, and disappeared. Your great-granddaddy's name is mud to most of the folks in the Gallegos family. How is it that you found me, anyway?"

Caleb turned to Eve, who took that to mean he needed her to answer their host's questions.

"In the records at the courthouse," Eve answered. "Caleb here thinks that his great-grandfather may have married your great-aunt Katherine while he was still married to a woman from the East Coast," she explained.

Ms. Gallegos appeared to consider this bit of news. And then she just shook her head. "I ain't never heard that story," she responded. "But that don't mean I don't believe it. We got more than a few skeletons in our closets, and a scoundrel like Caleb probably had lots more than any one of us ever heard about. The way he did Katherine, wouldn't surprise me a bit that he had several wives."

Caleb looked down at his hands that were folded in his lap.

"Wait, East Coast?" Ms. Gallegos asked. "You say your family is from the East Coast?"

Caleb nodded. "North Carolina," he answered.

Ms. Gallegos leaned forward, trying to pull herself up. It took two tries, but she soon was standing. She was shaking her head. "Caleb was from Texas," she said. "Lubbock, I think." She stood at her chair for a minute and then started walking out of the room. "Some of the men went looking for him when he disappeared. They went to Texas. Hold on, I got a picture of him," she added. "I'll get it."

"Oh?" Eve started to get up as well and follow the woman. "Can I help you?"

The woman waved her hand in front of her face as she moved out of the room. "Nah, Sister, just sit back down and I'll get it for you. It's hanging in the hallway with the pictures of the others who used to work the family mines. That Caleb could have made a fortune when he married into the Gallegos clan. Got greedy, though, and couldn't wait."

Eve leaned back in her seat on the sofa. She looked over at Caleb, wondering how he was doing hearing all this news about his great-grandfather, knowing that he was not only a polygamist but also a thief. They waited without speaking until Ms. Gallegos returned.

"Here it is," the old woman announced as she walked back into the room. She blew dust off the old frame and handed the picture to Eve.

"Caleb Alford and Katherine Gallegos at a summer picnic. This was taken just after they got married. I remember my grandmother telling me about it."

Eve took the photo and held it so that Caleb could see it as well. It was old, black-and-white, and looked like the pictures she had seen around the area all of her life. Ranchers, miners, the homesteaders from the late 1800s, this photograph of a New Mexican family reminded her of the pictures from her own grandmother's photo album.

Caleb handed the picture back to Eve. "Ms. Gallegos, are you sure the man in this picture is Caleb Alford?" he asked.

She shuffled over to her seat and sat back down. "Yes, sir," she answered. "That's my great-uncle from Lubbock, Texas. He married Katherine, stole all her money, and then disappeared. Everybody thinks he went back east, back to Texas. Oh yeah, everybody in the family knows about Caleb."

Caleb looked over at Eve, then to Ms. Gallegos, and then back at the photograph. He handed it back to the old woman. "Well, he may have the same name as I do, and he may have told everyone that he was Caleb Alford, but based upon all the pictures I've seen, I'm pretty sure that is not my great-grandfather."

FIFTY-SEVEN

"So what did you find on Epi's land?"

Eve and Jackson were at the office, just sorting through a few files and closing up some loose ends before heading out to the doctor's office in Santa Fe. They were going over both of the cases they'd been working on before she left for Las Vegas.

She had already told him about how things ended with Caleb Alford, about the visit at the Gallegos home and how he was convinced that the man who had married Katherine Gallegos in Madrid all those years ago was not his great-grandfather, that somehow this man from Texas had stolen the identity of his family member and that there just didn't seem to be an answer to what had happened to Mr. Caleb Alford.

She told him that their client had decided not to continue trying to dig up information, that he wasn't going to attempt to figure out who the man calling himself Caleb Alford really was or even the identity of the person who had sent him the beads. He was finished; he wasn't going to try to discover what really did happen to his great-grandfather.

"Gold?" she wanted to know.

He waved his hand in front of his face. "No gold," he answered her. "There was a bag of rocks," he added. "A few chunks of silver and turquoise. Somebody took the gold a long time ago."

Eve shook her head, surprised at the outcome of the search at the Salazar ranch.

"No gold," she repeated. "How did he take it?" She wanted to know, recalling how the old rancher seemed quite interested in finding the treasure on his property, how convinced he was that it was there.

Daisy was in her lap, and she was giving the cat lots of attention since she knew the poor thing had been neglected while she was away.

The Captain took a sip of water from the bottle he kept in his lap and kept talking. "I don't really think he ever cared about finding gold. It was just his way to get us involved. Just a way to get the answers he really wanted about his family. He had his father's body exhumed while they were digging. He thought his father had been killed.

Turned out he died from cancer. I never knew it, but he thought his brother had shot the old man before he left town. Epi didn't know how to ask for the body to be exhumed and the questions answered, so he decided to act like he was looking for gold."

Eve shook her head. "I guess it's true. You just never know, do you?"

He turned to her. "Never know about what?"

Eve shrugged. "About anything," she replied, scratching behind the cat's ears. "About why a person would marry somebody when they're already married, why a man would pretend he wanted to find gold when all he really wanted to find out was whether or not his brother killed his father, why a man would pretend to be somebody he wasn't."

The Captain cleared his throat. "Life is a great mystery."

"It is that," Eve responded, thinking about everything that had happened in the last few days. Daisy jumped down just as Eve and Jackson turned to the front door as it opened. It was Caleb Alford.

"Hope I'm not catching you at a bad time," the client said as he glanced down and saw Daisy heading to her water dish in the corner of the office. "I know I don't have an appointment."

Remembering his allergies, Eve got up to take the cat outside, but Caleb waved her off.

"Don't worry about that," he said. "I'm just here for a second, and besides, I took an allergy pill on my way over. I'm fine."

Eve sat back down, brushing the cat hair off the front of her jeans.

"I just wanted to come by and thank you both for your help. I couldn't have done everything I did without you."

"Sounds like we didn't really give you the answers you were looking for," the Captain noted. He was still at his desk. "I'm not sure we solved your mystery."

"Well, I guess we can't really solve all the mysteries," Caleb responded. He remained just inside the door. "I have no idea what happened to my great-grandfather. I don't know how he died or if he ever intended to bring his wife and family out here. I don't know about any of the choices he made. But the truth is we can't really understand why people choose what they choose. I guess we can just learn from them and maybe try and understand ourselves a little better."

Eve nodded. She was thinking about Dorisanne and Daniel, how she'd probably never understand the decision her sister had made to stay in Vegas.

"After all this searching and researching, I realized I haven't seen my son in a long time," Caleb noted. "And the truth is I don't know anything about him, what he likes, who he loves. I realize now that I'll never know what my great-grandfather was thinking. I can't ask him. But I can ask my son, and if he wants to know about me, maybe I can answer some of those questions he has. I guess I went searching for the wrong thing, set myself and you on a wild-goose chase."

"Goose chases are what we get paid for," the Captain replied.

"Yeah, I guess," Caleb responded. "And I don't really think it was a complete waste of my time."

The two waited.

"You know, I did meet Rochelle," he added. "If it took me a goose chase to find love, then that's a goose chase I'm happy to go on."

Eve looked over at the Captain. He was smiling.

"Well, that's a fact. Finding love and deciding to reconcile are both pretty good things," Jackson said, coughing as he spoke.

Caleb walked over to him. "I want to

thank you for everything," he said, extending his hand.

The Captain shook it. "I'm afraid I didn't do too much on this case." He pointed over to Eve. "She handled most of the load."

Caleb turned in Eve's direction. "Thank you, Ms. Divine." He shook his head, realizing his mistake. "Divine," he noted, correcting his pronunciation. "I don't know why I can't remember that."

Eve stood up. "No worries. We're sort of used to it by now." She reached out and the two shook hands.

"All right then, I'll be heading back east." He nodded at them both. "Thanks again," he said and headed out the door.

They both stood and watched as the client got into his car and slowly pulled away from the office.

Eve turned to the Captain. "You ready to go?" she asked, glancing over at the clock on the wall. "We'll need to hurry to make your appointment."

Jackson got up from his chair, heading toward the door. "I'm pretty sure with your lead foot, you'll get us there in plenty of time."

She gave him a gentle punch in the arm as she held open the door and he passed through.

FIFTY-EIGHT

Eve glanced around until she spotted Daisy, who had jumped up and was sitting in the Captain's chair. "Good thing he's not looking," she said to the cat as she turned off the lights and pulled the door closed and locked it.

She got into the truck, Jackson already settled in the passenger's seat. She started the engine and backed out. "You want to wear your seat belt?"

"I always do when you're driving." He grinned and pulled at the shoulder strap.

Eve hit the gas. The wheels spun in the gravel as she moved forward.

"Oh, Twila found her sister," he noted, unfazed by his daughter's driving tactics. He leaned down and set his water bottle in the drink holder between them.

"Is that right?" She slapped the steering wheel. "Well, how about that? The sisters finally meet."

"Yeah, she seems pretty excited. Found her in Nevada, little town west of Reno. She went up there and spent time with her over the weekend while you were gone." He coughed again.

Eve looked over at him, her concern about the Captain and his illness growing.

"Took some pictures — the two of them even look alike," he added. "If you can imagine that." He cleared his throat again.

She turned her attention back to the road and sped up. They drove without further comment about their friend.

"Dorisanne called," he finally shared.

Eve was surprised.

"When?" she wanted to know.

"This morning, just after you went out for coffee."

Eve nodded but didn't ask any questions.

"She says you were quite the hero."

A slight grin emerged, but she remained silent about her sister.

"She said you stole a motorcycle and almost got yourself killed."

Eve wondered how her sister had heard that part of the story. She had not told Dorisanne or Daniel about that bit of activity that had occurred in Pahrump before she found them both at the old house.

"She also said that she was sorry if she

disappointed you."

Eve could feel his glare on her. She kept her eyes on the road.

"I don't understand that," he said. "What does that mean? Why does she think she disappointed you? Is it because of Robbie and what he was involved in?" He waited for an answer.

Eve just shook her head. "I couldn't say," she replied, knowing that her sister's comment had nothing to do with the credit card theft ring or her husband's involvement with loan sharks. She knew that Dorisanne thought that Eve wanted her to move back home to New Mexico and make a life with Daniel. She had never asked Eve what she thought, but Eve figured out that her sister had read her face when they left each other. And it was true — that's what she was hoping for.

"Well, are you?" Jackson finally asked after a long, awkward pause.

Eve thought about the question, thought about how she felt about her sister's decision. "No, I'm not disappointed about anything."

Jackson tried clearing his throat, coughed a few more times, and Eve decided not to continue the conversation. In truth, she was still a little tired from the Vegas trip, and she was quite worried about her dad, so she was glad not to have to talk about Dorisanne and Daniel or anything else for that matter. She hit the gas and hurried along the highway.

It wasn't too long before she made the turn into the town of Santa Fe and quickly found the parking lot at the doctor's office, located an empty space, and pulled in. They had made the forty-minute trip in less than twenty. She felt a little proud of her accomplishment. When she put the engine in Park, the Captain reached over and touched her on the arm, surprising her. She quickly turned to him.

"Look, if this is bad, I don't want you to feel like you have to stay here." He pulled his hand away. "If you're ready to go back to Pecos, you go. You've taken care of me long enough."

Eve tried giving him her best reassuring smile. She patted his hand still resting on her arm. "Let's find out first what this is, then we'll decide what I'm doing."

The Captain studied her as she reached for the door, ready to make her exit. He leaned over, touching her arm again.

"What?" she asked.

"I don't want you to use me as an excuse for not going back to the convent. You did that before, and I suspect that's the way it had to be at that particular time, but it isn't going to happen again. You make your decision based upon what you want, not what you think I need."

She breathed out a long breath and then looked the other way. "What if I don't know what I want," she confessed. "What if I can't give Brother Oliver an answer? What if my life and the choices I make are as much a mystery as that missing miner or . . ." She hesitated.

"Or your sister choosing to stay with the man she doesn't love?"

"How do you know about that?" She jerked around to study her father.

He made a kind of laugh that then turned into another cough. "I'm crippled, not blind," he replied. "I knew she was in love with Daniel when she got married."

How could Jackson know about this and not speak about it, she wondered.

"And Daniel? Did you know then that he was in love with her?"

He shook his head. "Nah, I didn't figure that one out until a couple of years ago when he kept making trips out to Vegas for no reason. I knew he didn't gamble, and I knew he didn't like that city. Finally put two and two together." He didn't finish.

Eve just shook her head. "Are you going to tell him that you know?"

Jackson cleared his throat. "Nope. I guess I figure that's his story to tell."

"Well then, what about you?" she asked.

He seemed confused. "What about me what?"

"Are you disappointed about this? Are you upset at Daniel? Dorisanne?"

"Nah," he replied. "It's like you said. People make choices all the time. Some are the right ones, others maybe not. But it's not for me to judge what other folks do. I don't know the details people are trying to sift through in making their decisions about their lives. I ain't looking to solve that kind of puzzle. I can only try to work on my own choices. Try to figure out why I do what I do. That's hard enough." He coughed again. "And then there's what we have in our hearts," he added. "There's love."

Eve waited.

"Don't really think we have much choice about that one. We love who we love and we love what we love."

Eve sighed with great relief. She was glad to hear that her father wasn't angry with his oldest friend. "I think you should tell him that."

"Who? Daniel?"

She nodded.

"I'm not talking about Daniel."

She waited.

"I'm talking about you."

She shook her head. She wasn't following him.

"I'll tell Daniel what I think about him and Dorisanne, but I'm pretty sure I'm not the reason standing between the two of them getting together. If he's the one not moving that relationship forward, I'm guessing he's making his choice for other reasons, even if he's claiming it's me. And I certainly can't speak for Dorisanne."

"Okay, but why are you talking about me? What are you saying?"

"I'm saying that if you love being a nun, then be a nun; go back to Pecos and be about the things that give you peace. But if you don't love being a nun, if you don't want to be in Pecos, if you love this work, love being a detective, then you can say it's me and my diabetes or my old lungs keeping you here, but we both know that's not really the truth."

Eve slumped a bit in her seat. She knew what he was saying was true, and she knew that if she was waiting for what the doctors were going to say about his condition to help her make her decision to stay or go back to Pecos, then she wasn't really being fair to Jackson or to her superiors at the monastery.

"There are some mysteries we will never solve, but there are others we could find an answer to; we just sometimes don't want to search deep enough."

Jackson reached over and opened the car door, slid his legs out, and stood up. He leaned back in to say one last thing.

"But that kind of thing nobody can choose for you. You've got to choose that for yourself, even if it's a mystery to everybody else around. You choose for yourself."

He shut the door and coughed a few times and then slowly headed for the office.

Eve waited a second, watching him as he walked away. She glanced up at the rosary hanging from the rearview mirror of the truck, and then, somehow feeling a new resolve, she stepped out of the truck and followed after him.

Epilogue

January 3, 1891

Caleb was halfway home. He was tired and broke. The roommate had stolen everything he had, including his name. It turned out the man calling himself Red was running from a past and looking for a future. He wasn't from Oregon like he said he was; he was from Texas, Lubbock, Texas, and he was real trouble. The young man from North Carolina didn't realize it until it was too late: Red making debts, staking claims, and, worst of all, getting married — all under the name of Caleb Alford.

The miner walked along the wagon trail, the winter wind strong and biting. His coat was threadbare, his fingers and toes frostbitten. He knew his chances of making it all the way to North Carolina without any money and in the worst season for travel were slim, but he couldn't stay in New Mexico. He loved his wife, missed his family, and he was a wanted man. He had killed Red and left his body in the mine where they had worked. He knew it wouldn't be long before the law would realize he was the killer and come find him. He had to get home, had to get as far away from Madrid as he could.

Caleb felt for the bag he had in his pocket, the small one where he kept the necklace he had made for Claire. He'd wrapped it in a handkerchief, along with a note asking that it be sent to his wife in case he was found dead somewhere along the trail. It was the only thing Red Farley hadn't taken from him, and he could only hope that somebody would get it to Claire along with the news of his death and the news that he was trying to make his way back to her, trying to make his way home.

The young man stumbled along, knowing he couldn't make it much farther. He stopped and sat down by the frozen river, hoping just to rest and then keep walking. He leaned against a large stone, closed his eyes, and thought of Claire. He smiled, seeing her smile, hearing her voice calling him, feeling her warm arms around him.

"I'm coming," he said as the clouds gathered above him. "I'm coming home," he whispered just as the snow began to fall.

READING GROUP GUIDE

1. Caleb Alford was searching for information about his great grandfather's disappearance. As you reflect upon your own family history, are there any unsolved mysteries involving members of your family? Throughout the years, was there anyone who left home and was never heard from again?

2. In your family history, what stories interest you the most? Is there a family member from generations before who you feel connected to?

3. The book is about the relationship of biological sisters, the bond they share. Do you have a sister? What is your relationship with her like? If you don't have a sister, did you always feel like you missed out by not having one?

4. The story primarily takes place in Las Vegas and it's truly "a fish out of water" story for a nun from New Mexico. Have

you ever visited Las Vegas? What do you remember most about the city?

5. Sister Eve still seems unsure about her vocation as a nun. What choice do you think she will ultimately make? Why?

6. Daniel assists Eve in solving the mystery of the missing sister, what is his relationship with Eve? With Dorisanne?

7. Dorisanne left a book with clues in her apartment, who do you think she expected to find it? Do you think she imagined her sister would come to Vegas to search for her?

8. What does "family" mean to Eve?

9. We never learn how the contemporary Caleb got the strand of turquoise. What do you think happened? Who sent them to him?

10. What does riding on a motorcycle mean to Sister Eve?

ACKNOWLEDGMENTS

I am deeply grateful to the staff at Harper-Collins Christian Publishing/Fiction Division. Thank you especially to Ami McConnell, Daisy Hutton, Karli Jackson, Katie Bond, and Kerri Potts. A special thanks to Deborah Wiseman, the world's best copyeditor! It's awesome to work with you all.

ABOUT THE AUTHOR

Lynne Hinton is the New York Times bestselling author of *Friendship Cake* and *The Art of Arranging Flowers,* along with sixteen other books. She holds a Masters of Divinity degree from Pacific School of Religion in Berkeley, California. She has served as hospice chaplain, church pastor, and retreat leader. Lynne is a regular columnist with *The Charlotte Observer.* A native of North Carolina, she lives with her husband and dog in Albuquerque, New Mexico. Visit Lynne's website at www.lynne hinton.com and Facebook: Lynne-Hinton -Books.